PASCALE PETIT was born i
Wales and lives in Cornwall.
Indian heritage. Her eighth poetry collection, *Tiger Girl*, from
Bloodaxe in 2020, was shortlisted for the Forward Prize for
Best Collection, and for Wales Book of the Year. A poem from
the book won the Keats-Shelley Poetry Prize. Her seventh
poetry collection *Mama Amazonica*, published by Bloodaxe
in 2017, won the inaugural Laurel Prize in 2020, won the RSL
Ondaatje Prize in 2018, was shortlisted for the Roehampton
Poetry Prize, and was a Poetry Book Society Choice. *My
Hummingbird Father* is her first novel, published by Salt in 2024.

# PASCALE PETIT

# MY HUMMINGBIRD FATHER

SALT

PUBLISHED BY SALT PUBLISHING 2024

2 4 6 8 10 9 7 5 3 1

Copyright © Pascale Petit 2024

Pascale Petit has asserted her right under the Copyright, Designs and
Patents Act 1988 to be identified as the author of this work.

First published in Great Britain in 2024 by
Salt Publishing Ltd
18 Churchill Road, Sheffield, S10 1FG United Kingdom

www.saltpublishing.com

Salt Publishing Limited Reg. No. 5293401

A CIP catalogue record for this book is available from the British Library

ISBN 978 1 78463 311 0 (Paperback edition)
ISBN 978 1 78463 312 7 (Electronic edition)

Typeset in Neacademia by Salt Publishing

Printed and bound in Great Britain by Clays Ltd, Elcograf S.p.A

# CONTENTS

# PROLOGUE

*I rise out of myself and hover above my body on the kitchen table so I can watch what the doctor is doing. I am the hummingbird of colours no one should see, new colours painted on snow-soft feathers. Now I can watch the rolls of cotton wool the doctor keeps dabbing at my body, how they are smeared with sunrise.*

*It is dawn and I am escaping into the red mist my six-year-old self sees when she opens her eyes, the shimmer of dots, the walls of tree-doors that keep opening and closing, that bang and creak in the breeze. I can fly so fast that my wings blur. I can fly backwards, sideways, and on the spot. The doctor swats at me but cannot catch me. I can drink the nectar of my child-self's body. She thinks she is a flower that someone has plucked, petal by petal, until all that's left is the pistil.*

*She thinks the whole Amazon basin is a childhood. In the beginning, in the darkest part of the forest, Papa came up to her bed and forced his tongue between her teeth. She clenched her jaw and her front tooth cracked, the sides of her mouth split.*

*Later, the hummingbird will stitch her wounds with cobwebs, weave a nest in her mouth and in the secret places between her legs. She will mend every tear with moss and eagle down feathers, with leaf veins and hairs of the sleep sloth.*

*'Tukui,' she whispers, and her hummingbird listens.*

*I call the black jaguar with his coat of exploding stars – my new night, velvet-furred and smelling of moonlight through leaves. I call my white jaguar smelling of morning steam from the earth floor. I call my owl monkeys and they hoot an alarm. The pygmy marmoset crawls out from my hair. The ceiling echoes with scarlet macaws, their tails streaming behind them like fresh blood.*

*My parents' kitchen disappears when they come. Papa vanishes like morning mist wiped by sunrays. The doctor closes the door after him. He wonders if I am dead, this child he's wrapped in gauze like a bride, this girl with a face like a smashed mirror. The one who will never be able to bear children. He's stitched her with spider silk and orchid roots. He's used all his animal helpers. There is nothing left in his rattlebag, so he says a prayer and leaves.*

*Now I am in the forest of perpetual childhood. Now I can start painting my animals, animals no human has seen before. Their names are pain and beauty, hunger and camouflage. They hunt each other through the understorey. They climb the minds of trees.*

*I am releasing them into the canopy of my canvas.*

# PART ONE

# THE FACE IN THE FALLS

1997

T HE GIANT FACE that appears in the waterfall is her father's; Dominique knows this even though she has not seen him since she was a child. He turns from one side to the other, showing her each profile buffeted by gusts from the world's highest torrent. The scattershot spray around him is his sheet. He must be ill – his eyes are closed.

She is sitting on a high stool in a rough church, the wall behind the altar is missing, and it's here that she can see the tumbling veils of Angel Falls. Though they do not tumble, they hover in a white mist of micro-bullets. They spit like a white *tigre*, as glacial eyes open to meet hers. She realises that the falls are silent, because after the drop of almost one mile, all water has evaporated. She watches the meteors of spray rise back up and explode.

Two years have passed since she first saw Angel Falls. She has even canoed to the base. But this dream, she realises as she wakes, tells her she longs to return, and the dream will recur, but never show her her father again. Instead, she will climb Devil's Mountain, the tabletop *tepui* they drop from, that the Pemón people call Auyán-tepui – the House of the Devil. And she will dream of the summit, a vast fissured sandstone moonscape with its own life forms. She will dream of a school in one of the valleys, and she'll wake homesick for this uninhabitable place.

But what she has to paint is that face. It is not a human face and yet it is electrifying as that *tigre*, her mythical white jaguar, and terrifying as an angel. Yet how can that be? Is her father dead?

What she has to paint is how a week later, a letter will arrive from a father she has not heard from for thirty years. When she goes to meet him, he will tell her that a week before she received that letter, he lay in bed and could not sleep, tormented, having made one of his rare sorties from his apartment, to the hospital that day, where the consultant had given him the prognosis that he would live for only two more years at the most.

'As soon as my lawyer's office opened, I phoned him and had him come to see me, to send you the letter, letting you know where I live, asking you to come. You don't mind?' he will ask her. 'Are you angry with me? I had to have peace of mind, to make up for the lost years.'

The lost years.

Her dream of his face after years of not allowing herself to think of her lost father. He appears in the wildest place on earth, and even before the lawyer writes that her father is ill, Dominique knows, because she's seen it in her dream. She saw the face in torment, and its thoughts spat at her. She woke with intense longing, like being in love. But she cannot be in love because this man is her father. But that's what it will feel like – this summoning out of the blank.

## 2

# THE LETTER

THE LETTER TREMBLES in Dominique's hand as if she's holding Angel Falls – a kilometre-long cataract shrunk to the size of a page. She folds the letter and it's like trying to hold an archangel's wing in her palm. She unfolds it and it fills the room. She's creased it so many times that one line of Father's address is faint. What if her tears blur his phone number?

Now she's dressing, no time for breakfast. She's running for the tube to the French Consulate, which closes for emergencies at noon. They must renew her passport; she'll make them do it.

Now she has her passport and she's running back home, to the phone, to let him know she's coming.

A week ago, she dreamt of him: she was back in Venezuela, at the base of Angel Falls. His face appeared titanic in the tumbling comets. She looked into the vapour as his face dissolved and reformed. First, she saw the lace of a wedding-veil, shreds of skin behind a veil, then his face turned towards her, and she saw her father.

Dominique dials the number and listens to his phone ringing, and in the pause as she waits for him to answer there is this sound – far away and very near, as if she's also got the Amazon on the line. A series of low grunts inside her ear, then an icy roar – deeper and longer than a jaguar's. Howler monkeys swing through the space between them while time drops in light-year-long arrows. And she can wait. She has already waited thirty years. She is not afraid. Then a voice – French, formal, familiar, from the slash-and-burn past:

'I have thought of you every day,' he says. It's in French, so she has to check she's heard right.

He repeats, 'I have thought of you every day, *chérie.*'

Dominique tries to absorb this word as he asks, 'What time will you arrive?'

'I'm catching the Eurostar tomorrow at ten,' she says.

'Can't you come this evening?' he asks.

'I have to pack!' she explains. And she has to tint her hair and wash and dry her best clothes. And there is a mask she has to conjure, to hide her hunting-face.

When Dominique first arrived at the foot of Angel Falls, she was feverish. She camped in a tent on Raton Island. Before dawn she was up and out, in time for the first rays to pierce the saddle between Sun and Moon Mountains and hit the falls so they shone like fire. She stared at them transfixed as mist tumbled slowly, then rose back up and vibrated in the morning steam rising from the treetops, before it disintegrated and fell in forests of foam. If the falls look supernatural in ordinary light, they were now god-like, imprinted on her retina.

She will visit him with that letter lighting up her face – the world's wonder as her bridal veil. She will wear this Amazonian armour and it will be frozen at first, even though she's at the equator of her life. After a few hours sitting opposite Father – after he has answered some of her questions – her angel-veil will start to thaw. Behind it will be her rose-quartz face, blinding in the dawn light, like a mirror where he will catch glimpses of himself behind the shreds of glitter. The ice will heat up under the morning rays. The released vapour from her bride-visor will sting him. Gradually, he will see small black words in the falling haze, a life he must translate.

When Dominique reaches the Gare-du-Nord she rushes to the toilet and makes herself up, as if she's painting the cliff behind Angel Falls with foundation, highlighter, concealer, blusher, copper eye shadow. The full works. She wants him to regret not having known her. What time did she tell him she'd arrive? She can't rush. She must look her best. The light is so bright there are spots in front of her eyes, but it's a harsh light; she's not slept. Her eyes are puffy. How she wishes he could have seen her when she was younger.

The taxi stalls. She's going to be late. Let him wait! She keeps folding and unfolding the lawyer's letter as they cross the Seine by Notre-Dame into the Boulevard Saint-Michel:

> Yesterday I went to meet your father, Abel Emmanuel Grandin, in his home. Despite the many years of his disappearance, he asked me to come to Paris urgently to see him so he can make contact with you.

> Your father understands perfectly that your first reaction might be surprise and anger but he wants to put his life in order. He is dying.

> He wants you to visit him. He has asked me to give you his address. Here is his phone number. He would be so happy to hear from you.

As they enter the Quartier Latin, the taxi driver asks if she's visiting Paris for the first time. She explains she was born here and is coming back to meet her father who she hasn't seen since she was seven. He catches her face in his mirror as he says, 'Your father must be well off – this is a smart area.'

They draw to a halt at 7, rue Clovis.

Dominique glances up at the windows in case he can already see her. She pictures him looking out for her from his elegant apartment and can't believe she will soon be up there. She tries to look composed. It's hard to pay, as her whole body is shaking.

She pulls out the instructions Father has given her for entering his apartment block – the code to the courtyard gate, the number of his flat, the code she must key in at the outer door. But his name isn't on the panel. She rings other names. It's 3:15, siesta time and maybe no-one's home. She tries the concierge as Father had suggested, but there's no answer. Has she got the right address? She tries the second building and rereads Father's instructions, but they still don't make sense. Then she realises there's a fourth building at the far back of the courtyard. And there, in a bank of buttons next to the glass outer door, is his flat number, with his name. She presses it.

His voice!

She answers, 'It's me – Dominique!' She keys in the new code he gives her. The door clicks open and she hesitates. There's a frantic shadow at the top, attached to a lead, and she can hear whimpering, but he darts back in without realising she's seen him. She leaps up the short flight of stairs.

His apartment door is ajar and there he is – small, thin, in silk pyjamas and a bronze paisley dressing gown. She shakes his hand. He hugs her, pressing himself against her body. It gives her an electric shock. It's too soon for hugging. She notices the plastic tubes dangling from his nostrils, and how breathless he is. He is taking short desperate gasps before he can speak.

'Come in. It's a jungle!' he grins, waving around his room.

There is nowhere for her to sit. The room is tiny and chock-full of furniture and heaped boxes. She takes a narrow pathway through the clutter, as she has taken jungle paths. She is wearing her angel-veil and through it everything looks misty.

Dominique pulls out a hard-backed chair from under a pile of old newspapers and sits facing him. He hauls himself into his red armchair; a pink pillow propped behind his back. Between them there's a small table piled with cooking appliances and medicines. To her right is his narrow bed by the corridor wall.

'Let's eat,' he says. 'I didn't have lunch because I was waiting for you and I'm about to faint! You're very late.'

She glances at her watch and realises she forgot about Paris being one hour ahead. He obviously needs to eat. She's hungry too, but not yet ready to eat with him. She wants to sit and talk. But all he says as he serves the microwaved meal is, 'Wait . . .' and tries to catch his breath. This is what he will always say when she asks a question, but she does not yet know this. For now, she thinks he is going to talk until everything comes right.

While he is panting for air, she becomes aware of a pumping noise, she can't yet tell where from, it vibrates through her chair and up her spine. Later, she will locate the oxygen recycler – a machine inside his door-less toilet just by the front door.

He offers her vintage pink champagne and tells her he has had three crates delivered to celebrate her arrival. His eyes sparkle as he leans back to say, 'I didn't know if you'd come or not. I thought you might be cross with me. Are you angry?'

'Yes. But it doesn't matter now,' she reassures him. 'I've always wanted to have a father.'

He struggles with the cork, stopping every few seconds to pant, but won't let her help him. She waits patiently then asks what his days are like. Can he go out? He looks so alone, like a wolf in a forgotten corner of a zoo. It's hard to hear him say he hasn't left his flat for two years. She could have been visiting him all along! Every three months an ambulance takes him to hospital to see his consultant. These are his only outings. 'I can see the trees through the ambulance window. If it's spring, there's blossom. If it's winter, there's sometimes snow on the branches of the Bois de Boulogne,' he says, stopping to cough, '. . . though they look the same to me . . . my only glimpse of the outside world, apart from this window here.'

Dominique glances out. 'At least there's a fir,' she says.

'All I can see from here is this tree and those buildings and this section of the old Paris wall. Look – '

Dominique takes in his only view bleached by the late September sunlight. She's relieved to hear a home help comes every weekday to wash up and do his shopping, and asks, 'Do any friends visit?'

'No,' he replies. 'Not anymore. I lost touch with them little by little. I'm too proud. I didn't want them to feel sorry for me. Even my old pal, Pierre Oudin, whom I've known since the brasserie days, he was the last to come and I told him not to bother again. That was two years ago.'

He reaches across the small table and gives her his hand.

Because the angel mask guards her, she can touch him. She can let him hold her hand and she can let their hands lie there on the table while he looks into her, trying to glimpse beyond the tumbling falls of her face.

When a huntress first encounters someone else in the forest, she hears twigs snapping. The sound echoes from trunk to trunk. Time slows to a standstill. Beams slant in through leaves, splash her shoulders. Then fear comes, like a pump in the corner of a room. The huntress realises she is not in the forest of her father – she is *in* her father. He has swallowed her.

'Are you disappointed?' he asks. She is disappointed that his place is so shabby and cramped, but how can she be when she's met her father and there's light dancing around them? He fumbles with a package meal he's kept warm, and she tries to eat. 'I didn't have time to order proper food,' he apologises. 'But tomorrow Lucienne will bring some nice meals for us.

'With your big brown eyes, you look like my Bambi, *ma p'tite bichette*,' he says, looking right into her.

Did he call her his little fawn? Dominique looks down at her plate and the pattern starts marching towards her in rows of red ants. They crawl up her arms and neck into her mouth. They tickle her gullet and make her choke on her food. They swarm over her hot face. She tries to flick the burning ants off. Then he wipes his mouth with his serviette and smiles.

She takes the plates away, glad for an opportunity to escape, and retches into the sink. What just happened?

When she comes back in, she worries about where she's going to sleep since there's only one room, and eventually plucks up the courage to ask, then is alarmed when he suggests she sleep in his bed while he uses his armchair. Much to her relief, he decides that's not a good idea. She could stay in a local hotel, so he searches for numbers. 'Do you have a room for a little one?' Father pleads with the sixth, but they are all full. 'It's because of the fashion fair,' he apologises, going through the phone numbers on his list. 'Perhaps you'll have to stay here after all.'

'Ah . . .' he corrects himself, 'she's not a child, she's a young woman – she was *ma petite fillette* . . . but I am your neighbour. I'm just around the corner from you. Can you take care of her?' At last, it seems there's a room.

'I keep thinking you're a child,' he turns to her, chuckling. 'How old are you now?'

'Thirty-seven.'

'Oh! You must be married then?'

'I was, but I'm divorced now. I've been on my own for five years.'

'Do you have children?'

'No,' she says. He looks disappointed. She's relieved they've found a room. He isn't well enough to spend the night in his chair, and she's scared to spend the night with a stranger. It's unthinkable.

After his exertions on the phone, he slips into bed and she goes to the kitchenette to wash the dishes. She comes back in and settles in his armchair, studying the room, the boxes with medical labels piled to the ceiling, the nicotine-stained wallpaper, brown in the corners. She swings round and takes a long look at her father. He's even thinner than she thought. She follows the tubes from his nostrils to the machine by the door and finds his toilet. Dare she have a pee? There's no door, just the screen of a wall and she's too shy. She's dying for a cup of tea but there's no kettle, so she heats up a pan of water and searches the cupboards for tea and sugar.

'What have you got there?' Father asks, as she creeps back in.

'A mug of tea,' she answers. 'Would you like one?'

'No, I don't drink tea and can't have coffee, it's bad for my heart. You're so English with your tea!' He presses a button and the upper part of his bed rises. 'It's an electric bed,' he explains. 'I treated myself for my last birthday.'

She tries to plump up his pillows, and sits back down feeling awkward. His eyes keep closing. Maybe it's time to go. Dominique picks up her bags and kisses him on both cheeks. His eyes fill as he asks, 'You will come back tomorrow, won't you?'

⁂

As soon as she's closed the outer door behind her, Dominique takes a deep breath and orients herself, peering at his map. It's been the strangest day of her life, yet everything in the street looks normal, people going about their business. She makes her way to the Hôtel St Jacques in the rue des Écoles. Her room is up a twisting staircase to a sixth-floor attic. She sinks onto the bed and writes in her journal: *There's a cold sensation in my stomach I can't explain.* But her face is still burning.

# 3

# GIANT ANTEATER FATHER

*F*OR A WHOLE *year I am quiet as a flower. Birds come and go, dipping their long beaks into me. They speak petal, nectar, anther. My lips are honeyguides. My body thins to a stem.*

*The bees of memory come; the bumble bees hum a tune too deep for human ears. They land on my cheeks and crawl down my neck, emerge with full pollen baskets. All day long they turn pollen to medicine.*

*If I don't move, they think my face is a flower. I have learnt to keep quiet so they can work undisturbed.*

*Someone is drawing me. I want to ask: please draw me some eyes. I have been a mouth too long. My bed is the soil. I long to become human, but then the bees will stop visiting. Flowers don't remember the winter when they died. They resurrect with wiped minds.*

*Whole months of my childhood are blank.*

*Out of the blank wide as a Gran Sabana, the giant anteater comes, shuffling on his knuckles with his scimitar claws that can disembowel a jaguar with one stroke. He ambles towards a termite mound and pushes his long snout down a ventilation shaft, his sticky tongue ransacks the galleries.*

When he appears I become a fawn, father's little bichette, not much stronger than a flower, but at least I can run!

I run and run, searching for my mother, until I'm weak and collapse. That's when the fire ants climb up me. They swarm on my face and crawl into my mouth. My throat is on fire.

There's only one way to survive. I call the giant anteater and he comes. He is all alone on the Gran Sabana. He waves his flag of a tail as if to say, 'I'm coming to save you!'

I see his curved claws, his long snout. He approaches and I back away. 'I've come to save you!' he says, 'let me kiss your face fragrant as a flower.'

And before I can say no, his snout is in my mouth, licking the sides of my gullet, flicking all around my stomach. I see his small black eyes as he feasts, the way they close in pleasure.

## 4

# STICK INSECT FATHER

T HE NEXT MORNING, Dominique heads to the Jardin des Plantes, as her father told her to come for a late lunch – he feels too ill for visitors in the mornings. She strolls down the rue Linné and through the gold and green iron gates of the Jardin and makes for the Ménagerie, past marguerites and late sunflowers where she pauses, touching their burnt faces big as hers. She enters the zoo past the deer and their fawns, the sandy path crunches reassuringly and there's still dew on the railings. This is where he used to take her when she was little, he will tell her this afternoon, but for now it's hers. Hardly anyone else is here.

The first animal she sees is the racoon-like coati who, according to Amazonian myth, stole the world's first colours and gave them to the birds so they could paint their feathers. Alone in the small mammal house, it feels as if *she's* stolen the world's colours; everything looks fresh now that she's met her father. She makes for the Palais des Reptiles and finds a rainbow boa in a glass case. The last one she saw was on the highway to El Dorado, twisted across the sun-drenched asphalt, its spine run over in several places. This one is curled into a ball. His black mother-of-pearl scales rise and fall gently in his sleep.

At the centre of the Palais is a large glass tank filled with branches labelled 'Les Phasmes'. And there he is – her stick-insect father. She could break the glass and take him home in her coat pocket. Even customs would think he was a dead twig – he who has thought of her every day of his life.

# 5

# TASTE

*I AM FILLING my sketchbook with carnivorous leaves, a jungle under the magnifying lens of my eyes. The stems are giant stick insects of Papa's limbs. I wait for them to betray themselves by turning their faces to look at me. One leaf is a praying mantis with a hummingbird in her jaws. She chews, turning her great green eyes towards me, as if to say – look what you've drawn!*

*I watch as she nibbles the hummingbird's cheeks then saws through its brain. Now the hummingbird won't feel any more pain.*

*I am in the palace of carnivory. Papa's chair is ruby, veined green like a giant pitcher plant digesting him in its juices. His room is a swamp where leaves turn into insects and insects turn into leaves. I sit opposite him and have to watch him get thinner, my father with his lungs like burnt rafters in a green cathedral, his helper animals leaping along flying buttresses, green light filtering down from clerestories of the canopy where his fan whirrs.*

*He releases cages of songbirds to celebrate my arrival. They sing old nursery rhymes in time to the oxygen recycler. A parakeet squawks in a lost language. I think he has my father's voice – the rainforest at dawn, his words nesting in tree-holes lined with my baby hair as the smell of petrichor rises from the floor.*

*I am the tobacco shaman's daughter, I light a cigar and place the burning tip to their tails, their colours that streak through the room like flames. Their charred corpses litter his floor.*

# 6

# LUNGS

'TWO YEARS, MY doctor's given me,' he'd announced, after telling Dominique about the emphysema. 'But it could be any day. How often will you visit?'

'I'll have to think about it,' she'd answered. 'I'll let you know later, when it's sunk in. I'm so surprised to be here, but you don't feel like my father.'

He'd looked worried then.

'Thirty years is a long time,' she'd continued. 'I didn't expect to ever see you again. I didn't even let myself think about you. I believed you never thought about me. You couldn't have, you never wrote.'

'I tried to,' he'd protested, 'but your mother threw them away!'

'D'you know what it was like, getting that letter from the lawyer?' Dominique had said. 'My life will never be the same, now I know the impossible can happen.'

'Can I see his letter?' Father had asked. Dominique kept it in her pocket, but she didn't want to show it to him. If she'd unfolded its archangel wing in his flat, the feathers might have got dirty.

She's come to the Ménagerie to think. She can't just love him automatically. She can only like or dislike him. She thinks she likes him, but what is this cold sensation in her gut? Why did her face catch fire when he stared at her? Maybe she's just disorientated. She can be Daddy's girl now if she wants. But when he gasps and groans for air, she doesn't know where to look.

'Papa!' she cries out, seeing the time. She must hurry or she'll be late again.

Today she's going to ask him why he wouldn't let her contact him before, she promises herself as she presses his bell.

His voice crackles on the intercom. She still can't believe how familiar it is.

'It's me – Domino,' she answers.

'Come up!' he says.

She bounds up the stairs for the second time. There's his door. It's just an ordinary wooden door. But as she waits for Father to make his way towards her, it grows into a forest. When it opens, the Animal Master stands before her, one hand on his chest, straining to hold every last inch of air in his lungs.

He hugs her, and this time she doesn't get a shock. She can be hugged like this every day. She follows him down the path. Sunshine is pouring through the window. Dare she open it? She is one of the daughters of the world now. She struggles with the catch and it's stiff, but she persists, even though Father has started huffing. She turns to face him and smiles. It works, he smiles back and she looks for her chair.

He reminds her of the spirits the Pemón Indians say go to live inside the table-mountain after their death. That's where the Animal Master lives with his were-animals. That's why the oxygen concentrator pumps away in a corner of the room. They are in the heart of a mountain.

'How are you today?' she asks.

'Much better,' he says. 'Yesterday I was anxious and it was damp. Fog is the worst. When it's sunny like this, my lungs are clearer and it doesn't hurt so much to breathe.'

She can't imagine it hurting to breathe. It must be like trying to wade through rock. That's what ghosts do – pass through walls. She steals a glance at his body through the dressing gown and asks, 'Papa, why are you so thin?'

'My body doesn't get the oxygen it needs,' he explains. 'Only one of my lungs works properly, and even that's clogged up. Half of the right one has been cut out. They operated on it fifteen years ago. That's why I have to lie on my left side, because the right ribs are still sore from when they sawed through them.'

Dominique looks at his right side and sees the surgeon sawing a branch from a rotten tree. 'Did it help?' she asks.

'Not for long,' he says. 'I've slowly got worse. I could get about at first. I carried on with my work, and the *mairie* moved me to this room. I have to have an oxygen machine, but I also had a portable one then. So before, I could go out to the local shops trailing my oxygen on wheels!'

She pictures him trailing his oxygen, stopping to chat to neighbours. 'That must have been hard,' she says, 'but at least you could go out and get some air and meet people.'

'People? No one comes here now. That's why my toilet doesn't have a door – no one visits. The flat doesn't have a bathroom because I don't need one, I can't take a shower. Steam suffocates me.'

'So how do you manage?' she asks.

'The daily comes and washes me with moisturising wipes. I'm like a prisoner!' Dominique imagines Lucienne washing his naked body. 'But tell me what you've been doing this morning,' he asks, beaming.

She realises she can bring the outside world to him and chatters excitedly, describing the herd of deer at the entrance, the coati's antics, the parrot house, and the wolf enclosure at the far end of the zoo. Father gets animated then, telling her about the dogs he's owned. And does she remember the white poodle pup he bought Maman as a Christmas present, a little ball of fluff that cheered her up? But Dominique's still thinking about his dogs. Where did he live? 'Won't you tell me what you did, all those years?' she asks.

'Oh, I can't remember,' he sighs. 'It's muddled and I can only talk about it bit by bit as it occurs to me and as we chat. Let's eat – I'm starving. Then I'll tell you more.'

'Shall I cook something?' she asks.

'No,' he says, 'Lucienne has already prepared quails for us. Do you like quail?'

After they've eaten the birds, he shuffles down the path towards the kitchenette, stopping every few steps to catch his breath, perches on a stool and opens the fridge, inviting her over to sit beside him. Light pours on both their faces. Their cheeks touch. 'Tell me what you'd like for dessert, my little girl,' he asks. 'Ice cream? Ah, but I almost forgot! We have some petits fours.'

'What's that?'

'But you're not really French!' he protests. 'Oh, English food . . .' and he sniggers.

'But if I'm not French enough, then it's your fault!' she snaps, pulling away from him and almost tipping the stool over. 'I was only seven when you left. You haven't explained why you didn't come again.' The words have come out too fierce and he's coughing, loses his balance. She grabs his arm – has she spoilt everything? What if he fell?

She fetches the petits fours and Father divides them onto two plates – six each. Dominique bites into the first, still sulking, but her anger melting away with the flavour. They sit gorging and sip champagne until the room tilts. He looks relaxed and off his guard. Now she can make him talk. 'Tell me about your life with Maman,' she asks.

'I lived in a pension in the Boulevard Saint-Germain,' he says. 'She was so impressed. Django Reinhardt lived two doors down at the Hôtel Crystal.'

'Django Reinhardt?'

'Yes,' he boasts. 'I'd really lived, knew everyone in the neighbourhood – all the jazz musicians, and she was a naïve country girl who knew nothing about the ways of the world. She was a virgin.'

Dominique can feel her face burning again. Should she storm out? But if she did, she knows she could never return, and she has so many questions, so she changes the subject. 'Did we really live above a brasserie?'

'Of course,' he says. 'And the brasserie was ours. We sold beer to the Algerians. We were the only ones who would do business with them. D'you remember?'

'No, I don't remember anything!' she says, her voice shaking.

'Your mother could work harder than any man,' he says, '– she could load the beer barrels onto the lorries, even when she was pregnant with you.'

'Well, I know that,' Dominique says, 'because she told me you made her do all the work!'

'What do you mean?' he asks.

'Maman said *she* had to run the business,' Dominique insists, 'because you were still in bed at noon, spent afternoons making yourself pretty, that you'd be out all night at the casino.'

'But that's not true!' he shouts, grasping his chest.

'How can I believe you though?' Dominique says. 'Maman said she was trying to get rid of me, to miscarry!'

'There was the Algerian War, and the business collapsed,' he replies. 'Your mother lost confidence in me. That's what happened.'

'Oh!' Dominique says. 'Was that what happened? Did Maman make it up?'

'I don't know what your maman told you,' Papa says, 'but you must believe me! Think what would've been if we hadn't gone bust. You'd have grown up in Paris with me.' And he smiles.

Dominique can see Father is chauvinistically French and is glad she didn't grow up with him. How would she have turned out? Would she still have become an artist? Or would she have had to get a job? The prospect makes her feel trapped. But it's strange to think about this other person she should have become.

'I met your mother in the hotel where she was working as head maid,' he continues. 'I took her up to one of the rooms that were waiting to be cleaned and threw her on the bed and made love to her then and there. Before she could say no. It surprised her!'

'You did what . . . ?' Dominique asks.

'She was too pretty, with her peach cheeks and red ringlets in a halo around her face. I couldn't wait,' he boasts. Father's face has just got bigger, closer. The ice has rushed back to her stomach and she needs to go to the toilet but can't because there's no door between it and him. An image bursts into her head of the toilet they once had, with its hole in the floor, and walls painted dark red.

'What d'you mean you couldn't wait?' she asks.

'Your mother was too pretty and there was the bed . . .'

'I don't want to hear any of this!' Dominique shouts. But Father is clutching his chest again and coughing. *Please let me get back to how I felt before. Please,* she tells herself, *put your angel mask back on.*

Father has a coughing fit. 'You mustn't upset me, my heart is weak,' he pleads, 'because of the lungs. I only really loved her. The other women were just for hygiene.'

'Hygiene? What an odd expression.'

'Oh,' he shrugs, 'a man must have sex to keep healthy. As for my second wife, after your mother threw me out, I was on the rebound. That only lasted a year.'

Dominique doesn't want to stay any longer but knows he'd be hurt if she left so early, and there's still a question she's got to ask, 'Do I have half-brothers and sisters?'

'No,' he replies. 'There's only you and Veronique. I didn't want other children if I couldn't have you.'

She's both disappointed and relieved. She isn't sure she was prepared to meet new siblings. But what if she'd had a brother? Father rustles a paper bag on the table and takes out some pills. He looks tired and she'll go soon, but before she does, she wants to show him her paintings. She wants him to see how special she is.

She takes out a small lightbox from her bag and inserts the first slide. 'Ah flowers . . .' he says, 'I've always loved flowers.'

'It's a moonflower from the Amazon cloud forest,' she begins. 'Its pollinator is a hawkmoth with a really long tongue – two feet long.'

'No!'

'Yes, and it can only be pollinated one night in its life, when the moon is full. It has a powerful scent. The petals are pure white and translucent, with that green interior. I've seen one myself.'

'You've been to the Amazon?'

'Yes, twice already, to the most beautiful place on Earth. And I'm going again very soon.'

'So – you have some spirit?'

'Oh yes, I have spirit,' she answers. She shows him her painting of a ruby topaz hummingbird, its wings an explosive blur. 'They take two hundred breaths per minute, and that's just when they're resting,' she tells him, then realises it was tactless. But she will show him her triptych of Angel Falls. She pushes the slide into the light-box and pauses, holding it at first so only she can see it – her Lost World towering above rainforest. She strokes the treetops and the three views of its waters. 'This is the hardest piece I've ever done,' she tells him. 'I had to use gold leaf for the falls at sunrise, fire opal for the quartz façade behind them.' She can see he's interested and is making a big effort between breaths.

'I called my triptych one of their Pemón names – *Churún-Vená*.'

'Pemón?' he asks.

'Yes,' she says, 'they're the people that live in the Gran Sabana around the giant plateaux.' He looks puzzled but she continues. 'I worked on the three of them together. When I was concentrating, my paintbrush worked by itself.' She passes the lightbox to him. He looks impressed and peers through his glasses, wrinkling up his face to look closer. He's still handsome, with his eagle nose and large brown eyes magnified by glasses. Reflections of her colours flick over his cheeks giving them a flush so that he almost looks healthy.

'You're very clever,' he says. 'I'm proud of having a painter as a daughter.'

He's proud of her! All the flowers in his faded wallpaper have opened. Dominique thinks she must have misheard about his first date with Maman. Perhaps he was provoking her to get a reaction? Perhaps she will come at Christmas. It might be the last before he dies.

'Just before I go, there's one more painting I want to show you,' she says.

'Only one, *chérie* . . . I must have my nap now.'

'I only did it last week,' she says. 'The paint was still wet when I took this slide. It's Angel Falls again, but about a dream I had.' She slips the slide into the lightbox and hesitates, then thrusts it into his face, almost regretting it because he looks pained.

'But it's me,' he whispers. 'How did you know what I look like?' She stares at her painting and feels ashamed.

'I saw you in a dream. You were in the waterfall.'

'A week ago? That's not possible . . .' he says.

'I don't know why I dreamt about the falls or you,' she says. 'I never even thought about you. I wouldn't allow myself to.'

'How did you know I had emphysema?'

'I didn't. I saw you in the dream and when I woke I knew I had to paint you, even though it was the middle of the night. And when I started this is what came. I called it *The Summoning*.'

Papa frowns. 'But that must have been just before I asked the lawyer to write to you,' he says. 'I'd had a sleepless night and it was then, during that night I decided to contact you. I called him first thing and he came up to see me a few days later.'

He's floating upright in the mist that billows around him like swirling sheets. His chest is clamped open – the ribs parted to expose his heart and blackened lungs. Dominique thinks he's not so clever now. If he shocked her, she's now shocked him. She glances from Papa to the painting and back again. It's an exact likeness.

# 7

# HUMMINGBIRD FATHER

F OR THE SECOND morning she wakes and tells herself, *I have met my father.* For the second time she feels something is wrong and pushes it aside. She opens the blue and white gingham curtains of the small attic window that overlooks the courtyard. It's sunny and she's free until one when he wants her to come for lunch. She orders café au lait and croissants in her room and writes in her journal:

When the sun went in and storm clouds massed above Devil's Mountain, I could see Angel Falls was a hostile place. I scrambled up the slippery black rocks of the lookout point near its base and stared into the amphitheatre of swirling mists, my cheeks stinging from needle spray. Black clouds obscured the kilometre-high rim as the river at the base began to rise. Thunder seemed to come from the falls themselves then, and from the torrents and rapids of the river that I had to climb away from fast. I rushed down Churún River, back to Raton Island, before the falls swelled to fill the whole amphitheatre.

Papa is much too ill for confrontation. I can't just sit in front of him like a thundercloud. When I get back home I'll paint our conversation, and that's how I'll manage to be nice to him, the painting will be a storm-mask, and underneath the veil Father's face will appear, pierced by arrows of spray, like one of those voodoo dolls stuck with pins.

When she steps out onto the rue des Écoles, the cobbled pavements and the crooked back alleys are the maze of paths she saw from the Cessna as she flew over the labyrinthine plateau of Auyán-tepui.

She can't be in love with her father, but who can stop her? No one else knows he exists. When she gets back to London, she'll phone her sister and tell her what he's like, but until then she is his one and only. He told her she was his favourite and she thinks this is fair since Veronique was always Maman's.

She's surprised at how much she likes Paris. All her life she's remembered it as grey: the stone school where she was bullied, the cellar there and at home. And there are those flashes in the grey, like Papa trying to mend the TV. She can still remember the smell of burning, that lightning flash in their room, Papa thrown backwards onto his heels when it blew up, his hair standing on end.

Her memories of him are so few. All that's left are the stories Vero and she used to repeat to each other so that one day someone would believe them. But as the years passed and Paris faded, they had to admit they could no longer remember the real memories. All they could remember was what they had said the last time they had told them to each other. Paris was the place they were threatened to be sent back to when they were naughty, where there were no fields to play in. And what else was it she was so frightened of? Whatever it was, it was so bad that Dominique had not returned to Paris until now.

The sunlight in the rue des Écoles clears the fears away. This is the adult city now. She crosses the Boulevard Saint-Germain and heads towards the Seine, through a maze of even narrower cobbled back streets where medieval windows on third floors lean and almost touch. It must have rained during the night because the walls and pavements are steaming. The quaint rue de la Huchette is busy with tourists, but even though she dislikes crowds she walks along it, laughing at an alley called the rue du Chat-qui-Pêche, through which she can see the bouquinistes along the Seine.

Her very last memory of Papa before he vanished was of fishing with him. All that morning, he hadn't spoken to them as he waited for a catch, and Vero and she had grown bored and cold. She can still remember how oblivious he was, as they grew more and more desperate to pee until they had to shake his arm. How he'd just looked at them and asked if they could hold it until he'd caught his third fish. There were marguerites by the riverbank and in the end she'd crouched behind them, worried because the flowers weren't tall enough to hide her.

Whenever she'd looked up into his eyes as they walked home that afternoon, all she'd seen were the rapids, the stones, and currents too swift to wade in, where he still seemed to be searching for fish. This man, who had been their father all that summer, left later that afternoon without saying goodbye, while they were up in their rooms supposed to be having a nap.

She notices a hotel on the corner called Les Argonautes, rings the bell and is let in to the lobby where there are safari chairs and a chaise longue with jaguar skin upholstery, but is too shy to ask how much the rooms cost. Just around the corner is the quai Saint-Michel where stalls are selling the sepia books they have always sold. And there's the Seine, with Notre-Dame across the water, a few of its gargoyles spouting the last trickles of rainwater like the ephemeral falls on Auyán-tepui after rain.

Paris is hers now, not Papa's. He will never go out again. But as she crosses rue du Cardinal Lemoine to the boulangerie, she thinks she glimpses him dragging the portable oxygen cylinder on his last outing to buy bread. She enters the baker's and buys the baguette Viennoise he requested, holding back an urge to ask the assistant if she can remember him from two years ago.

Dominique pops back to her room to freshen up, peering into the magnifying-mirror. She tries sharpening her eyeliner pencil, blends two lipsticks to get the right shade, but it's no good. She sprays Shalimar on, wondering if Papa will recognise it and think of Maman. She grabs her photo albums, camera, bread – and she's ready for him.

Now that she knows the secret code to his building, his outer door springs open to her touch. He's given her the key to his apartment so she lets herself in, rattling it in the lock to give him warning. But he's waiting for her, sitting up in his red armchair, a big smile on his face. 'Ah! Lucienne has prepared lunch for us,' he says. 'You're just in time for hors d'oeuvre.'

She kisses him on both cheeks and perches in her chair while he sits smiling at her. 'This is the best weather for my lungs,' he says. 'On rainy days I stay in bed all day. But today, the sun is shining and now that you are here I feel a lot better. You are my new medicine.'

The cannula in his nostrils still shocks. She realises he can't smell perfume because he's breathing bottled oxygen. He looks regal sitting straight with his serviette tucked into his silk pyjamas. She fetches the champagne out of the fridge and gulps hers, thirsty after hours of walking. Father isn't huffing as much as usual, and her hopes are raised.

'Do you eat oysters?' he checks, frowning as he opens the fridge and brings out two plates, a dozen each on beds of ice and lemon, stopping every few seconds to catch his breath.

'Yes,' she says, prising one from its shell, but it won't free and she feels clumsy.

'This is how you do it,' he tells her. 'Let your father show you. Just do as you're told, like a good girl.' And he wags a teasing finger at her.

She's eaten them before and is annoyed with herself for falling into his trap. She drains her glass and he pours her another. There's an awkward silence. Part of her is still outside, wandering through the streets, feeling free. But that's selfish, she decides, and launches into halting French chatter: 'I love the Quartier Latin . . . I had no idea Paris was so pretty.'

'It's my favourite quartier,' he says. 'I've lived here many years. It's a very historic area. Did you take a proper look at Philippe-Auguste's wall out in the courtyard? It's one of the very few sections left. It's wide enough for an army to walk along!'

'I looked at it on my way in,' she lies. 'Have you lived here long? Were you always in this flat?'

'Oh no,' he says, 'I was in with the mayor, and I always found rooms in the best places. But we all lived near here together once, just by the Jardin des Plantes, when you were very small – that's where our brasserie was. Even before that, your mother and I lived in a tiny upstairs *pension de famille* in the rue des Boulangers, over what's now an Irish pub.'

'Finnegans Wake? I saw it on my way to the Jardin des Plantes yesterday, just off the rue du Cardinal Lemoine. It's boarded up, but I noticed it because of James Joyce,' she says.

'Yes, that's it,' he says. 'Number 9, I think? That was the first place we had on our own, after the pension in the Boulevard Saint-Germain. We were in love then – so happy we didn't need more space. It was the height of the jazz age and I edited a printing press in a bookshop.'

'So, you were an editor?' she asks, surprised.

'Yes,' he says, 'I was the first to publish Boris Vian – you know, the poet and jazz critic. I knew everyone. That was before our beer business. Afterwards, when I came back to Paris, I lived in hotels nearby for years.'

'Hotels? When?'

'Before I got ill. Oh, that must be sixteen or eighteen years ago. I lived in a charming one called Les Argonautes in the rue de la Huchette . . . later, I lived in a better one, the Notre-Dame, for a few years.'

'I saw Les Argonautes this morning,' she says. 'Near that funny alley – rue du Chat-qui-Pêche.'

Papa laughs. 'Oh yes, the fishing cat, that's me. Fishing has been a great hobby of mine. There was a good jazz café there – Le Chat-qui-Pêche.'

'What work did you do there?'

'I fixed things for people,' he says. 'When shopkeepers were in trouble, I helped them out. I was in charge of the Protection of the

Riverbanks of the quai Saint-Michel. People came to me when they had problems. I was good at sorting things out and giving them advice – if they couldn't get building permission, or afford the rent, were going bust . . .'

Dominique can't imagine him being useful. There's so much she doesn't know. 'You helped them?' she asks.

'I could always help *them*,' he says, 'but couldn't sort out my own problems! But fetch the casserole Lucienne has cooked for us, it's time for our next course.'

Dominique rushes into the kitchenette and when she gets there, stands by the open window, breathing in the scent of pine from the fir out in the courtyard garden. She can see the medieval city wall blinding white in the sunlight. Her father, helping people all that time she needed him. He was living in a hotel the day she got married, when he should have given her away. That had been the only time she'd cried about not having a father. It almost ruined the day.

She goes to the sink to splash her face with water, and when she looks up there's a small mirror on the wall, so old the silvering shows through. She never cried about him again after that day. How could she? She could barely remember him. It feels wrong staring so long into his mirror, where once, when he was still well enough, he used to stand shaving. If she keeps looking, she'll pass into its quicksilver world, into a quartz kitchen.

She brings the casserole in and sits back down, unable to look at him.

'Don't you like deer, *ma bichette*?' he asks. 'This is jugged venison, with chestnuts and apple in a wine sauce, it should really be cooked in deer blood as well.'

'That sounds delicious,' she reassures him, though she's still not sure she wants to be called his little fawn. She doesn't say deer are her favourite animal. She eats in silence.

'Living in hotels was so convenient,' he continues after a few mouthfuls. 'No meals to cook, no cleaning, no laundry. Even my shoes were polished for me.'

She nods, trying to smile. She shows him the skirt she bought this morning in the rue de la Huchette, happy to find one she really liked. 'I bought this near here,' she says, standing up so he can see it.

He grins politely. 'Very *gitane* – your mother would have liked that too.'

Dominique sits back down and remembers wearing Maman's green gypsy dress, her prettiest outfit.

'But it's time for dessert,' Papa says. 'There are pears in syrup in the fridge. Can you bring them, and fetch the pear liqueur too. Is there anything else you'd like?'

'What I'd really like is a cup of tea,' she says. 'At home I drink tea all the time.'

'You found some in the cupboard, didn't you?' he asks. 'But you English take cold milk in your tea and I don't have milk. I can't eat dairy products because they give me catarrh. Fetch me the pan and I'll show you how to attach the handle, so it won't be *la Comédie Française* this time when you boil the water!'

Dominique brings the pan and makes her tea, then settles herself down again, happy that he's in a good mood.

'You will come again soon, won't you? Perhaps you could come once a fortnight and stay at the little hotel again? Is it nice? The manageress sounded cute on the phone. Is she?'

'Yes, she is very *mignonne* – blonde and *soignée*. But Papa I can't come every fortnight, I'm working towards my first one-woman show, there're still paintings for me to finish, and I have to go to Venezuela in a few weeks.'

'Why go to Venezuela? Come and see me instead.'

'You can't expect me to! You don't even feel like my father yet.'

'At least promise you'll come at Christmas then,' he pleads, pursing his lips to breathe hoarsely. 'I get the *cafards* then.'

She doesn't like to think of him depressed, but won't commit herself until she's sure. The oxygen machine sounds so loud now she thinks it must annoy his neighbours. Papa is panting, his face screwed up. 'I'll let you know when I get home, very soon,' she says.

'I need to see how I feel after I've got back and can think properly.'

Papa opens his mouth but splutters and ends up coughing.

Dominique feels bad now. 'I wish you'd tell me more about your life,' she asks. 'It would help persuade me.'

'Do you think Veronique . . . will come to see me?' he asks, puffing hard.

'Yes, I think she will. She works full time so it's harder for her to get away.'

'Why? Can't she take time off?' he asks.

'She has to see her son whenever she gets holidays,' Dominique says. 'Jack lives with his father quite far away and Vero has to drive there to collect him then drive him back.'

'I have a grandson?' Papa brightens and his breathing calms. 'How old is Jacques now?'

'His name's Jack, he's five,' she snaps, not wanting to talk about Vero or her son.

'But why doesn't he live with his mother?' he asks.

She's not sure how to answer this because she doesn't want to discuss Vero's problems before Vero's had a chance to meet him, so she just says she's not sure and he accepts this, thinking it over.

Then he asks, 'Do you have her address?'

She stares at him open-mouthed. 'Do you mean that you'll write Veronique a letter,' she says. 'You said you can't write because it's too much effort.'

'Ah yes, it is,' he says, 'but I want Veronique to come and a letter will help.'

Dominique is furious. She's longed to own a letter with his handwriting, addressed to her. She's seen lists he's written for the home help, and she treasures the codes he wrote her on a scrap of paper for entering his flat. She realises he can write to her; he just doesn't want to. But she puts the thought to the back of her mind and gives him Vero's address, not sure she would want her to, but it would hurt him too much if she refused.

'Papa, you haven't looked at my photo albums yet, would you

like to?' She pulls out the two albums she made especially for him, late that first night before she came, so excited at the thought of showing him her life. He puts on his reading-glasses and peers at the cover of the first through a magnifying glass. She translates the title she's given it, *The Childhood*, and he opens the first page where there are black and white snaps of her as a sulky baby. He tries to pronounce the English captions under each photo. He looks completely rapt, drinking it all in.

'Is that Veronique?' he asks. 'She looks just like your mother with those corkscrew curls!'

'Yes, that's us on Gran's rockery,' she answers, glad he's studying this photo because she looks pretty in her pink floral dress, and Vero doesn't look as good for once. This must have been taken just after he disappeared. In the next photo Maman is in her blue housecoat, her auburn hair up in a chignon.

He sighs as he looks at his ex-wife.

Later she will paint his entranced face. Below it the childhood album will open, and her faded photos will wake, like humming-birds that have been kept in torpor for years, wrapped in swaddling clothes. As her brush moves over the canvas, the straitjackets will drop from them and they will stretch their tiny paper wings. Some will fly up to Papa's face. They will hover as more join in. He will hardly be able to face their jewelled crests. His eyelids will blink and droop into a daydream of needle-bills that she will paint with her sable brush. This room will appear whenever anyone looks at her painting. They will marvel at her hummingbird father. She does not want to close the album. She's so pleased she brought it, even though it was heavy to carry. This will be one of her best paintings.

The second album she brought contains wedding photos: her ex, their honeymoon, holidays. The years flash by as he turns the pages. Does he think she was attractive? He doesn't say so. There she is in her Victorian wedding dress. What does he think of her groom? There she is tanned, in a white bikini, then in black T-shirt and shorts in the Sahara, her jet hair dyed with henna. But she's had enough. She pulls the album from his hands and stuffs it back in her bag, and he seems relieved. He leans his head back on the pillow and closes his eyes. She waits for him to fall asleep but can't keep quiet.

'Maman never liked me,' she says. He jerks awake and opens his eyes again, making an effort.

'Are you sure?' he asks, concerned.

'Oh yes,' she says. 'Maman always said she wanted a boy. That's why I'm called Dominique. She wanted it to be Dominic.'

Father looks as if he knows. 'She should not have told you that,' he says. 'Your mother preferred Veronique because she has a strong character, and she's more vivacious. She has a strong character, and so did my own mother.'

'Just because I'm quiet doesn't mean I haven't got a strong character,' she argues. 'In fact it's me who's strong. I'm the one who escaped from Maman. Vero stayed to look after her. Maman trapped her and Vero got sick. So you see, I'm the strong one! Even though Maman said I was born on a Wednesday and am "full of woe". It's an English saying, "Wednesday's child is full of woe".'

Papa looks embarrassed by her outburst and says, 'You were born on a Sunday. That's why we called you Domino. It means Sunday.'

She stares at him. 'Then that means I'm "fair and wise and good". But why did Maman tell me I was born on a Wednesday? She said Veronique was born on a Sunday.'

'What do you mean, Veronique got sick?' he asks.

She's sorry that's slipped out now, and backtracks, muttering something about glandular fever to cover up.

'I understand how you hate your mother, because I hate mine with a passion,' Father says, looking intense himself.

'You mean Mamie Chérie?' she asks.

'Is that what she calls herself now?' he says.

'She died two years ago,' she tells him.

Papa looks straight at her as he shouts, 'I'm so glad! I'm relieved, she's dead! I can breathe! She's the reason I vanished all those years ago. I had to escape from her. She tried to destroy me. She *did* destroy me'.

'She disowned you, didn't she? She said you'd done nasty things.'

'Everything I've done that's bad is because of her,' he replies, glaring into the distance.

'I can understand not liking your mother,' she says.

'You can blame her for not having a father,' he says. 'She cuckolded my father and laughed behind his back. She was proud – always going straight to the front of any queue. No one dared stop her. She offended your mother, when she owned a couture shop but gave her second-hand coats. As for what she did to me . . . it was unforgivable.'

'Maman said that when you were first married, Mamie Chérie told her she was to turn a blind eye when you went off with other women. That was what men did and she had to expect it. Maman said you had fast cars and were a playboy.'

Papa laughs. 'It's true I had racing cars, but a playboy? Me? Hah! That's funny. They say the English have a sense of humour. I think your mother was making a joke. Oh yes, my mother liked causing mischief. She had peasant cunning. We came from Saumur you know, though my mother was of Basque origin.'

'Saumur by Tours?' Dominique asks. 'That's Eugénie Grandet country. I studied that at school. When I read about Eugénie's father, it made me think of living with Maman.'

'Surely she wasn't that bad? Not like *my* mother!' he says.

Dominique must make him understand. 'She wasn't a miser like Grandet,' she says, 'but that shadow-house they lived in was what it was like living with Maman.'

'We both hate our mothers,' Papa says, getting into bed, chuckling. 'So you see, you are a little like me after all.' And as she takes the dishes out, she can hear him muttering the phrase 'playboy' over and over, adding, 'What a tired playboy I am.'

She knows he's tired and must have his afternoon nap, but she can't let it go. 'I thought you disappeared because Maman was so horrid, and I could understand why you'd have to run away from her because I had to.'

'No, *chérie*,' he says. 'I was running away from my own mother. That's why I kept moving from country to country.'

'You should have stayed,' she says. 'Looked after us. Faced up to her.'

'No, I couldn't do that,' he admits. 'I don't have a strong character. You see, we are alike.'

'No we're not,' she argues. 'I've had to be strong!'

'I had to escape,' he says. 'I even changed my name several times. I lived in Algeria first, with a good friend in the Kabylie Mountains. Then everywhere, even in England once. Eventually I settled in Marseille. I had a nice house overlooking the sea.'

'So, what did you do there, to forget us?' she asks.

'I didn't forget you,' he says. 'I told you, I thought of you every day. I sold adult education courses. I went around collecting the fees. I was the area manager; it was a good job.'

Then he coughs and yawns, and she knows she has to stop so must ask her last question. 'Papa – if I come at Christmas, will you let me record your voice? Could I record your voice please,' she repeats, when he doesn't answer, 'so I'll be able to remember it.'

'After my death?' he says. 'Ah no, that's not natural. I can't talk to order.'

'Please . . .' she asks.

'You'll come for Christmas? Then maybe. I'll try. You'll come back tomorrow?' he says, searching her face. 'How long are you staying in Paris?'

'I'm going back tomorrow,' she says. 'There's a private view of a show I've paintings in on Wednesday.'

He holds his hand over his heart as he says, 'I thought you'd stay at least one week.' Then, with a long sigh, 'Will you come to see me before you go? What time is your train?'

'Noon,' she says. 'Yes of course I'll come to say au revoir.'

He turns towards the wall, the wall he must have stared at for two years talking to himself. She sits and waits for him to fall asleep. When he starts snoring, she takes out her camera and photographs the room, but the sun's gone in. He hasn't let her photograph him yet, and she doesn't feel she can do it while he's asleep. So she takes shots of his shelves, the boxes piled to the ceiling, the wardrobe, the huge television with the clock above it on the yellowed walls. He is a Grandin but not Balzac's Grandet who cooked crows to save money.

She tiptoes up to his wardrobe and prises open the door, just a crack. There's a mirror on the inside of the door. In the mirror she can see the reflections of suits. She longs to open the door more, but it creaks loudly and she's frightened she'll wake him. His shirts are packed in like ephemeral waterfalls rustling against each other, some made of black ice in icefalls. If she opens the door further, they'll spill out and flood his room. When did he last wear these clothes?

Dominique takes out her sketchpad and a stick of charcoal and draws his shape under the bedclothes. Her hummingbird father, so bony she might as well be drawing a skeleton. The bedspread has slipped down and she realises she's drawn him naked, so she takes out her sapphire crayon and starts doodling feathers on his skin.

*In the house of the hummingbirds, the hummingbird master wears a heart threaded on a rope around his neck.*

Her crayon scratches over the grey Ingres paper. She draws in time to the rhythm of the oxygen pump as he enters a deeper sleep. He's not going to wake for hours, so she packs her drawing things, puts on her coat and lets herself out.

8

# THE HUMMINGBIRD ALBUM

H ER STUDIO HAS changed. The sun is streaming in through the skylight, throwing panels on the white floorboards. She turns *The Summoning* around. That strange night a week before the letter arrived, she remembers waking up, words springing out of her mouth: *I must make my father appear, he'll come if I summon him hard enough.* She'd got out of bed and walked into her white studio and switched on the blue daylight bulbs. It was two o'clock in the morning but in the light of her room it was day. She'd pulled out a six-foot-high primed canvas. Violet shadows flickered over the surface. She'd picked up her brush and before she knew what was happening, three hours had passed and she had conjured him on the canvas – life-size and emaciated.

How could she have known what her father looked like? Yet, looking at the portrait painted that night, she can see that it really is him. She seems to be floating again now – a slow, silent fall, down to the plunge pool of morning. It's odd, gliding among the hours, to see them stretched around her in slow motion like water dropping from the top of the sky, water heavy as buildings with windows where a face appears, her father's face waiting for her arrival. There is the sound of amplified breathing during this slow descent to the canyon floor.

His face is imprisoned in a drop of water and distorted by gravity, the eyes wobble and split then reform as in a fairground mirror, the mouth opening and closing to say something above the roar of rushing air. She turns it to face the wall again so that he is facing the wall, just as he does when he lies in bed. Let him contemplate the cracks while she works.

She starts on *The Hummingbird Album*. On her table is the photo she found in L'Harmattan, her favourite bookshop on the rue des Écoles, crammed with ethnographic and travel volumes, where she spent her evenings after visiting Papa. She'd opened the Time-Life book on South America and there, facing her, were thirty-seven hummingbirds wrapped in rag pyjamas inside a suitcase. She'd read the caption that said they were alive and unharmed, being transported in the hold of a plane by the ornithologist, Augusto Ruschi. How he'd captured them with the decoy of a live pygmy owl, how aggressive hummingbirds were, and how it was possible to put them into torpor – a state they naturally fall into to conserve energy – by placing them in the fridge for half an hour. The pygmy owl was their main predator, which they mob to scare away, though Ruschi said hummingbirds even attack people, pointing their bills at his face if they got annoyed, hovering the whole time. He'd wrapped them in cloths so they wouldn't damage their wings, should they wake during the flight.

Looking at Ruschi's photo gave Dominique the same feeling she'd had watching Papa turning the pages of her album, her thirty-seven dormant years suddenly wakened by the heat of his room. Hadn't she imagined her photos to be hummingbirds?

Here on her table lies the photo she has stolen of the hummingbirds swaddled in their suitcase, carefully torn out of the book. It's a long time since she's done that – ever since her ex told her to stop shoplifting. That one day she'd get caught and end up in trouble. She'd stolen paints, make-up, jewellery. And even once, when she was feeling bold, she'd walked out of a clothes shop in Bond Street with a Chanel dress stuffed up her sleeve. She'd stopped stealing, and shops installed scanners so it became too risky anyway. But Ruschi's photo was hers as soon as she saw it. Hadn't her own photos risen from the gummy pages, to hover around Papa's face? *I have thought of you every day* he'd said, as the scallop-edged old photos in the album slipped from their cellophane skins and rose in the air in front of him.

# 9

# IN THE FOREST OF
# CHILDHOOD

WHEN I'M PAINTING The Hummingbird Album, I'm a child who's never seen a hummingbird before. My brush releases the nestlings from the pages where they've been sleeping. They dive into his face and emerge clean, these sepia days that roosted in virgin forest. They perch on his shoulders preening themselves, shaking the years from their wings like morning dew. They sunbathe under his bedside lamp, opening their tails and back feathers to let in the heat.

When they sing, out come notes that make Papa's neck hairs stand on end. He sees colours no one should see, violent and tender, smelling of milk and lightning.

Here is his face again – huge and blurred, as if made of falling water, and, in front of it, and all around his head, my hummingbirds hover. They sip his sap, while he is mesmerised by their colours, the whirr of their wings, the way they fly backwards back into the album leaves, then are still, having pierced time itself.

In the forest of childhood snakes are fat as cellars. They move so slowly that trees grow on them. When they are hungry, they draw hummingbirds out of the trees with their magnetic eyes and swallow my colours. Flashes that the snake swallows down the long low cellar of his body.

*In the forest of childhood, spiders are big as Papa's hands. The bird-eating spider still pounces on me when I fall asleep. Sometimes when I'm in his room, it's like I'm a hummingbird and he's torn my chest open and is gorging on me. I can't escape, trussed in his silk, his fangs piercing my heart.*

# 10

# VERONIQUE

A ND SOMETHING NOW pierces Dominique. She realises it's the phone.

'Hi Sis. Did you go to Paris?'

It's Vero! 'I was going to call you,' Dominique says.

'I tried calling you a few days ago,' Vero says, 'but you weren't there so I guessed you went to Paris.'

'I did,' Dominique says, 'and I'll tell you all about it, but I have to go out soon; I've got a private view. Four of my paintings are at the Chisenhale Gallery and the show's opening tonight.'

There's a pause. Then Vero says, 'Oh, and when are you going to get a proper job?'

'This is a proper job,' Dominique says, 'it's what I have to do. If I can't do it I'll die.'

'Don't be melodramatic. Life isn't a self-realisation trip,' Vero sneers, and Dominique tries her best not to get upset.

'So, tell me about our father,' Vero asks. 'He wrote and said you got a letter from the lawyer like me. That was a shock, wasn't it?'

Dominique realises that Vero knows about Papa. She's known for days! 'It is a shock,' she replies. 'I don't think I'll ever get over it.'

'It's been thirty years!' Vero says. 'You'd think he could have contacted us before now. It's a bit late, isn't it.'

'Yes! too late. But Vero, he's chained to an oxygen machine and has trouble breathing.'

'Why?' Vero asks.

'Emphysema, his lungs don't work properly – he's had it a long time. It stops him talking.'

'Oh,' Vero says, 'must be from the smoking.'

'He has to pause between words when it's bad,' Dominique says, wondering how much to say, she doesn't want to put Vero off seeing him.

'What's he like, Domino?'

'He has tubes in his nostrils. It's so frustrating because I wanted to know about his life. It was hard talking to him because my French isn't as good as it used to be, and even then, it was only childish.'

'It's better than mine though!' Vero says. 'I don't know how I'll manage. Doesn't he speak any English?'

'No. And he's so French! He's obsessed with food but he's thin – I'm just warning you. I expected him to be tall. That's how I remember him – tall, dark and chain-smoking.'

'Yes,' Vero says, 'I remember him tall too, and the chain-smoking.'

'He told me the doctor can't predict how long he'll live, but it could be two years max. And when Papa's cross with me,' Dominique says, 'he tells me he might die sooner, so I can't argue with him as it affects his heart.'

'It's a double shock, isn't it?' Vero says. 'He gets in touch and we find out he's dying, like he only got in touch so he could leave us again. Didn't you feel angry?'

'Yes, Vero, but I couldn't let myself. I had to keep it in when I was with him. But back at the hotel I felt odd.'

'Not surprising!' Vero says.

'It's like being in a film,' Dominique says.

'Yes, it's like a film,' Vero agrees. 'Someone's having a laugh at us.'

'Something's wrong though,' Dominique says. 'It's dreamlike, but when I'm with him too long I start to feel as if I'm doing something bad. As if I'm in a smelly room with a stranger.'

'A nightmare more like,' Vero says. 'He *is* a stranger.'

'He has cooking gadgets everywhere – a steamer and a table-grill

– I suppose because he can't walk easily into his kitchenette.'

'Was he a chef?'

'I don't know, but he knows how to cook. And there's so much furniture, boxes piled up to the ceiling! He's a hoarder.'

'How strange that he hoards stuff,' Vero says, then goes quiet.

'Guess what – he knew Django Reinhardt!'

'*The* Django?'

'Papa used to live in the Boulevard Saint-Germain, two doors down from him. He went to the Hôtel Crystal where Django was staying to interview him once, for a book he was editing about him.'

'I can see him doing that,' Vero says, 'he was very sophisticated.'

'He told me he ran a small press in a bookshop,' Dominique says, 'and published books about musicians. He said when he left boarding school he went wild in Paris.'

'Yes, I heard that from Maman – about him going wild,' Vero says. 'What does he look like?'

'All this time I thought he'd look like me,' Dominique says, 'that I took after him. He's good-looking though. Are you going to visit him?'

'I think so. I haven't made up my mind yet.'

'Vero, do go. He really wants to see you. He'd love to meet Jack too.'

'Oh, I don't know about that, I don't want Jack near him.'

'You could try asking him about the Hot Club,' Dominique suggests, 'and Club St-Germain, but you'll have to be patient, he can't talk much. He doesn't have any friends.'

'I wonder why?' Vero says.

'His only visitor's the daily help who washes him and does his shopping. At least write to him, or better still, phone.'

Dominique puts the phone down. Does she want Veronique to go? Yes and no – it would make Papa happy, but he won't be just hers anymore.

The next morning, she wanders into her studio in her pyjamas. *The Hummingbird Album* is gentler than she expected. She'd lain in bed thinking of the hummingbirds' beaks concealed in the feathery air, their hungry little girls' faces drinking Papa's eyes, an orphanage of them released from the album, like those white dormitories she slept in when she was four. It's true there's a hard expression in some of their black eyes, but most of them have a yearning look, like children waiting for their parents to arrive, getting more and more disappointed as the weekend passes.

His face is drained of colour, as if the birds have drunk him up. She wants to protect him from them. What was that children's home called? La Mésangerie – the Bluetit House.

And where was that kitchen she can barely remember? Perhaps it was their apartment by the zoo, when they had a brasserie. She can remember a balcony, a picture book with animals, learning about snakes and monkeys and a hummingbird with black eyes and colours that changed when she held the book up to the light. Perhaps her face could change like that.

All her life, she'd found out more and more about these little birds, as if her life was a forest of sleeping birds, of memories that must never be remembered.

But she mustn't let herself think this way. She must be kind. She will write him a letter. It will make him less lonely. She imagines Lucienne bringing it up from the post box in the hallway, reading out the name of the sender. He'll open it with his letter-knife and put on his reading-glasses, smiling but a little anxious. Dare she call him Papa in a letter yet? Should she say *vous* or *tu*?

She finds her French dictionary and starts again:

Dear Papa,
I'm snatching a moment to write to you. The important thing is that I spoke to Veronique yesterday. She was really happy to hear all about you, and I think that very soon she is going to write or phone.

As for me, I'm happy to have met you. I'm hoping to come for Christmas. It was such a big thing for me, meeting you, and it hasn't quite sunk in yet. I liked being with you and I believe I am a little like you. Your illness makes me sad.

The private view went well. A few critics came and told me they liked my triptych of Angel Falls. One of them said he could feel the canyon gusts on his face. It was strange standing there, seeing other people looking at it after you had looked at it.

I'll be going back to Venezuela in a week. Think of me up on the plateau in the Lost World – our lost world! I wish I could fill your room with trees to breathe for you. I think of it as a forest no one has mapped, where you are lost. But I found you after thirty years of searching!

So, Father, I hug you tight, and I'll phone soon.

Your daughter,
Domino xx

She seals the envelope and rushes to post it before she changes her mind. Today, she's going to paint *My Father's Wardrobe*.

# 11

# HIS WARDROBE

S HE PICKS A wardrobe-sized canvas and stands in front of it the way she stood in front of Papa's wardrobe, as if it's a secret door into a wood. She spreads a brown wash over the surface and turns the key, then prises the door open. A breeze blows in from her skylight. Suits stir in the draught. A scent of oak envelops her and guides her brush until depths appear between the trunks of trouser legs. Sunlight filters in through silk shirts, like green motes through leaves. All day they flicker over her face as she works. She wants to climb in and hide as she did when she was a child, stepping deeper into the clothes swaying on their hangers, the weaves of gunmetal wool and summer linens. The longer she paints, the darker it gets, suits pressed against each other like people in a lift that plunges her down through the years.

# 12

# HIDE AND SEEK

*T*HE DOOR CLOSES *me in. Darkness. There are steps outside and the sound of amplified breathing. Now light lasers in through cracks and knotholes in the wood. There's a mirror on the inside of the door. My moonlit face in the glass is a child's.*

*The steps stop just outside the wardrobe. A deep voice is counting to a hundred. I must not breathe. If I'm found I'll die, or something worse, but what could be worse? Something I mustn't tell, or the bird-eating spider will pounce out of the hole in the wood. She'll weave silk around me like a hummingbird caught in a web.*

*The footsteps fade and I let out my breath. Then they become loud again. I crawl into a coat. The door creaks open. The coat lining is scratchy and I pretend I'm in a hollow tree. Something creeps up my arm. I wait until my body is quiet. The door shuts again, the footsteps get faint. I can hear muffled cries, someone stifling sobs in a pillow. Then silence. It's safe to come out.*

# 13

# FATHER'S SHOES

DOMINIQUE BLINKS IN the light. It's as if the paint comes from inside her. Her father's days are in the wardrobe; his nights stored in inner pockets. And on the wardrobe floor, against trailing trousers, rest his shoes, their leather hides nestling against each other.

She spends the next few days preparing for her return to Venezuela. But every now and then she stands in front of *My Father's Wardrobe*, touching a shoelace, painting eyes into his shoes. They're twin brocket fawns, huddled against the trunks of trees – these tan shoes he hasn't worn for two years, that she strokes in her studio. Their tongues are silent as hers, as if someone comes at night to lace their lips. Two of her faces murmuring to each other in a mute language, two fawn selves she's smuggled into his room, to eavesdrop on his dreams.

She turns *The Summoning* around to marvel again at the likeness she captured. Papa wakes from his afternoon nap and mutters to himself that he has dreamt of his daughter arriving in his room. Then he remembers.

## 14

# KAVAC CAVE

DOMINIQUE LEANS AGAINST the pilot's half-open window. Beneath, plunged in shadow, lies the forested floor of Devil's Canyon, and up on the right, just swinging into view, she catches sight of Angel Falls. A second later and she can almost touch the spray, and for a brief moment is *in* his face – giant whorls forming and reforming like the dream that led her back here. The dream that made her rise as if still asleep and paint his portrait in the night.

As he'd lain in his bed, she'd woken in hers, and glided to her studio, picked up her brushes, and painted, shaking with excitement. She had never painted her father before. She did not know what he looked like, if he was alive or dead. But there he appeared on the canvas, and afterwards she thought it was she who had made him emaciated, his fingers gripping his chest to part his ribs like surgical clamps. Her father rising out of the rainforest haze, tall as the world's highest torrent. She could see his ashen right half-lung, and his left lung bare as a leafless forest. She'd picked up her hoghair and scrawled the title across the bottom, and only saw what she had written when she sat back on her stool. She knew what she had done, but it was not possible, he could not be summoned. She would never meet him. How could she? Yet here he was, half man, half ghost, and she had made him like that in three hours that passed the way a waterfall drops to the valley floor. She had taken away his power, without thinking, without choosing her colours – her brushes did that. The canvas was alive, a filmy weave like the cloud-forms in Venezuela's Lost World.

The Cessna banks at a sharp angle, and starts to spin, buffeted by one of the rogue gusts that could smash it against the cliff. The mile-deep lunge hits her stomach and she reaches for the sick-bag, but is too excited to let that stop her staggering down the aisle, leaning to gaze through the portholes on the starboard side to peer at her dream. She slides back into her seat, banging her hip against the arm. Then, there he is again, behind her, on the left - a god swaying against the rose rock, down to the glinting river among treetops of fluorescent green smoke.

The north wall of Auyán-tepui - Devil's Mountain - rears, its turrets swathed in mist. The plane swerves through the saddle between Sun and Moon Mountains at the entrance to Devil's Canyon, then cruises over Auyán-tepui's rooftop, skimming a maze of quartz towers. It's like flying through smashed glass. How can she feel homesick for a place she's never been to?

Again, she sees the plane's puny shadow like a gnat against sheer cliffs, flickering over gulches that pierce the plateau laced by ephemeral waterfalls. Far below, the claws of the lower talus slope clasp Churún River.

The canopy becomes broccoli again, as they circle over cloud forest broken by emergent kapoks, their tops bleached by lightning strikes. Flocks of scarlet macaws explode like fireworks. She stares at the slow-swaying crowns. The engine-hum surges through her like Papa's oxygen machine, making its exhalations and inhalations. She can hear Papa rasping for air, his face screwed up. She holds out her hand and her fingers graze the treetops. The forest is holding its breath.

The Cessna surges and once again they are hugging the plateau surface, her face glued to the porthole to take in the lunar land-scape. There's a city of columns, skyscrapers hemmed in by walls, a walled garden of cell-like apartments where the Mawari live - the Pemón's sky-spirits. One of them hasn't left his room for two years. He's thin as a stick insect, his skin green. No one could land here in this Paris-of-the-plateau, where orchids grow into diseased organs. But the Cessna is leaving the city enclosed in a valley and it's a distant skyline now, for here is a zoo of Mesozoic stone animals, a Jardin des Plantes with crystal greenhouses. Or so it seemed when they passed, for now the rock surface is bleak and flat, glinting with swamps, rockpools here and there, islands of pink sand in the black swamps, and succulents with blue scimitar leaves. Then the plane whooshes over the escarpment again and the sudden drop jolts her stomach as they swoop over the edge. Her destination is Kavac Camp, at the foot of the southernmost wall.

When the engine is switched off, its after-hum keeps her sealed in a bubble as she steps out onto hot pink sand. Children dash forward, their hands outstretched, begging for candy. They touch her pale arms and giggle. One of them holds out a pot-bellied baby parrot. Puppies yap at her feet. The savannah wind muffles every voice. When her ears pop the voices go up one decibel, but she feels as if she's landed on Neptune.

A Pemón steps forward and introduces himself as her guide. He has long straight black hair and a soft voice. He tells her his Spanish name is Juan as he carries her rucksack up to a window-less palm-roofed hut. Inside is a camp bed draped in a pastel blue mosquito net, a bedside stool with candle and matches. He gestures for her to keep the door open. As soon as she closes it she realises why – it's the only real source of light. A little light also slants in through the gap between the adobe walls and the palm roof, also letting the breeze in, making the hut surprisingly cool. The floor is beaten earth. At the end of her room a rough doorframe leads to her 'bathroom', fitted with a showerhead trickling cold brown water, a sink, and a gaudy cockroach.

She can see the escarpment through her door. Filmy white ribbons hang motionless down three rosy cliff tiers to the forest floor – waterfalls that form after afternoon storms. These are the legendary sky-ladders for the Mawari spirits to climb down from their mountaintop mansions. The holes in the quartz sandstone are their windows. She looks up at one and sees Papa waving to her from inside the pane.

If she walked up to the jumbled rocks at the foot of the top cliff, she would see a figure dart out, tethered to his room by a lead like a dog. If she climbed through the cloud forest, up the stairway of dwarf trees stunted by trade winds, she would meet her father again, as if for the first time. Her father with emphysema – the last tree in the world.

After we said goodbye, the back of my head felt his eyes, so I turned. And there he was at his window as far as the oxygen tube would allow. He struggled with the catch, as if the window was a pane of prehistoric glass that had never before been opened. Then he appeared, gasping but smiling, his oxygen tubes shining in the evening sun. He blew me a kiss and as he waved, rays refracted on the bevelled glass.

As she looks up at the window in the castellated façade of the mountain, his spirit climbs down the ladder and follows her across the courtyard, while his body collapses into his chair, choking. She stands outside her door under the moon – so huge and low its aureole fills the sky. One by one, fireflies start to flash from the forest edge, in sync with the sheet lightning on the plateau summit.

In the kitchen hut, Juan has prepared a chicken barbecue with plantain. He passes her a Cuba Libre and they drink gazing at Auyán for a while, then he leaves her to eat on her own. She flicks through the *Cosmopolitan* he's been reading to improve his English.

'You don't look like the other tourists,' he says, returning to clear away the dishes. 'Where are you from?'

'I was born in Paris,' she says, 'but my maternal grandmother was Nepalese from the Annapurnas.'

'You could be one of us,' he murmurs, and she knows it's a compliment. 'A Pemón with moonlit skin,' he adds, smiling.

She blushes, because he's looking right into her, and once again she thinks how soft his voice is. His eyes meet hers and linger before looking away. He offers her another Cuba Libre, but she's tired after the long flight and thinks an early night is best.

The howler monkeys wake her just before sunrise with their unearthly roars. At six there's a tap at her door, and Juan stands there grinning, waiting to lead her to a breakfast of plantain, rice and piranha served on a wooden board.

Afterwards, they set off up the first talus slope, crossing logs over streams. Soon, they're deep in the forest and its tripwires of roots. When they reach Kavac River, they bathe in frothy waterfalls crashing over slabs of red jasper. Juan climbs up onto a pillar and dives in, tobogganing down a stone chute, his whoops echoing off the rock. She sits on the bank and watches him show off.

They head upstream, where the air is suddenly sombre, and Auyán towers above them, cutting out the sun. The river widens into a black pool called Anaconda and Juan gestures for her to jump in and wade towards the gorge entrance. A violin bird breaks the silence, then just as abruptly stops singing as they swim through the narrow passage between the two high curving cliffs. Guide ropes have been placed for tourists to swim through the metre-wide creek. She clutches it now and again, panicking when she looks down into the inky depths. The passage is so narrow that she has to strain her neck to see the sky through the slit of the canyon. Juan swims up to her, takes her hand and they swim together, him ahead, leading her through the gorge.

Soon, she glimpses Kavac Falls – the source of the subterranean thunder, floodlit with a beam of sunlight from the hole in the cave roof. They haul themselves onto a bank in front of the spectre, their backs hugging the wet cave wall. Juan dives into the plunge pool and vanishes, leaving her alone with the cataract, the concave walls covered in moss and transparent white roots, as if the mountain's nervous system is exposed.

Suddenly he surfaces, laughing at her when she jumps, and yells above the waterfall. 'You okay? Now I'll tell you about the cave, but in Spanish.' She prefers it when Juan speaks Spanish, even though she can't understand everything. He tells her this is a special cave for young men. They come here alone and stay all day and night. When they leave, their muscles are hard as the cave walls, their minds deep as the plunge pool and their eyes cutting as the falling water. They have spent a night with Traman-chita - the god who lives on Auyán-tepui, more evil than the Mawari spirits. Traman-chita is the father of evil.

She's shivering now, and wants to go back, tired and running a fever. They return to Kavac Camp in drizzle.

When they get back, she rests in her room, worried that she's caught a chill, but when she joins Juan in the kitchen hut, he reassures her it's just the cave. He's caught a cold from there himself. A Cuba Libre will cure them.

After lunch she takes a long siesta then feels better. She prises her door open and walks alone over the first slope with its jumble of boulders shaped like rough-hewn furniture, towards Kavac River. She wades into Anaconda Pool then plunges between the gorge walls, a green vine snake swimming alongside her.

The gorge twists and she follows, hardly daring to peer up at the slit of sky, as she swims between the jasper walls and into the mountain, making for the cave-light where water hurtles like intertwined lightning bolts. She has to swim in the plunge pool, between the whirlpool and the churning foam. This is what the Pemón do before entering their spirit world. They come to this shrine in the mountain's bowels where the spray stings like buckshot. She reaches the narrow ledge beside the falls and hauls herself up to stay all night, shivering in her wet swimsuit and shorts. She's brought with her the memory of another phone conversation with Vero:

'I went to see Papa soon after you,' Vero had begun. 'It's such a shock, isn't it? And he's going to die! That's a double shock - I haven't got over the first yet! He wants to see his grandson, but I don't want my son dirtied. I've never told anyone this - Papa did something to me when I was five, the same age Jack is now. Jack would be able to tell just by the expression on Papa's face, wouldn't he? Children can sense things. D'you know what I mean, Domino?'

'Yes,' Dominique says, staring up the gorge walls at the hole of sky, far up but blinding as the past.

'When I was sitting facing him over that table, Papa stared at me as if he was looking at Maman. I couldn't look him in the eyes. I don't want those thoughts near Jack,' Vero had said.

'But he so wants to see his grandson . . . he kept asking me about him,' Dominique interrupted, trying to defend Papa.

'I just can't,' Vero had insisted. 'It was the summer holidays when we were little and living at Gran's. Papa had come to stay for the holiday to say goodbye to us. He crept into my room, up to my bed . . . lay on top of me and . . . French kissed me a long time. He thought I was asleep, but I was too scared to move.'

The walls of Kavac Cave bulge out now, their exposed roots like a memory long buried in rock.

'I've never told anyone this before. He was our father. He should have been protecting us,' Vero had added, and Dominique had felt sick. She'd opened up to Vero then.

'I'm glad you've told me,' she'd said, 'because when I was with him – I felt there was ice in my stomach, but when he stared at me, my face caught fire. But I can't get angry with him because it might give him a heart attack. I can't remember what happened to me though.'

'That's probably a good thing?' Vero had said. She'd confided in her sister then about things she'd discovered about him from Maman. 'Are you sure you can't remember anymore?' Vero had asked.

'I don't have a good memory like you. You were younger than me, but you remember more,' Dominique answered. And it's true, she thinks, because there's a part of her brain that's as impenetrable as this rock surrounding her, her sister's words pouring down from the canyon hole high up on Auyán's cliff.

After Juan had shown her the sacred waterfall in its cave, they'd scrambled up over to the top, to watch the water swirl down a plughole in the roof, then plunge into the abyss. They'd peered down at frozen rainbows, and when they thrust their arms in, the water was icy.

'I'd be careful if I was you,' Vero had continued, 'Maman's told me terrible things he's done, you know when she's off her head on one of her highs. She says she had to marry him after he date-raped her, because she got pregnant with you.'

'He kind of boasted about it to me,' Dominique had said. 'It must be why she hates me so much!'

'I'm not sure what happened,' Vero said. 'She's such a drama queen. All I know is I don't want my son near him, and I won't go to see him again.'

Dominique looks up, and sees the full moon framed by the canyon hole.

Those phone conversations with her sister were the first time she'd talked to anyone since she'd seen Papa.

When she'd got back home from Paris, she'd booked her flight to Caracas and hidden away until her trip. She'd painted and read her Amazonian books deep into each night. She wanted the names of the trees, of each species of jungle nightingale. And she wanted to learn the Pemón language, the words for storm, jaguar, spear.

She's learning their spells, wants to know their initiation rites for young men, how they become warriors. The more she knows, the better she feels. Kavac Falls is burning her cheeks and insects are crawling down her back. The foam whirls around her like flakes of Papa's face, just as all those years ago, he had thrust his face into hers as she lay in her cot and his bird-eating fingers felt her.

Papa's face keeps materialising then collapsing into the torrent, suffocating her. He's kissing her with his ice-cold lips. His hands are tarantulas crawling over her body. Dominique thinks she died at the age of six. That her life as a painter is an afterlife she's created from paint. The heart-shaped plateau of Auyán-tepui is her heart, broken by Devil's Canyon.

Here, beside Kavac Falls, it's safe to think about her painting.

How when she got back she'd propped it up, and this time felt no guilt looking at it. How it had painted itself in the middle of the night, the exact night when Papa lay tormented. First, his face had emerged, like the image on a shroud, painted in blood and ochre. Then his chest – open as to a surgeon on the operating-table. But he was floating upright. In the tobacco-brown shadows that surrounded him shapes grew – coral-necked vultures, jaguars' green night-eyes and milky eight-eyed chicken spiders.

She'd collapsed into bed and fallen into a chaotic dream. The next morning, she ran to her studio and turned the painting to face the wall. When she met Papa and found she really had captured his likeness, she thought it was her fault he was dying.

After Vero's phone-call she stopped feeling guilty. But did Papa deserve to suffer so much?

# 15

# TRUTH AND TELL

*IT'S PITCH DARK but already the pale-winged trumpeters call to each other on the forest floor. I listen to their staccato hum, which makes the inside of my mouth tingle. Soon, the titi monkeys will start screeching from their treetop roosts. Then the howlers will pump their throats with air.*

*Now I can paint animals no human has seen. Their names are hide and seek, truth and tell. They hunt each other through the understorey. They climb the minds of trees, trees that know what Papa has done, his secrets stored in annual rings.*

*Salto Kavac knows, coiling down its hole, roaring the mountain's tales to anyone who swims in here. The vine snake knows, waiting to lead me back to safety like a green rope thrown by the mountain gods. I'll wait until the spiders have retreated to their burrows.*

*All night the torrent bores a hole in my head making me ready for Papa – strong as the cave walls, deep as the plunge pool, my eyes knives of water. I'm back on Papa's knee and he's playing our boat game, singing our rhyme,* Bateau sur l'eau . . . *tipping me further and further down with each swing of his arms, until my face is drenched and the water is up to my neck.*

*But I can't swim, the torrent's arms keep pushing me. I break the surface to feel hard rain on my face pushing me back down. The river's rising up the walls. I flail my arms to stop being pushed to the bottom. Each time it takes me longer to reach the surface and call for help, but only my mountain voice answers. The water is in my mouth, forcing my lips open, pushing its tongue down my throat and against its hard bed.*

# 16

# TIGRE MARIPOSA

'YOU ALMOST DROWNED!' Juan says. 'Never go into the mountain alone!'

Dominique's on the sand, lying on her side, spewing water. He's kneeling beside her. 'How did you find me?' she coughs, bringing up more water.

'I knew I'd find you here,' he says. 'I dived in, but the river was rising too fast. I kept feeling the river stones with my hands; luckily, I know the canyon walls blindfold, every rock on the bed. You were lying on the bottom, I thought you were dead!'

'I'm sorry,' she tries to say, starting to cry. Everything is hazy and far away, the waterfall still thundering through her head. Juan wraps his jacket over her shoulders and they start back in the cold dawn light, Dominique stumbling and shivering all the way.

She sleeps through the morning, then after lunch they prepare to climb Auyán-tepui. Juan drives her to the village of Kamarata where she stocks up with dried meals, enough for a week, and four extra days' portions for emergencies. They buy a camp stove, then head back to Kavac to pack. She sprays her tent with water repellent, packs her rain poncho, ground sheet, first-aid kit, water purification tablets, and most important, her pastels and sketchbook in plastic bags, and stuffs everything into the rucksack. She straps her sleeping bag and mat on top then seals it all in polythene. Juan will carry the food, tent and camp stove. She pays him three hundred dollars upfront, then collapses onto a bench, exhausted.

Juan doesn't mention the Kavac incident again, he's back to his smiling self. *Tigre mariposa*, he calls the jaguar they hear cough but can't see, as they watch the moon moths flutter under the hurricane lamp. 'Why butterfly jaguar?' she asks.

'Their rosettes are black butterflies that lure girls into the forest,' he says.

Huge stars surround them like cinquefoils against the black velvet sky.

'I keep dreaming I live up there,' she murmurs, pointing to where the stars are eclipsed by Auyán's escarpment.

Juan shakes his head. 'No Pemón will willingly lay a foot on the plateau, Anwoná lives up there, the double-headed king vulture and king of the spirits.'

'But you've been up there, guided tourists before?' she asks.

'I've guided a group to El Oso, the first camp on the summit, several times and once went as far as the top of Salto Ángel when I was a porter helping my uncle.'

'I must get to the top of Angel Falls,' she tells him, looking straight into his eyes to show him how serious she is.

'I've always wanted to go back,' Juan says, 'but it's hard. It will be much harder for you. People have gone up there and never returned. I'm happy I'm your guide, though, and I'll help you because you're interested in our people.'

Dominique isn't interested, she's *enthralled* by Pemón myths, but she too is glad Juan is her guide. Looking into his eyes is like looking down from the plane onto the top of Auyán-tepui – into a wilderness where she wants to live.

He dashes inside and brings her some leaves to chew, picks up a hunting bow and starts to play it like a harp. As she chews the bitter leaves, she feels as if her bones are being plucked. Everything goes misty and slow then blacks out.

She wakes to find her head on the table, and Juan sitting cross-legged on the floor, his face painted with intricate red patterns. He's chanting in Pemón, his eyes closed. She stumbles up and mutters that she must go to bed and he snaps out of his trance and follows her as far as the door, where he takes hold of her hand, pulls her against him and starts to kiss her.

She pulls away, saying, 'I don't kiss!'

'That's a shame,' he says. 'You're strange but I really like you. But I'm sorry, I shouldn't have kissed you.'

'No, you shouldn't have,' she says, 'if you're going to be my guide.'

'Exactly,' he says. 'It would spoil the *taren* – the spell I'm making to keep us safe. But I kissed you before, when you were drowned!'

'You saved me?'

'Yes, I brought you back to life.'

She thanks him with a peck on his cheek and says goodnight, closing the door and fumbling in the dark for her matches to light the candle. How long since she kissed anyone? And enjoyed it? Perhaps a fling is what she needs. But no, it's not a good idea. She doesn't even know if he's married. And he's younger than her, perhaps only thirty. And what about Papa? Is she in love with her father? That's what it felt like, like meeting someone new and falling in love – the surprise of him appearing out of the sky. But it also felt wrong. She can't have fallen in love with him because he's her father. But she can't fall for anyone else. She decides to keep her distance from Juan and falls asleep, pleased with her sensible decision.

# 17

# ON AUYÁN-TEPUI

A T FIVE A.M. Juan knocks on Dominique's door. His face is still painted with red dots and waves, but he seems to have forgotten about the attempted kiss and shows no embarrassment. As she eats her porridge in the semi-dark, he tells her how the red dye comes from the urucu plant and will make him invisible to the spirits.

'Mawari was once the scissor-tail kite,' he says, 'our creator-bird of the dawn. The Mawari are what we call the souls he's captured. You might see them! We can fly as far as Uruyen if you like, a camp nearer the first wall, for a hundred dollars more – it would cut three hours off the trek across the savannah.'

She agrees. He's packed everything into his wicker carrier, and insisted on tying her sleeping bag and mat on top, which is a relief as she tested her rucksack and it was too heavy.

At Uruyen they set off up the first slope, through savannah grass taller than their heads, the puri puris – small black flies – biting them, until they reach the first river, where she has to remove her boots and wade barefoot over the sharp, slippery bed, clinging to her walking stick to stop the current knocking her over. Juan is waiting for her the other side, chanting his spells under his breath. When they reach the first steep cliff and she starts panting, she thinks of Papa. Is this what every day is like for him? Does he always have a pack on his back? Is he climbing up his cliff? Is talking a luxury he can't afford, just as she's conserving her breath by not talking? And as drizzle turns to rain, she becomes enclosed in her own hoop, Juan always just out of reach ahead, the rain harder but erratic, starts and stops, huge drops, some big as marbles, others like pins stinging her face, her boots sloshing in the red mud.

They reach their first camp – Guayaraca – where Juan pitches her tent under one of the two thatched roofs. Dominique throws herself onto her sleeping mat to recover, but when she gets up Juan has vanished. She boils water for tea and bathes in the stream nearby, washes her wet clothes and lays them out to dry in the sun, wondering where he's gone and if he'll return. She eats alone. When she goes to the bushes to pee, there's a grunting sound and for a moment she's terrified it's a jaguar or a peccary. But a hummingbird appears – the grunting is the sound its wings make. It whirrs up to her and hovers just in front of her face, its black eyes shining into hers, bill aimed straight at her.

Twilight is brief and with it the rains start again – a wall of sound around the unwalled roof. She's grateful for the ditch dug around the shelter and so are the frogs with their peeps and rings like doorbell chimes. She checks her tent for the puri puris, whose bites are itchier than mosquitoes, then drifts off to sleep, only to be repeatedly woken by thunder.

She wakes at 4:30, startled by Juan's footsteps. He tells her he spent the night with a group of Pemón in a shack further up the trail and has already had breakfast, so she boils some porridge and tea, and as the water boils, tells him about the hummingbird. He listens intently as she describes its glittering eyes and how it looked fearlessly at her as the wings made their peculiar grunting hum.

'What colour was he?' he asks.

'Green,' she says, 'with some copper-red in its breast, but I didn't get a chance to look properly as I was mesmerised by its bill.' The truth was that when she looked at the bird hovering in the air before her, she thought of Papa and her *Hummingbird Album* painting, how thirty-seven photos had risen into the air to beat their wings like hummingbirds woken after a lifetime's sleep.

'That was Tukui you met, one of the protector spirits of the tepui,' Juan says. 'It's a good sign that he appeared when I left you. He'll

protect you from the Mawari and Anwoná – king of the vultures.'
And he takes her hand, holds it palm up.

'What can you see?' she asks.

'I see a Gran Sabana here,' he says as he strokes her palm, deep valleys, and here is Churún River. The skin on his fingertips is dry and calloused, but gentle.

Dominique smiles at him, and again his face makes her think of the mountain, with the wavy designs and spirals like cloud-forms on his cheeks, how he himself is a protector spirit who's already saved her life.

'Our spirit world is like your left hand,' he says. 'It exists next to your right hand, which is the visible world, almost identical but different. Sometimes the two worlds meet.' And he places her left hand on top of her right, cradling them both in his. 'I think you're becoming one of us,' he says. 'Perhaps I should paint your face red against the spirits?'

His dye seems to have been freshly applied. He's handsome although his skin is rough under the wavy stripes. But it's his softness that attracts her.

She agrees to have her face painted, as she knows it will reassure him, and closes her eyes as he brushes dye over her eyelids and cheeks then down her nose to her chin. She steals a glance in a pool and likes the effect: he's turned her into an ocelot!

Then it's time to set off towards the second cliff. She hums a tune she remembers from childhood. They continue upriver, scrambling up the second talus slope. When they reach a rocky outcrop, she asks to take a rest. Every tendon in her legs aches.

'Watch where you place your hands!' Juan snaps. She whisks her hand off the vine she was about to grab, sees the scorpion and yells.

'Quiet!' he hisses, 'you'll wake the Mawari!' He points to gaps in the rosy sandstone just under the summit. 'Those are the windows of their houses. That's where we go after we die. Drink some water, you're dehydrated, which might make you visible to the Mawari.' And he passes her a flask.

She looks up and sees a bright shadow inside the quartz rock. She thinks of Papa at his window as she left him after that astonishing first meeting. He never looked out again after that, never struggled to get to his window to blow her another kiss, although she always turned around to check.

They trek two hours through more savannah, then a cloud forest of stunted trees covered in lichen and orchids, until they reach the second cliff, which takes three hours to climb with the help of knotted ropes. Juan stops mumbling his spells as even he has to struggle up the high sandstone slabs, reaching a hand down to haul her up after him.

They stop at El Peñon camp at the base of the top cliff. Juan puts her tent up under a rock overhang while she prepares lunch for them both. 'Why d'you want to climb Auyán-tepui?' he asks. 'I've never guided a woman on her own before. Where are your husband and children?'

'I'm divorced and I don't have children because . . . because I'm an artist,' she says, not wanting to discuss her history.

'How does that stop you having children?'

'I have to be a really good artist, not just part-time, and for a woman that's hard.'

'I've never heard of that before,' he says. 'You must be a very good painter, I think. You should have been a man!'

'I was supposed to have been a man,' she tells him. 'My mother wanted a boy. So, I did boys' things: sculpture as well as painting. I can weld and carve stone.' Juan looks impressed, so she goes on, 'I've wanted to climb Auyán-tepui ever since I saw Angel Falls in a book, and I knew it was on a mountain called Devil's Mountain, but I never expected Auyán to be so huge.'

'It's shaped like a heart,' Juan says, 'but we call it a pumpkin!'

Dominique laughs and adds, 'A Halloween pumpkin with a devil inside!' Seeing it as a pumpkin makes it almost homely.

'It's the home of our gods,' Juan says, looking serious.

'I climbed Mount Roraima two years ago,' Dominique says, 'but it wasn't the right tepui. I've had dreams about living on top of Auyán.'

'Roraima is the mother of our gods,' he says, 'and the tallest. She's surrounded by the storm dragon.'

Dominique pictures its impressive prow and the triangular summit like a sky-island. The storms and how her guide rushed her back down, thinking the gods were angry. 'Did you see the oilbirds?' he asks.

'Ah no, I wish we had,' she says. 'We were going to, but the swamp was too deep. The mud was up to my waist!'

'No one could live on top of Auyán, no humans, certainly not a gringa,' Juan says. 'But one gringo lived up there for three years – Alejandro Laime. He was a powerful man. He lived alone on Orchid Island sometimes, down in the canyon – a loner a bit like you. He used to wander around naked because he never bumped into other people.'

'I saw Orchid Island,' she tells him, 'on my way to the base of Salto Ángel, last time I came to Venezuela. I saw his hut just after he died. The guide said they dug up his floor and found twenty-thousand dollars in a tin can and that he'd found gold on the tepui.'

'That's not all he found,' Juan says. 'Laime saw the Mawari on the top and he went a bit crazy. He stayed at the top of Salto Ángel though. He said there were little green men up there.'

'I've heard that story,' she says.

'But they were the Mawari,' he continues. 'Once, he went to sleep in a cave and woke up the other side of Churún Canyon, with no idea how he got there. He said the little men carried him. Another time they carried him back down onto his island – Mawari can fly without wings. He's explored deep into Aonda Canyon as well, the narrower canyon the other side of Salto Ángel. His island is at the entrance to it, but no one else has explored Aonda, it's too rocky.'

The mention of little green men makes her want to change the subject, so she decides to tell Juan about her father and how he first appeared to her in a dream here, his head in Angel Falls. How a few days after the dream, he contacted her, and how she had never expected to see him again. Juan looks puzzled as she explains that the night she had the dream and painted *The Summoning*, was the night her father felt he had to phone his lawyer to ask her to come.

'So, you made him come?' he asks.

'Yes, I made him appear after thirty years.'

'You're a sorcerer,' Juan says, laughing, but she can tell he's impressed.

She pulls out her sketchbook and pastels, but he protests. 'Don't draw me, you might make me disappear!' He's sitting with his head quite close to hers and she can feel his warmth.

She's tempted to get closer, thinking he might try to kiss her again. Perhaps this time she won't pull away. But she reckons he must have a wife in Canaima, so she just looks into his black eyes and says, 'But you're already invisible!'

He looks into her eyes as he says, 'Only to the Mawari.'

'Can we go exploring this afternoon?' she asks. 'Doesn't your wife miss you when you guide?'

He looks away at the distant mesas wreathed in clouds. 'She died two years ago.'

'Oh, I'm sorry. What happened?'

'It was a Kanaima.'

'What's that?' she asks.

'She was attacked by a black *tigre* when she was working in our garden. We call deaths like that Kanaima. Kanaima is the evil spirit of the forest. He isn't up here; he only lives in the jungle. We call Canaima Camp after him because of the tourists, they're white devils.'

'Yes, I guess that's true . . .' she says.

'Kanaima can change himself into a snake or jaguar. We'd had a quarrel with another family and they made this happen to her.'

'I'm sorry, that's so sad,' she says. 'But you must at least have your children, where are they?'

'My oldest son is training with a tour company to become a guide,' he says. 'He saw his mother die the slow Kanaima death.

73

She had a bite on her head that got infected. My youngest is with my parents, he wants to work in Caracas as a teacher.'

Juan decides to take a nap, but Dominique's set her heart on sketching and she sets off up the trail along the wall and finds an enchanted gully. She sits on a rock in the sun and thinks about Juan's wife slowly dying from a jaguar bite. No wonder he's so superstitious and aloof. Then she thinks about Laime and his stories and how, when the guide told them to her on Raton Island at the base of Angel Falls, she'd had déjà vu. It was as if she knew Laime's stories and had lived on Orchid Island herself, had been that hermit who drew mad maps and diagrams to a Lost World she alone had walked on. And here she sits at the gate of that world, in a sunny garden, surrounded by unnamed bromeliads, tiers of them heaped on every branch like the debris on Papa's shelves. She can almost reach across to hold Papa's hand, at four o'clock when he wakes from his afternoon nap.

The next morning, she rises early, ready to scramble up the crack in the Paloma wall, the only gateway onto Auyán-tepui. There's just enough light to find the pan and boil water, then pull her clothes on, careful to shake each boot for scorpions and wolf spiders before putting them on. As dawn breaks, the fog clings and she has trouble keeping up with Juan who keeps vanishing ahead, eager to reach the top.

They use the knotted rope to haul up their gear, then she inches her way up the rocky 'staircase' between cliffs hundreds of metres high, their tops veiled in cloud. Her footsteps make a loud metallic echo as she hauls herself up onto the top boulder and looks down.

Below is a kilometre drop. She can see right across the Gran Sabana to the cloud forests that hug distant tepuis. She calls Juan to look, but he puts a finger to his lips. 'Please don't shout or laugh, it annoys the spirits. You could start a whirlwind that would uproot our village huts.' She's surprised he thinks she would shout, but guesses that's what tourists usually do when they reach the summit. 'It's still a long way before we reach El Oso,' he urges. She's reluctant to leave the view but realises he will have to set up camp for them so follows him over a landscape of crevasses. She leaps over a metre-wide crack and walks between the towering rock formations. They have to use the rope to descend into valleys of cymbidium orchids and the less spectacular but jewelled miniature orchids clinging to rock faces.

At El Oso, Juan sets up her tent and warns her he won't stay.

'But what about Angel Falls?' she asks.

'I'm returning to El Peñon camp tonight,' he says, 'and I'll come to collect you in the morning. It's too cold up here and that cold I caught at Kavac has got worse.' He's shivering, but she senses that there's more to this change of heart and she's disappointed.

'Well at least let me stay here all day tomorrow so I can do some drawing, Juan. It's what I came for and the views from this rock are like my dreams, I didn't expect that there'd be jungles up here too.'

'These are sky-forests,' he says.

She pictures forests floating on clouds. 'Why do you want to go back now?' she asks.

'I know you'll laugh,' he says, 'but I saw the footprints of a Mawari on the trail in the sand and I can't stay any longer. I'll come back in the afternoon tomorrow and guide you back down.'

'You're leaving me on my own here for the night? What if a jaguar comes?' she says, suddenly nervous.

'There aren't any up here,' he says. 'You can come back with me now if you prefer, you choose.'

She decides to stay, even though it's starting to rain and his story about the Mawari has made her jumpy. She sets up the camp stove under the tarpaulin and boils some rice as it starts to pour down, giant drops clattering then suddenly stopping and starting again. She throws herself into the tent and falls asleep, woken every now and again by the rain.

At dawn she pops her head out and finds the rain has evaporated. She fries an egg for breakfast then digs out her sketchbook and pastels, the rock slabs sparkling in the slanted rays. But first she goes to the nearest rockpool, tears off her sweat-soaked clothes and dives in. The water is freezing.

She crawls out refreshed, dresses, then continues exploring. The wind has died down, and it's so quiet she can hear the blood pumping in her ears. Plants with blue strap leaves deflect the sun's rays, but she can't identify them. Her feet no longer leave prints. Has she vanished? No, she reassures herself – it's just that the wet sand has stopped and she's on a rock floor, approaching a maze of crazy piled-up furniture – hundreds of stone tables and chairs. She squeezes through a narrow passageway lined both sides by what look like cloisters, and enters a cobblestone labyrinth of alleyways.

At the far end is a sunlit valley like an ornamental garden. She rests on a quartz rock and takes out her pastels. She's brought a pad of Ingres paper, tinted grounds on which to record – what? She sits with a white pastel raised, as if waiting for her model to arrive.

She starts tracing a curved beak as something catches her eye through an arch opposite. It's a large chick with downy white feathers and a naked black head, and it's gazing up at the sky, making long growls.

When she looks up, a white vulture is gliding out of the sun, its black-tipped wings streaming with rays. She knows it's a king vulture by its naked rainbow head. She crouches, still as a corpse. She wants him to come close. And he does. His flight feathers whistle as he lands next to her, waddling towards the nestling.

*Glup*, grunts the father. The chick responds with croaks. There's time to look at the father properly – his piercing silver eyes circled by red, his coral wattle, vermilion and violet bald head, his pearl feathers, the black tips. And that swollen crop, dangling on his breast where his last meal is stored, which he now vomits up for the chick – a feast on the marble tabletop.

She's amazed to see she's filled five pages. Five pages that were charcoal grey are now caves of colour. And at the centre of each page – the vulture father in his kingdom. She's astonished to see it's three already and she's supposed to start back at four.

She backs out of the cloister through the narrow passageway chanting: *I am Revenge: sent from the infernal kingdom, / To ease the gnawing vulture of thy mind.* Shakespeare? Must be. She thinks of the king vulture's Latin name: Sarcoramphus papa – Father of the Coffin, and of his family name: Cathartidae from the Greek Cathartes – cleanser.

☙

'Hola, my friend, you survived the night, I was worried. Did you see the Mawari?' Juan asks.

'No, but I did find a king vulture's nest!'

'You saw the king vulture father?' he says, impressed. 'Tramanchita sometimes appears as him and sometimes he's Anwoná. Do you know the legend of the king vulture bride . . . ?'

'No, please tell me . . .'

'Let me tell it as we climb down,' he says, 'but be careful where you place your hands and feet. Soon the bushmasters will wake, and we must get to El Peñon before nightfall.'

As they scramble down, climbing backwards, there's no time to take rests. His voice drifts in and out of hearing. But it doesn't matter, the story she's hearing is her story, and when she gets back to London she's going to paint it. But first she must see Papa for Christmas, she's going to tell him the myth and see how he reacts. What he has to understand is that the king vultures are so beautiful they must be gods. That today she saw the king of the Lost World and it's given her the strength to visit him.

# 18

# THE KING VULTURE BRIDE

SNOWFLAKES CLING TO Dominique's lashes like down as she climbs the stairs to Papa's flat, knocks, then inserts the key. She pulls her chair out from under the window as he sinks into his red armchair and smiles with relief.

'Is it snowing?' he asks, 'I hadn't noticed. Look at that snow in your hair, you must be frozen. When did you get back from Venezuela?'

'I came straightaway, as promised,' she replies, 'caught a direct flight from Caracas to Paris.'

'And how long will you stay?'

'Until the thirtieth. We've got a week together. How are you?'

'Happy, now you're here.' He pauses to catch his breath. 'Why do you have to go to a jungle? Even one mosquito drives me crazy. Why don't you just go to the Midi? There's no need to go anywhere else – France has everything.'

It's her birthday but he hasn't mentioned it yet. Perhaps he's waiting to surprise her. She looks at the walls, and tries to describe the Lost World. 'If you saw the table-mountains you'd understand. They're otherworldly, not Conan Doyle's dinosaurs – stranger than that.' But she's not going to tell him about Kavac Cave or climbing Auyán-tepui. 'The Pemón have wonderful myths,' she says.

'I love myths,' he says. 'At school I studied Egyptian myths and always wanted to go to Egypt. You see – we *are* alike!'

She inspects his features carefully and now she's sure he doesn't look at all like her. All her life she was convinced she would resemble him. Wasn't that why Maman hated her so much, why she was always punishing him through her?

There is one way they are alike though: they are both loners. He will never go out again. She is all he has. She must at least cheer him up this Christmas. How long is it since he spent Christmas with someone? How long since she spent Christmas with someone? But at least she's learnt to set it aside for painting time when she knows no one else is working. It's a special feeling, as everyone eats their Christmas lunch while she works on a new canvas, like she's alone on the plateau, walking on a sky-island in the clouds.

'The best Pemón myth,' she begins, 'is the tale of the vulture bride. Her face is rainbow-coloured like the king vulture's, and she lives in her father's house on top of the *tepui* – that's the Pemón name for these mountains.'

'Her father's house?' he repeats.

'Yes,' she says, '*tepui* means house. Their first shaman, Maichak, decides to contact the vulture father, so he sets a trap. He smears himself with grease and lies down next to a rotting tapir. When the vultures land he waits for the most beautiful one to arrive, thinking it's the king who feasts first. But it isn't the king, it's his daughter, who transforms herself into a woman with whom he falls in love.'

'Ah! A love story?'

'Yes,' she says. 'Maichak asks her to take him to meet her father in the sky-world. She agrees, on the condition that Maichak won't look at the king vulture's face. She sticks white vulture down over Maichak's hair and leads him onto the plateau to her father's house.'

'Like those snowflakes on your hair?' Papa says, but Dominique ignores him.

'From behind a screen, the king vulture father commands Maichak to perform three trials. The last of these is the hardest – he has to carve a shaman's stone stool in the king vulture father's likeness.'

'Like your painting of me?'

'But no one has seen the king vulture's face,' she continues, 'so how can he carve his portrait? A hummingbird comes to Maichak's rescue and tells him that the vulture father has two heads – one is a man and the other is a king vulture.' Papa is frowning, but she has to go on. 'The Pemón have these spells called *taren*. And the king vulture's chant goes something like this,' and she tries to recall what Juan recited:

> 'I am the Vulture-Father,
> I eat death,
> I am the Two-Headed-Father,
> I am the Bald-Father,
> I am the Multicoloured-Feather Father . . .'

She can't remember any more, so they both look out of the window at the whirling snow.

'It's going to be a white Christmas,' Papa says, and then laughs. 'I'm not completely bald! And my face isn't multicoloured like a vulture's!'

But it is, she thinks. He's sitting with his serviette tucked in his silk pyjama collar. He's wearing the lambswool scarf she sent him for his birthday, and it looks like a king vulture's creamy-white ruff. The cannula trailing from his nostrils is a wattle.

They tuck into pâté de foie gras – an entire duck's liver smeared on slices of baguette. There's a steamer on the small table where he's heating up white asparagus.

'Wait,' he keeps saying, 'it's not ready yet.' While they wait for the spears to cool, he blows on them. At last, he drizzles Béarnaise sauce over the white tips.

It's delicious but she's cold and jetlagged and longs for something hot. She drains her champagne and pours herself a cognac, after offering Papa one. 'All that's finished now,' he says, 'I can't drink any more. But champagne – that's medicinal. It's so funny your mother said I was a playboy. Hah! What a joke! I can't even have

80

sex anymore.' And he laughs then gives her a funny look. 'And are you going to bring a brave young man to meet your two-headed father?' he teases. 'Your old invalid, the vulture?'

'There's no young man,' she says, embarrassed, then fumbles in her rucksack and brings out two tape recorders.

'What do you have there?' he asks.

'Tape machines to . . . to record your voice.'

'But you've got two. Is that one for each of my heads?'

She laughs nervously and places one near him on the table. 'Can we try it now?' she asks.

'No, no. I can't talk into a machine. It wouldn't be natural.'

'But you promised . . .' she pleads.

'I think you misunderstood,' he says. 'Maybe if you came more often, then later on, when we get to know each other better perhaps, who knows.'

She stuffs the machines back into her rucksack and clears away the dishes, clattering them in annoyance. He protests as usual, saying Lucienne will do it, that she hasn't come here to work, so she sits back down and watches the snow blowing against the window, wondering what to talk about next.

Papa clears his throat. 'Veronique phoned,' he announces, looking animated. 'And she wrote me a letter and she came to see me. Can you reach that file up there and find it?' Dominique brings it down and fishes out the envelope with her sister's large handwriting. Papa wants her to read it aloud, so she does, instantly envious of Vero's chatty casual tone and how she writes half the letter in English. 'She's going to visit me again in February,' Papa says proudly. 'Do you think she's disappointed in me, this place? I'll have to ask Lucienne to clear the mess! But I almost forgot, Domino - see that box over there? Can you pull it out?'

She lifts the huge cardboard box and unwraps it as instructed.

'It's for my grandson, for Christmas. Do you think he'll like it?'

'What is it?' she asks.

'Table billiards! I bought it online - it was expensive. I always played billiards. So did Django. That day I interviewed him he insisted we played a game. Can you take it back with you?'

Dominique turns the box over; she can't believe he's asking her to drag it back with her. She could barely manage her luggage, what with the drawing things and camping stuff from Venezuela. 'No, Papa, I can't take it back. It's big and it's heavy,' she says, lifting it up to show him. 'Who do you think I am, a courier?'

'But you're strong!' he protests, 'you've climbed mountains!'

'I may be strong,' she says, 'but I'm small and this is huge.'

When she doesn't give in, he sulks, turns the TV sound up, peers at the news around her head so she has to push her chair to one side. The screen is enormous and above it the large wall-clock ticks. The bright overhead light hurts her head. She's tired and uncomfortable. 'What about the neighbours?' she tries, hoping he'll turn it down. But he's forgotten about her and his eyelids start to droop. He switches it off, gets into bed and turns to face the wall. She moves into his armchair.

Suddenly he has a spluttering fit. He sneezes repeatedly, spits into a jar that's already half full of yellow mucus, then to cap it all, lets out a loud fart. She's had enough. She says she has to go and lets herself out into the night.

She makes her way out of rue Clovis passing the now familiar lycée garden behind iron gates in the rue Descartes, the little crossroad with its Poisson Curieux and Violon Dingue bars, their names that always make her chuckle. The steep rue de la Montagne-Sainte-Geneviève with its red-lit restaurants that make her homesick, even though she's never been inside them. She repeats their litany of names to calm herself: Au Dromadaire Gourmand, La Madeleine de Proust. A passing couple kiss, and she thinks of Juan. How normal they look! She'll never be like them, and it's all Papa's fault! She wends her way down to the Hôtel St Jacques to check in to her attic room, stopping off to buy a bottle of Mouton Cadet at the Nectar wine shop.

❧

She wakes late on Christmas morning, and rushes up to go to the Jardin des Plantes, hoping it's open. At rue des Boulangers she glances up at the windows above the Finnegan's Wake pub. That's where they lived and where he said they'd been happy. She can't picture Maman being in love with him – all those years she wouldn't let her mention him because he'd done vile things to her. 'When I'm dead you'll find out,' she warned her, that time she dared ask what he was like. 'I've kept all the letters in that trunk for you to read.' And she pointed to the black leather trunk she kept locked in her bedroom. 'You'll understand everything then,' she added. 'Every letter I've sent has a carbon copy. That's why I typed them all. So you would know what I went through.'

So, is he lying? Or does he really believe Maman was in love with him? He's not considerate, expected her to drag back a huge box for Jack as well as all her luggage. Perhaps he deceives himself. Walking down the crooked cobbled street on this deserted Christmas morning, she can almost hear them giggling up in their rooms. Two small rooms, he'd said, but they didn't need more. A peacock cries from the gardens. She peers into a broken ground-floor window, the thick small panes of glass like lorgnettes. It's dark and smells of oranges when she leans in. She remembers a party, jazz playing on the gramophone on the bare floorboards. A game with oranges, pulling out the shrivelled stalk, but they used to give it a special name – its *navel*, Papa tickling her belly button as she peeled it. There she is held up in his arms, dancing on his shoulders.

She greets the iron entrance gate and the old cedar tree on the first bank of the Jardin des Plantes. The sandy path crunches as she veers towards the Ménagerie, passing two untethered scarlet macaws displayed outside.

She finds herself walking down L'Allée des Rapaces, lined with tall outdoor cages. And perched on pillars in a corner cage are two king vultures – a male and female. They could be the king vulture father and his daughter. A rat carcass lies on the ground beneath them, as they warm themselves, wings out in the winter sun. She takes out her sketchpad and searches for pastels to match the corals and violets that jewel their heads and necks. Duller shades than the ones she used on Auyán-tepui at the king vulture nest.

The rat smell reminds her of Papa's stuffy room. Papa! she says, realising it's almost lunchtime. Time speeds up when she's drawing.

It's snowing hard, so she makes for the zoo nursery, where she knows there are seats. The glass roof is covered with snow, making it prematurely dark. This is one of her favourite places, and today there is a new occupant – a baby king vulture, on a fleece in the corner of a toddler's playpen. He has stubby white winglets and keeps falling over onto his head.

*I am the vulture shaman*, Dominique whispers, *it is I who eats death. I am the double-headed daughter. I eat carrion and warm my belly. And my children will have warm bellies . . .* And as she makes her way towards Papa's flat, her belly fills with river stones, she's breathing water.

❧

Papa has been worrying that he won't feel well enough to enjoy Christmas Day. He opens his presents like a child, and seems pleased with the French-English dictionary – not too small and not too big so he can hold it easily and look words up. He also likes her moon orchid watercolour, but she will have to get it framed and hang it for him. She looks at the yellowed walls and can't imagine it there.

'Guess what I found in the Ménagerie?' she says. 'Two king vultures, *and* a baby in the nursery.'

'So you see,' he says, 'you don't have to go to Venezuela. France has everything, even your garish vultures. Why do you talk about them so much?'

'But don't you think it's a strange coincidence?' she insists. 'I saw two just last week, on the plateau. And here they are in our zoo. It's as if I conjured them with my spell.' She stares defiantly at him but he blinks and looks down. Is she too intense for him? He would rather she just small-talked. But she needs to know. 'Please Papa, talk to me about your life.'

'But it would take me a long time,' he replies, 'and many visits. I can't talk just like that. It will be gradual, bit-by-bit. You should come to visit me every fortnight. Why can't you do that?'

'But my work!' she protests.

'You're an artist . . . you can work when you like,' he says.

'I've twenty canvases to finish for my show in May. It's my first one-woman show. And I have to anyway because of the grant I got from the Arts Council.'

'They pay you to paint and travel?'

'Yes.'

'You won't come until May?' he pleads.

'No, I can't. I need my painting. It's all I have.'

'But you have me!' he says.

'Oh Papa, I don't, I'm here and I'm not. My real self is in my studio painting my waterfalls so I can visit you. You have no idea how hard it is for me to be here.'

'But I'm your father!'

'Eurostar is expensive,' she adds lamely.

He snaps back that it's just eighty-five francs and makes small whimpering noises then clasps his chest. 'Look how you've made my heart beat too fast,' he huffs. 'You shouldn't say things that upset me. You'll give me a heart attack.'

'I'd better leave you to rest,' she replies.

'You do as you like. I'm not much fun for you. I should have given you more brothers and sisters to play with. You should be out dancing! When I was your age I was always dancing. So did your mother. She was so light-hearted before . . .'

'I used to dance,' she interrupts, 'but I'm thirty-eight now. It was my birthday yesterday.'

'I know it was,' he says. 'Here . . .' And he rummages in his papers and brandishes a cheque. 'This is your birthday and Christmas present. You can take it to that bookshop you like so much and they'll accept it without a card, as they're my neighbours.'

The cheque is for two hundred francs. So he did remember her birthday. She feels she has to stay longer now. She sits quietly while he naps, takes out her sketchpad to look at her drawing of the baby king vulture. She can't understand why Papa won't let her sketch his portrait. He says it's because he's too ill and won't look his best, but why can't he understand how important it is to her?

He's snoring loudly now, so she opens her box of crayons. His head is covered in black fur. She draws him sleeping with his eyes open. She is staring at the face she has been forbidden to see. His pyjama top is open and she can see down to his chest, where silver hairs sprout.

19

# BLACK JAGUAR

E VERY TIME DOMINIQUE gets lost along the Ménagerie's paths, her feet lead her to the Fauverie, an octagonal art deco big-cat house at the end of the zoo, next to the nursery and the noisy quai Saint-Bernard by the Seine. It's surprisingly crowded for Boxing Day – fathers with their children, couples. She is the only one alone.

The big cats are hiding behind fibreglass rocks at the back of their cages. She starts at the far left, by the nursery, where the pumas are kept. In the next two cages there's Luna the gold jaguar and a black one called Pataud. Next to them are North China leopards, then a lion, larger than even the panther, and lastly a snow leopard.

Yesterday she only glanced at them, as she wanted to see the king vultures. But today she realises these are the crown jewels of the zoo. And although the lion is the most impressive, it's the black jaguar that holds her. Its coat is a chocolate brown through which the black rosettes glow.

*Their rosettes are black butterflies that lure girls into the forest,* Juan had said, when she asked why their Spanish name is *tigre mariposa.* And as she's thinking this, she realises that the jaguars are mating, that the black one is a male. The keeper smiles at her, so she retreats onto a bench, watching from a distance.

The female snarls and springs away then rolls over. Juan had said that jaguars can be Kanaima – a shapeshifting devil. That shamans can turn into one by painting the corners of their mouths with V's, and placing hairs from a jaguar's ears into their ears so they can

87

hear as sharply as one. 'If you file your teeth,' he'd said, 'you'll turn into a were-jaguar.'

'Some daughters turn into were-jaguars in the forest of their fathers,' she'd answered without thinking, and Juan had looked puzzled.

She feels powerful today – strong enough to face her father, whatever is waiting for her. It's as if she's painted black quatrefoils on her skin under her clothes, and jaguar lashes have been stuck onto her own, a lustrous mascara that makes trees transparent and helps her see into his heart.

She imagines she is lying on a rough table under a kapok tree, between its tall buttresses. She knows she must keep still so the jaguar will come, and Juan has painted her skin black with the genipap dye with red urucu rosettes.

## 20

# WERE-JAGUAR

*T*HE DEEPER I *go the more I remember. The dark is thick as jaguar pelt, grips me by my scruff, its tongue on my nape. I can smell its breath – hot and rank with rotting meat.*

*I call the black jaguar with his coat of pulsars, smelling of starlight on leaves. He prowls the heavens, devours planets as if they are balled serpents. He bites the neck of Earth and it unravels, the mantle trails blue and green blood.*

*I call my owl monkeys asleep on the tree of life and they hoot an alarm. The tree Roraima, mother of all waters, whose trunk is hacked. The dragon curled around her buttresses stirs and the storm begins. Her tongue is a tree of lightning bolts, her strikes are smouldering stumps. Her scales are fireflies flickering over the savannah. She releases her fire-rivers – thunderheads mass over the land.*

*The pygmy marmoset crawls out from my hair as if it's the last refuge. My monkeys leap from branch to burning branch, their paws scorched. My howlers, clever capuchins, my spider and squirrel acrobats, my bald uakaris of the flooded forest, leave phosphorescent trails where they leap. My last golden lion tamarin's fur is foxfire.*

*Here is cotton wool from the kapok's silk-cotton pods. Here is the bat that sucks the sour-smelling flowers until I am numb. The scissor-tail kite offers his tail as surgical scissors while I lie face up on the table.*

*I am splitting myself in two so I can watch from the ceiling as the doctor mends me. The cotton pads are red as kapok blossoms. Here is the hurricane lamp casting a hole of light over the kind nurse, who sits nearby, sewing boy's clothes for my doll.*

*The sword-billed hummingbird is a living needle, mending my wounds with moss and orchid fibres.*

*The black jaguar licks my face. He licks my teeth and tongue, removing all trace of Papa. When he's finished, I'm clean. I can leave my childhood. Papa vanishes like morning mist wiped by sunrays.*

*The doctor closes the door after him. He wonders if I'm alive, this girl he's wrapped in gauze like a straitjacketed hummingbird, this girl with monkey tails she refuses to comb, whose caves are scarred. She's pretending she's dead now; it's safe to leave her. The doctor packs his bag, says goodbye to her mother.*

*When I next see Papa, after thirty years have passed the way a waterfall pours from a plateau one kilometre high, he will see the jaguar hairs in my ears, the V cuts at the sides of my lips. And he will be frightened of the woman I have become, who bursts into his room trailing air from virgin trees.*

# 21

# THE NOTRE-DAME SPARROWS

## STILL SECOND VISIT, CHRISTMAS
## 27TH & 28TH DECEMBER 1997

DOMINIQUE CROSSES THE Pont-au-Double onto the parvis of Notre-Dame. She makes for a stone bench to gaze at the cathedral she had passed in the taxi from Gare-du-Nord. Part of it is shrouded in scaffolding, but the façade is free and a gleaming creamy-white, newly cleaned like her. It's so huge she doesn't know where to look first – at a bewildered looking Eve or shamed Adam, above the great door and portal sculptures of the kings of Judah and the Last Judgement.

Further up, grotesques leer down at her – gargoyles with long arched necks and gaping mouths. Higher still, on tower balconies, she can see tiny people moving behind the chimeras of the Grand Gallery. One day she will climb up the towers. She peers up at them as if they're the ramparts of Auyán-tepui with its eroded stone idols.

A crowd has gathered around one man in front of the cathedral. She approaches, curious. His arm is outstretched and birds flutter around him, diving up to his hand. They hover there, beating their wings, then dart back down to the low privet. As she gets closer, she can see the birds are sparrows. The closer she gets, the more arrive; the box hedge is thrumming with them, and starlings, a few opportunist pigeons. Then a woman accepts the crusts and peanut shells the man offers her, and she waits to be honoured by the birds. The sun is warm, in spite of winter. They are tame, these sparrows that pluck crumbs from the privet, scratching for insects under the pungent twigs, just by the verdigris statue of Charlemagne on his horse, with his tapering double beard and long hair.

The birdman has noticed her and beckons her over to pour bird-seed into her hand. Dominique steps onto the low wall surrounding the box hedge and holds out her hand, feeling self-conscious when no birds choose her. Then a female sparrow lands. Her tiny claws clutch her fingertips. The sparrow picks up a seed, throws back her head and balances it between her upper and lower beak, which is yellow and peach inside, cracks and munches it, then bends down for another. Dominique keeps her hand stock still. A male lands, and the female flaps her wings angrily to dispatch him. Another lands, and she flaps her wings even harder, as if to say: *She is mine.* Every now and again her small black eyes dart up to Dominique's face, then down again, to survey her banquet. A starling tries to join in and the sparrow protests – off he flies. She feeds for half an hour, batting off intruders, and Dominique's arm aches. She inches her free hand under it to support it, all the while keeping her arm steady. The sparrow feeds slowly, balancing one seed at a time between her lower and upper bills and swallows, stops, darts a glance at her benefactor then down to her palm until she's full. Then she leaves. But for years, Dominique will feel her tiny claws scratching her fingers.

She searches for an unoccupied stone wall to sit on and tries to sketch her hand with the sparrow, the sensation of her claws, the beak with the poised seed inside, the beak that's gold at the back and buff at the front, the peach tongue and the seed. She holds her hand up as she did when she was feeding her and draws her downy breast. As she draws, she thinks of Annette Messager's installation *Les Pensionnaires* – The Boarders: forty or so stuffed sparrows in knitted jumpers and crochet caps, laid out in a vitrine as if put to sleep. She's always loved this piece, but now that she's had a sparrow perch on her hand, she thinks it's cruel. When she gets home, she'll have a look at the booklet where Messager describes the rituals she went through, of taking them for afternoon walks, their dust baths, and how some of them caught cold and they all had to take a nap. Some had to be punished by taking exercises on little machines.

When Dominique thinks of Messager's boarders, she's reminded of La Mésangerie – the orphanage she was sent to south of Paris when she was four, all the infants in their beds for enforced afternoon siestas, laid out like bluetits in a bluetit-house. Two years she was there, like Messager's sparrows, forced to go through daily rituals by the nurses.

The sparrow she draws will be alive. She concentrates all her efforts on this, the seed in her beak is a sun in that peach interior. She is only a juvenile, but strong enough to fend off intruders.

Dominique crosses the square onto the rue de la Cité. Didn't the taxi pass an orchid house just here – La Maison de l' Orchidée? There's a vast hospital across the square, the Hôtel-Dieu, which she will later learn was once a hospital for the poor. She passes the police headquarters, another imposing building, and heads for a glass-covered metal pavilion, where she finds herself among giant succulents in a rare-plant house, surrounded by the scent of lilies and gardenias, winter-flowering jasmines.

❦

'So, what have you been up to this morning,' Papa asks.

'Admiring Notre-Dame,' she answers, not wanting to mention the jaguars she's discovered, or the sparrow. She can still feel her delicate claws on her fingers.

'You must go up the towers', he says. 'There are four hundred steps – you like climbing don't you? I went up when I was young, with your mother. She was soon out of breath, but not me!' He holds his chest and heaves, then resumes pursed-lip breathing between words. 'My daughter the climber . . . you can see all of Paris from the top . . .'

'The Eiffel Tower?'

'Yes, the Eiffel Tower near where we lived, my *chérie* . . . and even Sacré-Coeur.' And he clutches his heart as if the basilica is in there. Dominique sees gargoyles peering from his shoulders, leering at her, one of them with its tongue lolling out of its mouth.

'Behind the Notre-Dame parvis I found an orchid house . . .'

'Ah – the Marché aux Fleurs!' he says. 'You went there?' He forgets his chest and takes a deep breath, longer than she's ever seen him take. There's a weak smile on his face as he looks past her, deep in thought. 'I took your maman there often. She loved to smell the flowers . . . and I'd buy her an orchid. They were expensive but it was worth it just to see her face.'

'I love orchids,' Dominique says.

'I know, *chérie*, you paint them.'

'How are you feeling today?' she asks.

'I'm breathing easier now,' he replies. 'Later in the morning it's better, and today is a fine day.' He reaches over and takes her hand then raises it up. 'Let's drink some champagne to the past,' he says. 'To those days!' And she goes to where he's pointing, to the crate. She returns with two glass flutes and he pours, with much ceremony, pausing every few breaths to regain his strength. Then he picks up her hand once again and holds it up as if feeding birds.

'My child, tomorrow is Sunday when you must go to the Marché aux Oiseaux.'

'The Bird Market?'

'Yes, where that flower market is, as if by magic, you'll find birds on Sundays. Cages of them. All kinds: lovebirds, parrots, canaries, parakeets, cockatiels. They even sold hummingbirds once.'

'I love birds,' she says.

'Then you must go,' he says. 'And you'll find animals there too. You like animals, don't you? Wait a moment – ah yes: chipmunks, silk hens, rabbits, puppies! That's where I bought your maman her white poodle. It made her so happy!'

He beams at his daughter, then lets go of her hand, and Dominique thinks he's thinking that she doesn't look like Maman. He wants

Veronique, not her. But she wants to prolong the moment, so she tells him about the sparrow.

He laughs. 'They're for tourists, they've always done that,' he says. Then he's mumbling under his breath and she realises he's reciting a poem. He stops to catch his breath, then begins again, slowly so she understands each word.

When she hears the words *mon amour*, she listens harder. Is he reciting a love poem to her? She wishes her French was better, because he's talking about the birds in the market, and between his coughs and struggle to breathe, he's saying that he's bringing her flowers from the flower market.

After a long pause, he looks at her in a way that makes her uneasy, and says he's gone to the scrapyard, searching for heavy chains. Then, as if that isn't enough, he's looking for her in the slave market. The slave market? Surely she's mistranslated? But he did say *esclave*.

She gets up to go into the kitchen, not wanting to hear any more of his stange poem, and when she comes back, he's telling her that he didn't find her in the slave market after all, and he looks bereft. A tear rolls down his cheek. She's never seen him cry before and wonders why he's so upset.

He turns his face towards the window, and Dominique thinks that he's gone back to the bird market, still healthy, no oxygen in tow, and he's searching for a bird to buy. While she can't help feeling that she's a sparrow feeding from his hand.

'You must know this poem. "Pour Toi Mon Amour",' he says. 'It's by Jacques Prévert. I know it by heart. You are my little *moineau*, I bought you at the bird market and gave you to your mother, so she couldn't fly away!'

Who is the sparrow and who the feeder? Is she his untamed daughter, pecking at any seeds he will feed her, darting a look at his out-of-focus face, trying to understand those words he coughs out? Or is he the sparrow with his thin limbs and skeletal body? Does he fly in his sleep, out of the window and across to Notre-Dame, he who spends most of his life dreaming? Does he breathe easily in his dreams? Is there a reprieve for his sparrow soul? 'Rats with wings,' one tourist called them. Her father the winged rat, resting in a gutter.

'Tell me more adventures,' he urges. 'That way I can imagine I'm taking a walk.'

'Then perhaps you won't want to come with me into the crypt?' she asks, wondering whether to tell him about her visit under the parvis, into the archaeological site under the Notre-Dame square.

'Yes, tell me,' he says. 'You'll find the whole history of Paris under there.'

So she tells him what she learnt about the Parisii tribe, who first settled on the Île de la Cité, and how the first king of Paris was Clovis. 'So that's why your street is called rue Clovis!' she exclaims, and he nods. She looks at him and sees that he is a king in his armchair, with his kingdom spread around him, up on shelves, so many cooking appliances at his command, as he nibbles his rillette.

'Did you see the thermal baths?' he asks.

'Yes,' she replies, 'there was a frigidarium and a caldarium.' But she also remembers the garbage pit, the narrow cellars excavated under the old hospital for foundling children. And a book she bought about subterranean Paris, the tunnels and oubliettes, trapdoors and catacombs. She sees a rat inching along them, injured.

Papa has a pained expression. He shuffles up and falls onto the bed, pulls the sheet over his shoulder. And she knows that her stories have worn him out, that even following her in his mind has exhausted him. A ceiling in his lungs has collapsed. But as he lies there, staring at the wall, making wheezing noises while he takes shallow breaths, she remembers reading how students hold parties underground, in ghost stations and caverns, how free they feel where there is no law. She wonders if Papa went there when he was young and wild.

He turns around and faces her, reciting the poem again: 'I went to the bird market and bought a hummingbird for you, my love.

You must look it up,' he says, 'you'd like it. Do you know Jacques Prévert? Look him up on the internet.'

'I don't have the internet, Papa, but I will look him up in the bookshops.'

He sinks back down and closes his eyes, his lips reciting the poem soundlessly. Then his lips are still and he's asleep. It's time for her to leave.

⁂

The next morning is Sunday and she's back on the rue de la Cité early, heading towards the market. She braces herself for disappointment. The idea of a bird market is so dreamlike and perhaps Papa made it up. But already she can hear parrots squawking. And there they are, hundreds of colourful birds in cages: peach-faced lovebirds – a dozen nuzzling; budgies squashed in a cage, one on top of each other; pearl-grey cockatiels with filmy crests; turtle doves; fire-red rosellas; yellow headed amazons. There's a cage of Japanese sparrows, a small flamboyant Venezuelan bird, but she can't make out the scrawl of the label. A couple of red and green parakeets are quarrelling with each other; one keeps turning his body around in the confines of his cage. He lunges at his cage-mate and emits a piercing squawk. There are red-crowned parakeets labelled 'kakariki' that make a kaka-riki sound, and African greys, more subdued.

The more she looks, the more she sees Papa's features in their faces. He is wearing feather pyjamas and the air of his room is echoing with shrieks. He sees her face beyond the bars – huge, out of focus, inquisitive, peering at his plumes, trying to see into his mind. He closes his eyes, but a flash pierces the lids. She's taking a photo of the parrot. Then a hand thrusts in and slams the hatch shut. His neighbour, who lived against him like a shadow, is in someone's hand. A few yellow feathers float down through the air. Then the neighbour is in a small cardboard box and taken away by a customer.

In front of the rows of caged birds are empty cages for sale. Some with perches and exercise wheels, water vials. There are stalls selling birdseed for every species and she scans the labels: macaw feed, parrot mix, wild bird grain. And all around are lemon trees, oliviers, hibiscus, lantanas, tiers of gardenias, lavender and ornamental peppers.

She pauses at one birdseed stall, wanting to buy some grain for the Notre-Dame sparrows, loses her nerve and is about to leave, but the seller spots her and asks what she wants, so she tells him. He fills a small bag with multicoloured seeds and off she goes back to the parvis, to the wild birds.

She fills her hand with feed and holds it up, feeling foolish again at first. But soon a male sparrow lands on her fingers and starts pecking. A female joins him, her tiny feet scuttling across her thumb. More fly up and there's a scuffle. Only a female is left. Dominique wonders if it's the same one as yesterday. She talks to her as before. It's not quite the same as the first time a sparrow landed on her hand and stayed as if she trusted her, and her fingers tingled from the sensation of tiny claws clinging on, the way the bird seemed to respond to her voice as she chatted to her. Though now she has three sparrows clinging to her, chirping at each other. One stays, and one flies off. A new one lands and is frightened off by a flurry. A starling tries to land and they all vanish, back into the low privet, which is a-rustle. More males choose her today, but the females are daintier, with their cream-coloured breasts and brown wings.

Each day, after visiting Papa, she goes back to handfeed the sparrows. As he sits opposite her, munching his Viennoise baton, Dominique thinks of them and can bear being with him.

One morning, she decides to go to the Musée de l'Homme, and that afternoon sits with Papa. Although she's small and he's her father, his head is shrinking, while hers is stuffed with the trophies she spent hours examining, the books she bought in the bookshop about the Shuar tribe of the Jívaro and their *tsantsas*. It's like sitting in her sand world, where, even as a child, she towered over her castle. The castle that she built, where Papa is imprisoned.

## 22

# AFTER VISITING THE MUSÉE DE L'HOMME

ON NIGHTS WHEN Maman takes too long to fall asleep, even with the help of medicine, I take my animals out of my toy box in the cellar. They glow fluorescent as black scorpions that glow lilac under the beam of a blacklight torch. I play with the ultraviolet sleep sloth, the night monkey and pygmy owl. I bring out the jaguarundi and tayra, agouti and tapir, my capybaras and bush dogs. I line up my poison dart frogs according to their colours. My parrots perch on me and squawk for joy. If you ask me to, I can recite the names of all the animals that live in the Amazon, exactly how many are left. I arrange them above the pillow on the mattress. I guard them and they guard me.

There is only one doll among them. I have given her your name, Papa, and dressed her in boy's clothes, her face wizened.

I walk through flames which do not burn, down the right fork of the cellar. I take my boy doll to the very last meter door and open it, enter a part of the forest where fathers are not allowed. The electric meter ticks like the big clock on your wall – our moon.

I kiss you, and when our lips meet, my animals talk. Oh Papa, the stories they know! They have taken datura to gain superpowers. Grandmothers have suckled them and mashed manioc with hallucinogens, fed them the pulp mouth to mouth.

My animals know the stories of the trees – those armies of forbidden ant-words patrolling the forest floor where it is never day, the twilit understoreys, the middle storeys where every letter has a prehensile tail! The canopies with their coral trees! And the emergent giants – those kapoks and ironwoods where mama harpy nests! As we sit here, she crashes through the ceiling and plucks the sloth. Let sleep always be plucked from you when she hunts!

When I say that we passed through the meter door, I mean that we passed through its branches of knowledge, the libraries wound inside the bark, rings upon rings of scrolls. Every night I read its pages. There are as many killing songs as leaves, as many curing songs as flowers. They rustle above us, raining notes.

It is always dark in this backroom cramped as a wardrobe. After I've kissed you, the pelts of my animals sway above us, dangling from hangers. Are you frightened, Papa? Will death be like this – a haunt of animal spirits? I've brought you here to tell you a story. Let my words crawl down your ear canals like fire ants!

Let my words coil around your brain and eyeballs the way a humming-bird wraps its double-tongue inside its head!

The Shuar warriors of the Jívaro say there's only one thing to do with a tormentor. They say that afterwards I'll be able to sit with you as if you're a doll that I can dress and undress, feed and bathe.

I sit here holding your hand, thinking that it isn't enough to shrink your head. I use water from Fire River, hot sand from its bed and I sing to my materials.

Even head-hunters would be shocked at how quickly I slit the sides of your limbs. How I discard your meat and ask my animals if they are hungry. The anaconda-canoe carries your organs to the feast, while

*I sew your hollow skin with bamboo needles and palm-leaf fibres. My stitches are as kind as the nurse who made your doll clothes. Papa, I iron your skin with a lullaby of river flames. The badness bubbles out. I don't stop until you've shrunk enough to be my doll.*

*I seal your lips with chonta pins to lock in your soul. I close your eyeholes with thorns from the baby kapok, plug your nostrils and ears with beeswax. How the bees stung me when I climbed up to steal it! When I told them what it was for, they helped me.*

*I light a fire. Can you smell my fire, Papa? It smells like supper cooking. It was always after supper you'd tell me to go to the cellar. We are here now and you lie beside me waiting to play.*

*I thread red toucan feathers from your ears, trail white strings from your smile. But still your soul lingers, whispering that I must undress. So I undress you – your miniature sex that can't hurt a mouse. I bring you to a part of the forest where only children are allowed. Walking here, I listen to what your soul has to say.*

*I am laying you out surrounded by hummingbird amulets, as the children gather around, touching your tiny fingers.*

# PART TWO

## 23

# THE LADY AND THE UNICORN

D OMINIQUE HAS NOT been able to visit Papa for almost a year. She knew she should, but felt too angry, she doesn't know why. Except, after her visit to the Musée de l'Homme, it was as if her body knew. Her body knew what books to read; it remembered the blank parts of her childhood. After she read about the Shuar head-hunters, she started to feel stronger.

In the end, she makes herself go, but arrives in Paris two days early so she can enjoy the Latin Quarter first, without having to visit Papa.

She wanders around exploring the cobbled streets of the Left Bank, then eats at L'Autre Bistro on the rue des Écoles, at a street table, so she can watch the comings and goings. She has the whole of tomorrow to herself, to explore her Paris.

By eight she's at Notre-Dame with her sketchbook, craning her neck up at the devils around the central portal of the west façade, who are leading the damned to hell. Above the door, in the half-light of the December dawn, she can just make out an angel and a devil weighing Papa's soul. For the moment, the angel is winning, but the devil is pulling the scales towards him. She cranes her neck further up at the gargoyles and the chimeras on the tower balconies. One day she will see them up close. Today, she's going to sketch the damned.

She pauses at the box hedges to watch the sparrows but doesn't have time to feed them, makes for the Pont-au-Double then down rue Lagrange and rue Monge, down rue Linné towards the Jardin des Plantes just as it's opening. The stone lion gnawing a dog, and the one eating a man, carry on with their eternal meals at the entrance to the maze. She sits on the bench opposite the plane tree and draws its stilt roots. The only other people in the garden are joggers. Papa is probably still asleep or dozing. He is remembering that Domino's coming on Saturday. He hasn't seen her for eleven months and this upsets him. He tells himself to be grateful she is coming. Does he realise she got upset last Christmas? Is he aware how hard it is for her to see him?

There are feelings she has to push to the back of her mind. Yet she must see him. His soul is being weighed and she can help. But today is Friday and it's still only eight and the sun is shining, as it always is when she comes to Paris. On the other side of her root-sketch she draws a tree-man. One moment the page is white and the next there are these lines – long, loud lines. She will never show them to anyone. She wants to make more, light as sunrays, heavy as a weighing-scale. She wants to draw leaf men with red shadows. Not lions gnawing the dead from the maze.

Her feet lead her to the zoo as they always do. Around the paths she goes, checking on old friends. Then she sits on a bench and before she knows it another drawing has appeared. The title makes her laugh: *The Zoo Father*. She cannot escape him. It's as if these animals are his masks. The paper feels alive. Some of the lines even leap. Others are asleep – maybe they will never wake. Here is the leopard pacing in his cage, back and forth. He turns then starts over again. Behind him is a bed of straw. She wants to draw things that bite. That are caged. That are both Papa and *fauve*. If she draws the puma with his long sandy nose and gives Papa his innocent eyes, she can make Papa love her like a beast, in the now, with no past.

*Tigre mariposa*, Juan had called the jaguar they heard cough but didn't see, that night after she almost drowned in Kavac Cave, and they watched the moon moths flutter under the hurricane lamp.

Her feet have led her directly to the jaguar cage, to find them mating again. The black male has mounted the gold female, his cinquefoils becoming black butterflies as he thrusts. She sits on a bench and watches, while they go through their ritual several times, him mounting, grasping her ruff, her snarl followed by his snarl, then her springing away and growling, only to roll over and invite him back.

She tries to capture their movements in charcoal, but the marks won't mate with each other. And she's hungry. It's time for crêpes and a coffee in the pavilion café, the canvas flapping in the breeze. She takes out the small map Papa tore out of a magazine of the district and ponders where to go next. And decides on the Musée de Cluny. She's avoided it up to now, but the crypt under Notre-Dame with its excavations from Roman times and the Middle Ages made her reconsider. Cluny has the original Adam from the façade. That would be worth seeing. And while she's there she might as well see *The Lady and the Unicorn*.

When she finds the museum at the end of the rue des Écoles, she sits in the courtyard, staring at the impressive medieval building. Here too there is a well and she peers into it, right down to the bottom. This is a city of wells. Once there were thirty thousand, she remembers Papa telling her. This one has a gargoyle jutting out of one side.

She follows the signs and enters a darkened room where she's surrounded by red tapestries – six of them, high and wide. But which one is *The Lady and the Unicorn*? She glances at each in turn and sees there's a unicorn in all of them. He's not the unicorn she's familiar with in films; he has strange eyes – half human, half horse – and his hooves are cloven like a goat. The lady is light itself.

Then she sees the bird perched on the lady's hand in the first tapestry she studies, its wings raised – she's about to feed it! Dominique laughs – is it a sparrow? But it could be a hawk or a parrot. The unicorn rears to the right of the lady, a lion on the left. The lion has escaped from the Fauverie. They and the lady's maid stand on an island and are surrounded by animals – a monkey, a genet, rabbits, a goat. Dominique bends down to look at the monkey and sees the caption, that this is 'taste' and realises that each tapestry represents one of the five senses.

Sight is a hand-mirror to show the unicorn his reflection. He is as charmed by it as he is by his mistress. He sits with his front paws on her lap, and Dominique watches his eyes light up with curiosity. His paws have raised the hem of the lady's dress, revealing her petticoat. The lion looks around, protecting this moment. The genet is in front of them, watching the lion, and a lion cub is having a conversation with a rabbit in the upper field.

The unicorn's eyes are like Papa's when he was looking at her photo album, when he lifted the cellophane film from each page and studied the snaps of his family and the woman he fell in love with, her luminous skin.

And look! In the 'touch' tapestry, the lady's hand brushes the unicorn's long white horn, near the base. She is dressed in black, like Maman on her wedding day. A hare has leapt to the lion's feet. Above them, on the red upper ground, are a cheetah, a leopard and a genet.

The Fauverie is open, its beasts roam Papa's flat when he's asleep and dreaming of being young. Though later, after he's woken, it feels far away as the Middle Ages. There were orange trees, a pubescent oak, animals bustling through red foliage, flowers everywhere. He can almost touch them. He can still hear her play the harmonium. He remembers there were six of these women in his dream, but whether they were his daughters or his wife he can't remember. He has had recurring dreams of the red forest with its mythical beasts. The lion that doesn't roar. The unicorn with his long spiral horn. The slim lady in her brocades. And the music of the harmonium, which puts the unicorn in a trance.

He wakes and they vanish. He tries to fall back asleep, to that red room where his lungs don't hurt and there is a hunt with no bloodshed. He thinks it might be the Jardin des Plantes. Domino is there in the rose garden. He is sure of it. She is not in London. He wakes hard, into his grey room. He would cry but tears won't come.

Then he remembers. Tomorrow, Domino is coming. He swings his legs out of the narrow bed and snaps out of his siesta.

The phone rings and he's jubilant: it's Vero. Even better!

In the fifth tapestry the lady is weaving a chaplet of carnations. Both the lion and unicorn face her, and smile, as if the scent alone could make them happy. She looks at the flower she is adding to the garland and inhales it. Seven centuries later, she is still engrossed in the scent, a sad expression on her face. Dominique can only watch her in her embroidered world, this virgin enclosed by a silk forest of flowers that take millennia to die. So why does she think the garland is a wreath?

Now Dominique is ready to examine the sixth tapestry. The lady is on a wide island-rug, in a blue damask tent embroidered with gold flames. Inscribed on the canopy banner are the words 'À Mon Seul Désir'. The lion looks as if he's about to devour her but restrains himself. The unicorn watches her, adoring, as she pulls a necklace out of the casket her maid holds open. Dominique does not know what this sole desire of hers is; she and her companions are still surrounded by a bestiary. Dominique thinks of the jaguars mating. Perhaps she has removed that heavy necklace and is placing it back in the jewel box?

She thinks the jewel box is Papa's soul. It is not in his body, his body that she day-dreamed she shrunk to the size of a doll.

It is here, in the Musée de Cluny. It is a medieval soul surrounded by a medieval zoo. It is guarded by a virgin, a unicorn and a lion. The maid is Lucienne, who washes and feeds Papa, passes him all he needs.

And this is the beauty of these tapestries. They have different meanings for every visitor.

Dominique sits on the bench in the centre of the darkened room for hours, and it's as if she's on an embroidered island. The tapestries float in the twilight. The unicorns and the lady's six faces shine, absorbed in their allegories. The bird is always perched on her hand, waiting to peck at the sweet she is about to offer it. What

Dominique is certain of is that innocence is in this room. This room where there is a casket containing her father's soul for safekeeping.

Papa listens to what Vero is saying in her halting French. She can't get hold of Domino. Does he know where she is? Is she there?

She is in this red room and no one knows where she is, no one in the whole world. She is an anonymous tourist in her father's city. Today is fatherless. She is sitting among the tapestries. There is no man in them, no man in this red forest with its harmonious creatures. The music that the woman plays is church music, but the notes are silk flowers dotted on the wool lawn. The unicorn listens. Only he can hear it. His muzzle is open and Dominique can see his red mouth and white teeth.

## 24

## AN ANNOUNCEMENT

T HE NEXT DAY, Dominique arrives at the appointed time at Papa's, 3 p.m., as if she's come straight from the Gare-du-Nord. He hugs her, then says:

'I have something to tell you, but not yet.'

He won't say anymore, and changes the subject. She can tell he's hurt that she hasn't come for eleven months, but he's too glad to see her to let it ruin the day. 'Tell me what you've been doing all this time . . .' he starts, and instantly she feels guilty.

'My show opened last night,' she says. 'A hundred people came to the private view. It's my first one-woman show, and I'm pleased with a few of the paintings. But my work is out of fashion. No one wants nature. Certainly not nature "not from our neck of the woods" and I don't want to paint London, or anywhere in England. It's too crowded and tame. I like wilderness.'

'So now, it's all finished, and you can visit me more often?'

'No!' she says. 'It's just starting. It's only my first show. I have to follow it with a second that's better. I have to be the best. And it's harder for a woman artist to get on.'

Papa looks hurt. 'Don't you want to ask me questions,' he teases, 'about my life?'

She realises she's given up trying to squeeze information out of him. She's dismayed to see his condition has deteriorated. There's a mini fridge by his bedside that wasn't there before. 'Because it's harder for me to walk now. I get breathless after two steps,' he explains, following her glance. She feels really bad now, and doesn't know where to look as she sips the champagne.

'Dessert?' Papa asks. 'If you look in the fridge you'll find some nougat glacé.'

She beams at him. He knows it's her favourite, and she rushes to serve it, but he doesn't want any himself. 'My stomach's shrunk,' he says, patting his robe. And he watches her as she eats.

When she's licked the last spoonful he smiles again, a curious expression on his face. 'I have something to tell you,' he begins. 'Do you remember I said I had some news? I can tell you now you've eaten. If I'd told you before, it would have spoilt your appetite. And I haven't seen you for eleven months – I didn't want it to come between us. I wanted to have one meal with you beforehand.' He looks straight at her.

Dominique thinks how Papa resembles the unicorn with this strange expression on his face. He's opening his mouth, and his lips are poised and trembling slightly as if a hummingbird is struggling against them to escape:

'You no longer have a mother.'

The words fly into his window and crash against the pane. To her surprise she bursts into tears. Then it occurs to her he might be joking. She doesn't believe him. But she can see he's serious.

'You no longer have a mother,' he repeats. 'She died yesterday.'

'When?' Dominique asks, realising that it might have been when she was in the Musée de Cluny. 'How did she die? And how do you know?'

'She died late yesterday morning,' he says. 'She was in hospital, having an operation, and it went wrong. She never came round. Your sister called me. She said she had a hunch you were in Paris and that was why she was calling me, to talk to you.'

A hunch, Dominique thinks. Vero was right. How could she know? She hasn't been here for almost a year. But Vero's like that, amazing intuition. Maman died when she was in the Musée de Cluny, bathed in the red light from the tapestries. The lady was her mother, miming her departure from the world and its senses, young again, untainted by Papa, bursting with health.

'But why didn't you tell me as soon as I arrived?' she asks.

'I didn't want her to spoil things for us,' he says. 'It won't be the same now. You won't spend so much time with me, and we'll have to talk about her. And I thought you'd need a good meal before getting bad news . . .' he adds lamely.

'That was selfish. It's not something to hold back, fathers don't do that!'

'Yes, I know,' he says, 'but I don't have you for long, and haven't seen you for almost a year. Did I do the wrong thing?'

'I'm your daughter. I need a father!' And she starts collecting her things to leave.

'Please don't go, Domino, you're all I have! Vero refuses to come again.' He clutches his heart and whimpers for breath. She glares at him, but it looks like he really might have a heart attack, so she sits back down. And the news is starting to filter through.

'Last time I saw her – ten months ago – she was in hospital,' she tells him. 'She was playing a power game with me, even when she was ill, even when she was asleep, and I sat by the bed feeling like a child who hasn't been dismissed. I couldn't leave until she woke.'

'Will you cry when I die?' he asks. 'You cried when I first told you, so you must have loved her.'

'Loved her? No, that was shock. I felt sorry for her, she was always so ill. But love – no. I hated her. I still hate her. She hated me, that's why I need a father!' Even as she's saying the words, a sob slips out and her nose is running. She scrabbles for a tissue and Papa passes her his handkerchief.

'It's clean,' he assures her. 'But will you cry when I die?'

'Of course I will. I don't hate *you*,' she replies, not sure. She hunts in her bag for Vero's phone number, and Papa hands her the phone.

'You must phone Vero straightaway and find out what happened. You'll tell me everything she says, won't you? I loved your mother once too. I'm sad that she's dead as well. It's bringing it all back.'

She settles herself on the edge of his bed and dials. Vero answers immediately, as if she's been waiting by the phone.

'Sis? Are you at our father's?' Vero says. 'I called you at home first, and when you weren't there or your studio, I guessed you were in Paris, but I couldn't get hold of you yesterday or this morning.'

'Are you alright?' Dominique asks. 'I was in Paris yesterday. I came two days early so I could look around on my own, without having to spend all my time with Papa. No one knew where I was, no one in the world. Tell me what happened. How did Maman die? Papa says she was in hospital.'

He watches her intently as she chatters away in English. He looks like the unicorn gazing at his reflection in the mirror.

'She was in hospital having an operation for her ulcerative colitis,' Vero says. 'They weren't sure she was strong enough to have it, but things had got so bad. So, we thought it was worth trying. Just before she went into the operating-theatre, she got frightened, as if she knew that was it. I squeezed her hand and told her I loved her. She said she loved me. I'm so glad I said it. She went feeling loved.'

Dominique tries not to feel envious of how close they were, to feel happy for Vero that the last time she saw her was loving. 'So, the operation didn't work?' she asks.

'The surgeons told me it went okay,' Vero says, 'but in the recovery room her bowel perforated. She never came round. At least that way she didn't suffer. The funeral's Tuesday. Will you come?'

'Of course I'll come,' Dominique promises, at the same time wondering if she'll go just to be sure she's buried. 'I didn't say goodbye, Vero, but it's good that you did.'

'We have to sort her things as well,' Vero adds, trying to be practical. 'Remember that trunk she was always harking on about when she was angry with you? It says in her Will that we have to open it and read the letters when she dies.'

A vision of a large black leather trunk comes into Dominique's mind, and how Maman always pointed to it when she sat on her bed during her midnight talks. She'd always wondered what was in it, if it really did contain all the letters they'd sent her as children. There came a point during Maman's talk when she'd mention it, just before the end.

Dominique catches Papa looking peeved and realises she's been talking to Vero for thirty minutes and must stop. 'I have to go now, Vero – Papa looks annoyed. He always gets cranky after dinner. I'll have to stay in Paris a few more days, as he'll be upset if I leave early. It was strange – he didn't tell me she died until I'd been here an hour, and we'd finished eating.'

'How odd!' Vero says. 'How could he keep that from you?'

'I know! He's like that,' Dominique says. 'I'd better go, I get back to London on Monday and I'll catch a train to you then.'

She holds the phone to her ear for a few seconds after Vero has rung off. She feels powerful, being able to talk in English without Papa understanding, but he's got a strange look on his face.

'Well? What did Vero say? Did you find out? Will you tell me everything?' he asks.

She's aware that she's withholding part of the story as she repeats what Vero told her. She doesn't feel he's earned the right to know what happened to the woman whose life he ruined. Instead, she just tells him about the septicaemia, and how she died while still asleep.

'I suppose everything's spoilt for us now,' he replies. 'Will you still stay in Paris until Monday?'

'I didn't love Maman,' she reminds him, 'but I can't believe she's dead yet. I can't think. I'll let you know what I'll do tomorrow. Anyway, the funeral isn't until Tuesday so I could leave on Monday as planned. I don't have to be afraid anymore,' she adds, trying to take it in. 'I was scared of her, even when she was really ill and weak.'

Papa's face brightens then looks sad again. He's breathing hard and coughing. 'You see,' he splutters, 'I knew this would happen once I told you the news. That we'd have to talk about her and you wouldn't be interested in me anymore. Perhaps I shouldn't have told you!'

Dominique glares at him but he just smiles and asks her to take the plates out. 'I have to go now,' she says. 'I can't believe you could even think about keeping this news from me.' Then she kisses him goodnight, wanting to reassure him as he looks so pale, but thinking that she has a right to be upset about her mother's death.

When she steps out onto the street she feels light – joyful but grieving for the mother she never had. She can't hurt me anymore, she tells the Violon Dingue, she can't even phone or write. She shivers as she thinks of the last time she saw her, how even Vero was ashamed about that last power game.

'I know what you're up to, Maman,' Vero had scolded her, 'and I think you should stop it and behave. Just eat the chocolates Domino has bought you and stop playing games.'

Dominique had looked around the ward at the other patients and their relaxed visitors. And when Vero went out to have a smoke, Maman looked at her hard until her daughter blinked and looked away. 'You're ashamed of yourself,' she'd said. 'You're too evil to be my daughter. And too plain. Vero takes after me.'

Dominique had sat there, unable to think of a reply and angry with herself for not being able to stand up to her. But Maman had just stared harder. 'I know what you're thinking,' she'd said at last, her eyes shining. 'I've been thinking about my Will. When I get better, I'm going to change it. Vero has been such a good daughter.'

Walking down the rue des Écoles, it all comes back. How she'd felt like a fifteen-year-old schoolgirl again, in her dirty-white uniform blouse and the shapeless grey cardigan Maman had a neighbour knit her for her birthday. She always liked to taunt her about her Will. Dominique was an artist and needed the money. And she knew that. It was her last weapon. It was when she lived with her that Dominique had decided to become an artist. She would recreate the world, step into her true life through her canvases, into a world she loved. Her paintings were the real her. This person walking down the rue is a shadow.

It was a sunny evening, the trees bare in the Lycée garden. She thought of Maman lying in the hospital morgue. She was free. *Her mother was dead.*

But it didn't feel real yet. How strange that Papa had been the one to break it to her. He who hadn't seen his wife for thirty years, whom Maman had never let her mention, however much Dominique longed to know what he was like. It was as if she'd known all along that her daughter would sit in his small room in the Latin Quarter eating a delicious meal while he watched her face and thought about his news.

It had fluttered in his head like a hummingbird longing to fly out of his mouth. But he kept his mouth closed when he stopped eating and gloated in the luxury of having his daughter opposite him, her hand almost touching his over the small table. He watched her swallow one mouthful of nougat glacé after another until there was nothing left in her bowl. He wanted to prolong the moment, perhaps with another glass of pink champagne, but at that point his conscience got the better of him. He opened his mouth and the hummingbird flew out into her face.

Dominique thinks back to when she sat in the red room bathed in innocent light. Her untouchable mother up there on the wall – six of her radiant faces, before she had children, before she met Papa and the threads unravelled. She thinks now that Maman's soul slid into the lady and spoke to her in that silent circular room.

The next day she tells Papa she will stay until Monday as planned, and he pretends to be happy. But he knows that her thoughts are elsewhere, however much champagne he pours. She goes through the motions of cheerful chatter. He smiles obligingly but shakes his head. 'It hasn't been the same since I broke the news,' he says. 'It's right that you should be thinking of your Maman now. She threw me out you know. It wasn't my fault what happened.'

'What d'you mean, it wasn't your fault?' Dominique asks.

But he's adamant, 'No! It wasn't my fault that you didn't have a father. She wouldn't let me see you. She sent me away and didn't even write and give me your news.'

'But I needed a father,' Dominique says. 'She didn't love me and I needed you.'

'You have me now, *chérie*. You have a father now.'

'No, I don't. I can't love you just like that, without knowing what happened. You won't tell me. You don't talk about your life.'

'I've told you all there is to say,' he says, folding his hands.

'But I need to know what you were doing those thirty years,' she insists. 'You haven't told me anything. You haven't earned the right to be my father yet, you're a stranger!'

He struggles to his feet and then he's towering over her, his hand raised, and for a moment she's a child. She must make herself large as possible and wave her arms as if there's a puma on the path. She must shout for her life. But the words cower in her throat and come out too high:

'How dare you slap me!'

Papa laughs. 'Oh, I was just pretending, a little slap like when you were little.'

'It always hurt!' Dominique shouts.

'You've upset me,' he says, gasping for breath and clutching his chest. 'Look what you've done now. You mustn't fight with me or you'll give me a heart attack.'

'You can't hit me anymore, I'm grown up!'

But he's rasping now, taking strangled breaths and panting. 'Pass me those pills,' he gasps. She passes him the bag and he struggles with it and tries to reach his water. She waits quietly. There's no point saying anything more. In any case, he's forgotten her as he takes his pill and slips into bed. She might as well go. But he turns around and asks: 'Will you come back to see me soon?'

'Yes, I'll come back tomorrow to say *au revoir* before my train leaves,' she says.

'No, I mean will you come back to Paris very soon?'

'I can't say yet, Papa. I don't want to upset you, but I have to take it in that Maman's died. I'll let you know.'

'I can't force you,' he says bitterly, 'but I'm not going to live long and if you want to know what my life was like, you'll have to visit soon and often. Then I'll talk when I can. It hurts for me to speak. You said yourself you didn't love your Maman, but it looks like you did.'

She denies it because she doesn't want her ruining her life, even when she's dead. Papa's still alive and she's on an adventure; wherever it leads she is willing to go. *Whatever I don't say to him now, I will never say.* He may die soon. Maman's death is inconvenient so she tries to switch it off. She'll think about it later when she gets home. Or better still, even later, after Papa dies. Then it will be her time again. Go away, Mother. Don't bother me. You were always dead. No one kisses bodies in the cold-room. If she did accidentally touch her, she was always icy. And Dominique shrank back as if she'd stroked the cheek of a corpse.

'Maybe I'll come back in the spring,' she promises him. And she thinks of the lady with her unicorn and lion, making a perfumed wreath, so absorbed in her task that nothing breathes. She will return to the tapestries and puzzle over them again, but the lady will still be fastening that carnation onto the garland as if it's memory itself, while all around her the forest watches. The unicorn rears on his hind legs and holds her banner.

'I may be dead by then,' he mutters. But Dominique can't see how she can bring herself to come earlier and there's that black trunk to open, all those letters to read.

## 25

# THE BLACK TRUNK

'Do you like the green?' Vero asks, waving at the wall. 'It goes with the yellow door, doesn't it?' Dominique tries to take in her kitchen, but she's too aware of the back door that leads to Maman's annexe. 'Do you like this table?' Vero persists. 'It's new. And the tablemats, they're from Provençe. Maman liked those.'

'Yes, very colourful,' Dominique says. 'How are you?'

'Oh, you know,' Vero sighs. 'I bought a Givenchy dress last week and it was funny not having Maman say she liked it. I'm used to her okay-ing everything. I wanted her to come and tell me it was great when she got out of hospital, do all those things mothers do.'

'What things?' Dominique asks.

'Little things,' Vero says, 'like saying I look nice in my new outfit, or that this meal tastes good. Not that she could eat much with her stomach. But she still told me it was good even if she couldn't taste it. She was like that.' Vero looks pale and Dominique thinks that perhaps she should try to take Maman's place for a few days and asks her to show her the Givenchy dress.

Vero dashes upstairs and returns twirling. 'It's very Audrey Hepburn,' Dominique says, hoping she's said the right thing, aware that Vero can't really afford this. But Vero looks pleased and rushes back upstairs and returns in her jeans. 'You've always been so pretty,' Dominique reassures her, 'you'd look good in anything. Can I see Maman's annexe now?'

'Oh okay. It's through here, you remember?' Vero opens the back door and they pass through a utility room with a washing machine and a freezer. Vero fumbles with the lock and Maman's white cat leaps out yowling. 'I forgot to feed her,' Vero confesses.

Dominique can barely look at the furniture. It's exactly the same as when she lived in Maman's house – the dresser, the large table, even the ceramic knife-rests laid on the tablecloth. It's as if Maman was waiting for her to come home.

And she has. Here she is. She can smell Shalimar through the mould. They pass into the living room laid out like a bedsit. Maman's bed is unmade, the blankets pulled back as she left them before she went into hospital. A pile of bills is on the coffee table and next to them her reading glasses, an ashtray with a cigarette butt smeared with red lipstick. Dominique glances around, expecting her mother to be behind her, and catches sight of black bags piled in the corner.

'I've started clearing out her clothes,' Vero explains.

'Already?' Dominique says.

'She couldn't do anything towards the end,' Vero says.

Dominique thinks of her having to look after Maman and feels guilty. She should have helped. She only visited them once after they moved here, when Maman was in hospital. But she couldn't step into this house while Maman was in it. 'That must have been difficult,' she sympathises.

'Yes, it was,' Vero says, 'but that's what children do, isn't it? Let's eat then we'll open that trunk. I think I know where the key is.'

They eat in Vero's kitchen. She's made coq au vin and potatoes which aren't quite cooked. Dominique is hungry after her journey, but the food sticks in her throat. 'Sorry, I think I overdid it with the salt,' Vero apologises and Dominique realises that's what's wrong. She gulps the red wine down, hoping it will relax her. 'I must look for that key,' Vero says, getting up.

They go back into the annexe and Dominique sits on Maman's rocking chair as Vero rummages through boxes and drawers. The cat jumps on her lap and Vero laughs. 'Don't let her dominate you!' she teases. Dominique isn't sure what she's talking about at first, then she realises she means the cat, because she hasn't got up to help her search for the key.

Vero goes back into her house to find a cigarette, leaving Dominique on her own. It feels strange being in Maman's room, as if she shouldn't be there. *But I was all along,* she thinks, as she catches sight of her school photo on the mantelpiece. Why did she keep that one? It's the plainest she's ever looked, and that trapped expression on her face as if Maman knows Dominique will never escape. She can't bear to look at it, so she turns it face-down.

When Vero comes back in, Dominique reminds her she's only got tonight to see the trunk so perhaps they should try to force the lock. Vero scowls. 'Oh, I don't think we should do that. It doesn't feel right.'

Dominique takes a good look at her sister and reminds herself that her hair is not quite red as it was. She has Maman's strong nose and full red lips. But Vero's not as outgoing as when she was a child. She's become withdrawn, just like Dominique used to be when she lived at home. Dominique lets her search another half hour then puts her foot down. She's come to read those letters. Tomorrow will be the funeral and then she'll go home.

Vero reluctantly brings in a crowbar and forces the trunk. It springs open and letters tumble out. 'You start that end and I'll sort them this end,' she suggests, and they bend down and thrust their arms in.

More letters tumble out onto the carpet. Many are airmail, so light they seem to glide. Dominique tries to open one and realises it's never been opened. She tears at it and scans the translucent blue paper with faint typescript. 'Look! It's Maman's letter to Monsieur Kwan. She never sent it,' she says.

Vero frowns at her. 'I don't think we should read it, it's private,' she says. But it's too late, Dominique's already read halfway down and she's not going to stop. She sits back down on the rocking chair with it.

'Vero – he was her boyfriend. She's telling him she feels too 'guilty about us to see him again and won't pay his gambling debts.'

'I knew he was her boyfriend,' Vero says. 'It was obvious.'

'But d'you remember how Gran didn't have enough money for food for us,' Dominique says, 'and all along when Maman was in Paris, she was paying his gambling debts. She's telling him that she can't do it anymore because the guilt is killing her.'

Vero stands up and turns to face her sister. Her face is white. 'And who are you to come here and judge? We never see you. We've hardly seen you for years. It's all right for you with your arty London friends, but I've had to stay here and look after her. Someone had to! What do you think it was like being with her when her meds made her shake so hard I'd have to help her eat? How dare you talk about her like that!'

'But can't you see?' Dominique says. 'Here's the evidence. She was having a glamorous life and pretending she didn't have children.'

'I'm not going to listen to this,' Vero shouts, her voice shaking. 'I don't think it's right for us to read her stuff.'

'Well, I'm going to read them all,' Dominique replies, 'that's what Maman wanted.' But as she says it, she realises she's frightened of Vero, just as she used to be frightened of her mother.

When Vero leaves, slamming the door, Dominique tries to calm herself. She's only got tonight to read everything and it's already nine. She glances around at the room. It's as if Maman's here watching her, as if Vero's shouting has summoned her. *We've hardly seen you* – that royal *we*. She switches more lights on and kneels in front of the trunk, plunges her hands in and scoops out an armful of papers, tips them on the floor. Perhaps she'd better start from the bottom.

And she finds the letters she wrote to her mother when she was five, some neatly written, well behaved, then wilder ones with words misspelled. Illustrated with drawings of ducks and flowers and ships. Sent from the children's home – La Mésangerie. Loving letters, filled with kisses. She is trying so hard to make her love her. *Ma toute petite Maman*, she begins. Underneath these letters – Maman's small leather-bound diaries, which Dominique flicks through, searching for her name, but all she comes across is one entry: *Vero's birthday. Visit the kids* – among the endless lists of things to buy, nail and hairdresser appointments, pencilled lists of how many accessories she owns: 67 shoes, 34 belts, 32 handbags.

Then more unopened letters, from Papa to Maman. Dominique rips them open. So he did write to her after he left them. Begging letters, wanting her to take him back, promising that he's found them a home and is buying furniture she'll love, a real rose cottage for his country girl. Begging her to tell him how his girls are. And there, in his writing, is Dominique's name. Him asking *if Domino is better, less unhappy with Gran. I loved that holiday in her house*, he goes on, *with the roses and the garden the children could play in. I really liked your mother. She was so kind and warm. And Domino seems happy there, no longer a silent child.*

And underneath his letters, Maman's letters, also unsent, sealed in skin-thin envelopes. Like the organs of a ghost a vulture daughter has to eat to survive, the thin blood from Maman's typewriter that she must drink, sour in her mouth. All the things he's done to her.

Their first date in the hotel where she worked as a chambermaid. How he pushed her into a room that was being cleaned and threw her on the bed, and laughed but kept going when someone burst in on them.

*That's how Domino was made*, Maman wrote to him. *I had to marry you when I got pregnant, but I didn't love you. I never even found you attractive with your cow-shit eyes and sallow skin, not like my handsome Dylan in Wales who I had to break my engagement to, too ashamed to explain why.*

Cow-shit eyes and sallow skin – the exact words Maman used to describe Dominique.

The more pregnant she is with Dominique, the more he hurts her in the early hours when he's returned from nightclubs. How she had to get up afterwards and go to work in the beer business while he slept off his hangover and then spent a leisurely morning at his toilette. The beer barrels she lifted onto the lorries, hoping it would make her miscarry.

Underneath those skin-thin envelopes, longer letters to friends, asking to give evidence so she can get a divorce.

'Papa raped and abused her,' Dominique tells Vero, who's just come back in.

'I know,' Vero says. 'She always talked about that when she was off her head. She recorded it on tapes and I've thrown them out.'

'You shouldn't have done that!' Dominique says, raising her voice.

'They were mad,' Vero says. 'She was a drama queen. She used to talk like that when she was high, before she crashed. Disgusting stuff I don't want to talk about.'

'Why not?' Dominique demands.

'It's best to forget it and not bring up the past, Sis,' Vero says. 'It's not healthy. Can't you just forget her and stop dwelling on what she did to you?'

'I don't think it's healthy to just forget it, and in any case, I have to visit Papa and being there reminds me,' Dominique says.

'That's why I won't go again,' Vero says.

Dominique agrees, just being in that room with him and that musty smell, the sound of the oxygen machine. Looking at his face and watching him deny that any of it was his fault.

It's midnight now and Dominique is running out of time. 'I'm going to have to pile this lot into bags and take it home with me.'

'You don't want to do that – I'll burn the lot!' Vero says.

'But Vero, all our letters to her are here. And her letters to Gran, and Gran's letters to her. Even that primary school we went to in Wales – there are letters from the headteacher, worried about you. There are your letters too.'

'You haven't read them, have you?' Vero asks, scowling again.

Dominique blushes. 'I just read a couple. Your spelling was just as bad then as now. Your writing's just the same,' she teases, trying to make light of it. But she intends taking them with her, along with the others.

Vero flounces out and Dominique goes into the kitchen to search for some carrier bags and starts sorting. Some letters are in duplicate, triplicate. She typed them to keep a record of her sacrifices for her children.

At one o'clock she finally gives up and climbs down the steps into Vero's kitchen. Her sister is sitting there, puffing on a cigarette in her dressing gown, nursing a fresh mug of tea. 'You're not taking those,' she says, her voice rising, and bars Dominique's way. 'You have no right. You're a visitor here. We never see you. Who d'you think you are with your arty ways, coming into our house and riffling through Maman's things!'

'No one talks to me like that anymore, and who's *we*?' Dominique snaps.

'We?' Vero says. 'Why, your *sister* and your *mother*!'

'Maman's dead! We're burying her tomorrow!' Dominique shouts.

Vero flings her tea at Dominique. She ducks and the mug hits the wall and smashes on the floor. But it has splashed her and scalded her cheek. She stands there too scared to move. This was what Maman used to do when she lost it.

She forces herself to walk away, rushes up to where she's supposed to sleep and starts bundling her things into her bag. She doesn't know where she'll go. It's too late to catch a train and she doesn't know the area, but she can't stay here. She'll have to sleep on a bench outside somewhere. She's crying because Vero's made her feel a bad person, but mostly she's angry with herself that she couldn't stop her. She stumbles downstairs with her bag and carriers bursting with letters, hoping it's not raining, but Vero rushes to the front door and bars her way again.

'I'm sorry, Sis. I'm sorry I threw the tea. I shouldn't have. Is your face alright?' And she strokes the red streak on Dominique's cheek. 'Please don't go now. Let's calm down and think about this tomorrow.'

'No, I can't stay here!'

'Please stay, I promise to be good, and there's nowhere for you to go.' Vero's face has softened, so Dominique agrees. But as she follows her into the kitchen for some Savlon, she tells herself she will never stay with her overnight again.

# 26

# KING VULTURE DAUGHTER

WHEN I RIPPED *my way out, Mother took one glance at me and said I was ugly. She called me her vulture chick, always falling over in my playpen. She stuck a mirror in the corner, said no one would love me.*

*As soon as I could I fled from home and painted my face with sunrise – orange and violet, coral and rose. I dipped my wings in pearl mists. I made my own day, my own night, a bride who married silence. I glided among storms and bathed in waterfalls. I married colours only I could see. When I fly, my shadow scares jaguars!*

*Only when I become the king vulture daughter can I make my colours come. My bed is an untidy nest on a rock and in it I lay the eggs of new paintings. They crack out of their shells. I tell them they are beautiful. Their winglets are clumsy, but I teach them to fledge. I am a good mother.*

*Once, I had a mother. She would call me into her room at night, talk until my eyes were puffed slits. The air turned black and filled with red spots as she came to the end of her talk. It was then she pointed to her leather trunk, which lay locked like a carcass.*

*'When I die', she'd say at the very end, when I wanted to die, 'I want you to open that trunk and read every letter inside. Then you'll know how I suffered, and how evil your father was.'*

*I am the king vulture daughter, the one who makes the first gash. I plunge my head under the black leather lid, feast straight on the guts and heart. I gulp every word with my red beak, reading with my red circled eyes. My claws pierce organs, tearing open each envelope. I am so hungry for the truth, acid streams from my beak.*

## 27

# SIGHT

A S SOON AS Dominique reaches her studio, she empties all
the letters onto the floor and sits in the centre like the baby
king vulture in its playpen. This is what Maman wants her to do.
She won't feel guilty.

She reads deep into her mother's life. There are diaries for every
year in Paris. There are stories she wrote for therapy in the psych
ward. There's crazy writing in coloured crayons all over envelopes, lines scrawled over other lines, about Vero being Jesus and
Dominique Satan. It takes her days to read everything before she
picks up her brush.

She starts pasting the translucent Xerox sheets onto the canvas,
a sky of overlapping words like rain. Airmail-blue envelopes, cellophane windows, familiar addresses over foxed pages. She carefully
prises off the brown and black leather covers of her mother's small
diaries and arranges them in the foreground into the shape of a travel
trunk, ribbed like a carcass bursting with flies. Years inscribed in
gold lettering here and there.

Around the black trunk she pastes the letters she sent to her
mother from Gran's house, letters with drawings of the garden:
roses, pinks, sweet peas, in careful rows. She buries Maman in the
soil until she can no longer hear her. She stands in front of her
painting as she stood at Maman's graveside, while the priest lowered
her coffin past the roots, deep into the clay soil of a Welsh hillside.

It was in her mother's house that Dominique learnt to make paint
speak, her adolescence distilled into colours. Each had a voice she

listened to, upstairs in her room, as Maman called and Dominique learnt to slip through the mouth in the centre of her palette - which hummed when she placed green against red.

Letters of rose-petal pages. And at their centres, among the anthers and stigma, the marital bed. White petals open for the first time from sepal-envelopes Dominique has torn. Petals with writing on them in blue ink like insect blood. Letters tears have dropped onto, as their secrets bloom. Some fat as scarabs, their pincers raised to sink into her fingers.

Only now, when she's glued them on this canvas, can she face them. There's a father just beyond the painting's edge - she can hear him approach but he never arrives. He's a father-flower she can only see if she slows herself to the pace of plants, then she sees his tendrils piercing the canvas, his roots around her mother's body, so that even in her death, Maman is in his clasp. As long as there is an inch of flesh on his wife he will feed.

Dominique, who has learnt to make paintings so real they have skin, must watch him eat her mother like bonemeal.

Her parents are a garden. As long as she works on it, weeding and pruning words, fertilizing with her sable brush, she will not have to take Prozac.

She no longer has a mother. Her father is dying. Already she is planning the canvas plot where he will lie so she can visit. He has told her he's afraid of hell flames, even though he doesn't believe. He knows he has done wrong. And now she knows just what he has done. Her mother's letters have opened their buds and shown her the marriage bed with its anthers and the broken stigma.

# 28

# A WASPS' NEST

THREE MONTHS PASS. She locks herself away in her studio and works deep into the night. And when she stops, she reads her Amazonian books and almost every morning a new idea comes. The sun falls through her window and plays on the canvas, lozenges of light like notes written by the sky for her to read.

This morning she gets up at five and skips breakfast, anxious to start. She's read her book on the Kayapó deep into the night, the wasps' nest bristling in her dreams. She sees Ira Kayapó's drawing of the structure of the nest, its sky layers over the earth layers of the Kayapó cosmos, how they also see the nest as a man's crystal head.

She has to paint her face above her cheeks with the black dye from the genipap fruit and below with the red dye from urucu seeds. With gum Arabic, Dominique stiffens her hair into a spike on top of her head and paints the tip yellow as they did – a single gold macaw feather to represent a wasp's sting. She plugs her ears with grass to stop the wasps entering the ear canal.

There are days now when she feels more like an insect than a human; it's so long since she's spoken to another person. She is a Kayapó boy about to become a warrior. She weaves a latticework ladder. She plays her cassette of chants as she climbs towards the wasps' nest she's made from Maman's letters. It hangs from a beam by her skylight and glows as the rising sun ignites it. There's a hum inside. Maman's words sting anything that invades their territory. The nearer she climbs, the louder the humming gets, and as her hand reaches the hive, a swarm flares out and attacks her face.

She faints from the pain and starts to fall, but manages to cling onto the rung, her fists swollen like boxing gloves. The more the wasps sting, the braver she becomes. She has to harden herself to confront Papa. He must see that she's stronger than Vero – only she has read Maman's letters.

She could not stop reading her Kayapó book; it was like medicine. As if she was a boy who had undergone the wasp ritual, a boy whose mother is now bathing the weals on his face and chest with sap from healing leaves.

Dominique has not cried since Papa announced Maman's death, and even then, her tears broke out of her before she could stop them. She will not cry now. She will make herself tough as a warrior enacting the battle between wasps and giant rhinoceros beetles. She punches the nest of her mother's letters, the black and blue inks smudged as Dominique soaked and shaped them into hexagonal galleries. She has to smash it until it breaks. The fragments will be stuck onto her next painting. She is going to call it *Punched Wasps' Nest*. Maman's words will be rearranged in new configurations. Dominique will draw on them Papa's eyes, his mouth without his teeth like when he's just woken up from his afternoon nap.

Her arrival in his room will be a dream he will want to escape from. You've hurt me, he said, that time she'd accused him of not being a father. This time he won't be able to slap her. She will be an Amazonian spirit who lets herself in and watches the wasps humming in his head, making his almost bald scalp glow in a painting of macaw-reds on palm-greens, of wasp stripes.

She picks up the fragments of the nest – his letters that lay in their envelopes like larvae in their brood cells. That flew out to sting his daughter's fingers. So many winged words Dominique alone released. What else can she do with them but turn them into art? She has to stop the buzzing in her head. She won't eat until this painting is finished. She works with her eyes half closed, so the surface is a blur and the picture comes right.

The flame-reds burn into her retina next to the plume-greens.

There are plumes of endangered hyacinth macaws. Only men wear headdresses of their feathers as they goad the boys up the liana-ladder. Who will go up first? She's painted her face red and black so no one will know she is a girl, as she starts re-climbing the long ladder, its rungs far from each other. She will be the first to paint this way. The ladder sways as she works, her eyes are slits, her mouth open in concentration. If there's a street beyond her window, she doesn't hear it.

# 29

# TWO DOMINIQUES

DAYS MERGE INTO one another. How long since she saw Papa? How disappointed he must be that she doesn't come every fortnight to keep him company in his last months, his fridges stuffed with mouldy treats. The oxygen machine puffs in and out. It's his only friend. Why can't she make herself go? Even if she did, it would only be to get ideas for paintings, now that she's on a roll. Her head keeps buzzing with Maman's letters. What if he didn't do those things to her, things Dominique can't paint directly.

Dominique will send him a letter telling him why she can't visit. She will include photos of her new paintings and when he looks at them, he'll know that she knows. He will have to confess. The paintings are so hard to make and so easy.

After hitting the wasps' nest of her letters over and over, her hand swelled up and throbbed. She avoided catching her reflection but knew she looked wild. When the painting was finished, she stayed in bed for several days, feverish but happy.

Then she read about the Sateré-Mawé and their Tocandeira rite. How the elders raid nests for soldier ants with a sting like a bullet. How they weave them into palm gloves with their stings pointing inwards for a dance to turn boys into warriors. They place the gloves over the boy's hands and he has to bear the stings. He dances, stomping on the ground to prevent himself crying out from the pain, buoyed up by the drumbeat.

Dominique weaves herself a loose glove from raffia. She sticks pins into it like a pincushion and wears it to paint her ant glove painting. As she throws a wash over the background, the pins prick her hand. The harder she works, the deeper they stab. She can smell formic acid like lemons, can hear the drum. Her brush stomps over the canvas – a series of dots. She works faster – stripes appear. She is in the warp and weft, biting off ant-heads. Genipap words wriggle in urucu circles – a maze of threads leading to Paris, which she writes as Rapis.

Isn't that what Nostradamus called it in his prophecies? She is a child in the mirror heart of her birth city, stomping on the earth floor of the cellar, counting up to a hundred and rocking herself back and forth, from the past to the future, from the future to the past, away from her father. He wears a black cloak over his head. He thinks she doesn't know who he is, but she can smell his smell. He is swarming over her face like ants.

They are stinging, both of them, as they do their daughter-and-dad dance at the bottom of the world where the entrance to Rapis is hidden. Down she goes into herself, the worker ant with her sharp pencils with their dream colours tearing the paper. The colours flow – black for the cellar, red for fire, yellow for the lightbulb.

This is where the dream starts that she will dream all her life: Papa, who sometimes splits into two, with his cloak. One holds her, the other . . . what does the other do? This part of the dream is missing. A window appears in the cellar. She can see his two silhouetted heads cloaked against glass. Then there are two of her. One is outside the window, one inside. Now she is the one inside, watching over the reflections, the glass people and what they are doing.

What they are doing hurts but feels numb. She can taste ants' blood in her mouth.

She cannot feel anything below her neck. Her hand hurts.

The window has burst and shatters around her like spray from a torrent. The boulevard outside the window is a gorge. What are the elders doing? Their singing makes the houses sway. She holds her hurt hand to her face, which is also swelling.

Father has vanished. He will stay vanished for thirty years. He will get his lawyer to write to her from the heart of Rapis and she will have to return to that cellar, the drumbeat of the oxygen recycler in the corner of the room. Its hiss and stomp. She will be grownup and unable to split herself into two, for one of her to stand guard and keep the cellar dark so she will never remember it.

She takes off the pincushion-glove and sees streaks across her canvas where her hand has bled. She has painted a man with two heads, each one wearing a cloak. She has painted a girl of six flying through the air and a girl of six lying on the floor. The flying girl reaches the cellar ceiling and hovers just below it. She glides over to the corner and looks back at what the two fathers are doing: one holding her other self down; the other in shadow.

She is safe in the corner of the ceiling among the cobwebs.

The cellar starts to crack into a nest of giant black ants.

Her hand is infected, but before she calls the doctor there is a letter she must write.

She remembers how the doctor came and laid her on the kitchen table while her other self floated just below the kitchen ceiling and watched what he was doing. Her other self saw wads of cotton wool. Her other self waited until the pain went numb. It was only when that happened that she could vanish.

Only to return in dreams, so many dreams, when Dominique would split herself in two. She felt less lonely then, in those dreams when *she* was there, the one who knew everything.

Before the doctor – the letter. She uses a black pen:

Dear Papa,
I am sorry I can't see you even though you are dying.

She crosses out *I am sorry* and starts again:

Dear Papa,
I can't see you even though you are dying. I have paintings I

must paint. It's only in my studio that I don't feel depressed. I'm off the Prozac now and I don't want to take it again. I want to get better. The reason I can't see you is because you won't admit you've done anything wrong. If you apologise I will visit you.

Then she stops. She can't write the word. So what's the point of writing to him if she can't tell him she knows he raped Maman? She won't mention what he did to her. He will tell her she has a vivid imagination, that she always had one as a little girl. He will bring out a drawing he has kept all these years and show her the cellar and how his artistic daughter drew two of him in it. He will use it as proof that her imagination is too vivid. He will point to the window and laugh, saying that cellars don't have windows.

How Dominique wishes she could find that drawing. In Maman's black trunk she found many of her childhood drawings when she was five, even younger, but not this one she remembers doing after school when the teachers kept her in, while she waited for Maman to pick her up and she was late. She remembers Maman blanching when she saw what Dominique had drawn, how she told her daughter she had too lively an imagination for a six-year-old. She threw it into her bag and Dominique never saw it again. She cried all the way home along the Boulevard de Grenelle and stopped just as they were crossing the road.

Cars screeched to a halt, one after the other. A blast of horns. Everyone looking at her. Dominique picked up the crayon she'd dropped and Maman smacked her hard, then shook her, threw her in the cellar when they got home.

Afterwards, she drew only flowers and chicks, things Maman praised. She starts her letter again:

Dear Father,
When Maman died, I read all your letters to her and her letters to you. I've read letters she wrote and didn't send. I've

read letters you wrote and she didn't open. I've read letters from her friends and from her doctors. She had to break off her engagement with the man she loved, too ashamed to say why, and marry you because I was conceived then. That's why she hated me, because I reminded her of you and what you did to her, and how she could have been happy with Dylan instead. I ruined her life. She didn't even fancy you. You weren't her type. I know you are dying and it hurts for you to breathe, that my company would make your last days more bearable. Only if you admit what happened and talk about your life will I come.

Then she looks at her painting *The Ant Glove*. It has the wildness of a six-year-old's drawing, as if painted by an artist who doesn't care what she's supposed to paint or how. Not like her usual tight lines, worrying what the critics will say. It's not entirely figurative, with all those dots and stripes and that swaying window shape and that girl with her distorted face, her mouth open, her too-big hand reaching out towards the surface as if drowning in a whirlpool. The father above her – high as a waterfall, his mile-long uncloaked body. And in the window, the little girl's reflection. Her mouth closed, her eyes open, burning in the swirls of the gorge-dark.

Dominique finds her camera and takes a picture of it to enclose with her letter.

# 30

# A PHONE CALL

A LETTER ARRIVES with a Venezuelan postcode. It's from Juan, in English.

Hola Domino,

When are you coming back to Venezuela? I miss you. I'm mostly working as a waiter at Canaima Hotel, do occasional guiding. My English is getting better now. Last week I guided a group to Kavac Camp. Remember your snake? He was there again, swimming by me. He reminded me of you. Salto Kavac is just the same, as you say – the spirit of the cave. I think of you when the mariposas come at night under the lamp.

How is your painting? One of these days I'll come to London and see all of them for real. I hope you'll want me to guide you again, and if you come, I promise to stay on Auyán-tepui! Even with devils. You were brave to stay there and I admire you. No gringa has stayed there overnight on her own before.

I'm sending you a kiss.
Tu amigo
Eimasensen (Juan)

She's amazed he's signed with his Pemón name. The Pemón don't tell tourists their real names. He had told her, but she'd never dared call him that. She can hear his soft voice and see him sitting behind

Hacha Falls in Canaima Lagoon, after they'd walked behind them. She'd sat on a rock recovering from the thundering water, while he stayed in the cave behind them. Through the water-curtain, she could see him reciting something, which he afterwards said was a spell to keep them safe from the devils on the tepui. He'd stayed behind Hacha Falls for hours.

She can picture him in London, wanting to take her dancing.

After they'd watched the moon moths under the lamp again, he'd switched on his radio and started to teach her how to dance the merengue. He'd taken her back to her room and kissed her at the door, but she'd pushed him away.

She'd regretted it afterwards. But he was only thirty-two, six years younger than her, and perhaps he was just trying it on, thinking that she was rich. But whenever she was near him, she'd felt this warmth. He felt like home. And now this letter, maybe he was serious? She should go back and see . . .

※

The phone has been ringing for a while and she catches it just in time.

'Domino?' It's Papa! 'Chérie . . .' He stops to catch his breath and she tries to gather her thoughts.

'Papa, I was going to write to you. There's something I have to say.' But she can hear that he isn't so well. 'How are you?'

'I'd feel better if I knew you were coming,' he says. 'I just got back from the hospital for my check-up, that's why I don't feel well.' The hospital is the other side of the Bois and even in an ambulance the journey must be too much for him.

She takes a deep breath and starts: 'Papa, I'll come as soon as I can, but you must understand that it's hard for me. It's hard for me to be with you. After the things Maman wrote that you did.'

He goes silent. 'Are you there, Papa?'

'But chérie, that's nonsense.'

'I wish you wouldn't say that,' she says.

'I can't breathe!' he gasps.

And she feels cruel. She's pleased he's phoned, so she almost relents. Then steels herself. She must say what she feels. She must talk about her feelings but not blame him, because he won't be able to accept that. She decides to compromise.

'The hospital told me I haven't got long now,' he says.

'How long?'

'They couldn't say,' he says. 'It could be one month, or a year if I'm lucky! Will you come?'

'It upsets me to be in that room with you – I have to tell you that, I hope you understand?'

He goes silent again, then says, 'Yes, I understand it must be hard after all these years.'

'I will try to visit you soon,' she says. 'Will you let me take some photos of you this time?'

'Yes, you can take your photos if it makes you happy.'

'Will you talk about the time when you were with us when I was six?' she asks.

'I will try,' he says, 'but come quickly, before it's too late. Your father misses his little girl. He is a tired old playboy. And there are two crates of champagne left. We will celebrate!'

He has a coughing fit and she knows he can't talk anymore. She puts the phone down and checks her diary. Three weeks' time – that's when she'll go.

# 31

# BOULEVARD DE GRENELLE

## 4TH VISIT TO PAPA, TUESDAY APRIL 1999

DOMINIQUE LETS HERSELF into Papa's flat and he's waiting for her. The small table is laid.

'I wasn't sure you were coming,' he puffs, 'but you're here now and Lucienne has done a big shop for me. Are you hungry?'

'Yes,' she says, 'but how are you feeling?'

'Oh, I'm never so good in the evening, but much better for seeing you.' And he kisses her then falls back into his chair. She eyes the starter, which looks like raw mince and egg yolk. 'Can we eat now?' he asks, 'I'm starving.'

She walks over to the window where her chair is covered with a pile of old magazines and brings it over while he tucks into his hors d'oeuvre, then stops to open a bottle of champagne. She wonders if he'll mention her letter, which she did manage to post in the end, but he's smiling at her as if he didn't get it.

'Did – did you get my letter?' she asks.

'Let's eat,' he replies. 'Do you like steak tartare?'

'I don't know, what is it?' she asks, prodding the mince that looks uncooked. She takes a taste and realises it's completely raw.

'It's made from the best fillet beef, mixed with capers and shallots,' he explains. 'Ah, of course, the Anglo-Saxons don't have this; it's a delicacy here. You should come to live in Paris. Would you like that?'

'Did you get my letter,' she repeats.

'Yes, *chérie*. It was wrong of you to read all those letters of your mother . . .'

'But she insisted,' Dominique says.

'She was wrong to do that,' he says. 'They're private, and only one side of the story.'

'You could tell me your side?' she says, dropping her fork and staring into his eyes.

'Let's eat and forget it,' he says, looking away. 'The past is the past. Why do you want to bring it back? You can't change anything. I can't change anything. I can't even leave this room.'

'But will you talk about when we lived in the Boulevard de Grenelle?' she asks.

'Ah, the Boulevard de Grenelle,' he says. 'Yes, I remember. You used to play under the Eiffel Tower with your scooter.'

'But it wouldn't work properly because of the chippings,' Dominique says. 'It was incredible we lived just by the tower. And there was a puppet show under it.'

'Yes,' he says, 'the marionettes were just a booth under the tower then. I'd take you there.'

'I went back there, last time I was in Paris, but they've moved them to a small theatre in the Champ-de-Mars now – Marionnettes du Champ-de-Mars. I even went to see a show, sitting on a children's bench at the back.'

'Why did you do that?'

'To help me remember,' she says. 'I suppose it's just for children, but I enjoyed it.'

'You're my little girl,' he says, smiling at her.

'And it all came back . . .' she says. 'Except, I thought the puppets were outside then. I remembered standing watching Toto the clown who opens the show, and he still does!'

'All puppet shows have a Toto,' Papa says.

'Asking children if they've been good,' she says, 'or if they're so scared they've wet their pants.'

'That's right!' he exclaims.

'The other children were laughing,' she says, 'but I was scared like I was six again. Toto with his rubbery neck, and a hand inside his gown, an invisible man speaking for him.'

'A man's hand up his backside?' Papa says, choking on his food.

'Then Guignol the Punch appeared . . .' but she stops, because Papa is looking pale. So she moves on to her other discovery, the merry-go-round. 'The other side of the Champ-de-Mars I found the merry-go-round I used to ride on. It was so strange to find it still there . . .'

'You mean the *manège?*'

'Yes!' Dominique says. 'Do you remember it? It opened in 1913.'

'It's the only hand-cranked merry-go-round left,' Papa says.

'It's called the Chalet Mickey Manège now and has the same roof and wooden ponies. I used to choose Cricri or Lucky . . . or Zorro, and they're still there!' Dominique says.

'You used to play *jeu de bagues*,' Papa says, laughing now. 'But you never did get those rings over the hooks.'

'Cricri the coffee-coloured pony,' she continues, 'and Mallo was green. I loved Lucky because he was white like a unicorn and had a friendly smile.' She thinks that now is the time to get more information. 'Papa, didn't you work in some kind of car factory then?'

'That was when our beer business went bust, I had a series of jobs. There was a car showroom I worked in for a while.'

'What number did we live in in the boulevard? Wasn't it by the market? I tried to find it when I was there but didn't know the number. I walked up and down, hoping to guess right . . .'

'Let me think . . .' he says. 'It was number 77. That's right – 77! I can't remember if it was the second or third floor.'

'It was the third floor, I think,' she says, almost sure, trying to think back to the stairs and the old-fashioned cage lift. 'But it could have been the second. There was a woman on the ground floor, Madame Aubert, she used to look after us when Maman was working late and we'd sleep in her flat. I don't know where you were then.'

Papa looks tired, but she's thrilled to have the number of their flat. As she forces the raw egg down, she repeats it to herself so as not to forget.

'You were a very cute little girl,' he says suddenly. '*Mignonne*, but very naughty.

'Yes, Maman used to put me in the cellar sometimes for being too quiet,' she says.

'You were sly, and teased your sister,' Papa says. 'You used to steal her toys, and blame her whenever something got broken.'

'No, that wasn't me!'

'You used to fight with her and pinch her,' he says, pinching his fingers together to show her. 'You made her cry.'

'But it was Veronique who stole *my* toys, who blamed *me*,' she replies. 'I was unhappy.'

'Why?' Papa looks at her, concerned.

'I was bullied at school,' she says.

'But you should have told me, I would have sorted them! Your Papa would have gone to the school and stopped it.'

For a moment she basks in this scenario, her father looking after her, going to the school. Has she remembered it wrong? 'They used to put me in the cellar at school too, for not standing still when the first bell went in the playground. I never understood what I was supposed to do! They'd turn the light out and lock me in. They told me to count to a hundred before I could switch the light back on.'

'It was a strict school, that's true,' he says.

'When I told Maman about it,' she says, 'she did the same thing at home. Do you remember the cellar in our block?'

'No, that's not right. You're mistaken,' he says. 'Your mother would never have done that. She was too soft with you. I used to have to pretend to smack you to make up for it.'

'Yes Papa, I remember you smacking me with your slipper on my bottom. I was frightened.'

'Oh, but I was pretending, I hardly hit you properly. But let's change the subject to something more cheerful.' Papa is looking smug. He announces a treat for their main course – twelve Bourgogne snails in garlic butter. He takes them out of the microwave and hands her a snail tong and fork.

'Usually these are served for hors d'oeuvre, but I thought we'd have a dozen each for our main course, to celebrate your arrival. Now, let your Papa show you how to eat them . . .'

'I do know!' she says, annoyed. 'They're one of my favourites, I've had them many times.'

'You mean you get snails in London? Things have changed.'

'Ever since the Common Market a lot of French foods are there,' she explains. She pours them a second glass of champagne and relishes the snails, wondering if she dares ask Papa more questions.

'Where did you live when you left us?'

'After your mother threw me out, I went abroad, to Algiers first, then the Kabylie mountains with the Berbers. I stayed with customers of ours from the beer business and they treated me well. I was happy there.'

Dominique glares at him. 'Without us?' she asks, trying to imagine him in the mountains.

'When I returned to France I changed my name, many times, and kept moving,' he says. 'I lived in Lille, Cannes, Lyon, Nice, then settled in Marseille for twelve years. I had a house overlooking the sea and a German Shepherd – Garrap. He adored me.'

'Why did you change your name and keep moving? Were you making sure we didn't find you?'

'No, of course not!'

'We couldn't,' she says, 'though Maman once said that a friend of hers spotted you in Marseille.'

'No, chérie, I wasn't hiding from you. I wrote to your mother many times and asked if I could see you, but she refused. She wouldn't even tell me how you were or send a photo.'

'You asked for photos?'

'If I was running away, it was not from you or your mother, it was from my own mother. She set the police on me; I can't remember what I was supposed to have done.'

'She said you stole from her,' Dominique says. 'And that's why she disowned you.'

'I was running away from her,' Papa says, stabbing his snail. 'I hated her. She ruined my life. She made me go to that boarding school in Tours. You'd be shocked if I told you what those Jesuits did to me there.'

'You went to a boarding school?'

'Yes, my mother sent me there. I couldn't tell her about it for a long time, and I've never told anyone else. They would laugh at me too!'

'You can tell me,' Dominique says, 'I wasn't so keen on Mamie Chérie.'

Papa looks away as he says, 'All I will say is that when I went home at Christmas, my loving mother found blood on my underwear.'

'Oh,' Dominique says.

'She laughed – oh, she thought it was hilarious. All that Christmas she mocked me for bleeding like a young girl.' He pauses to catch his breath, still not meeting her eyes. She winkles her last snail out of its shell.

She remembers the photo she found of him as a ten-year-old climbing a tree, posing in his short trousers, wearing white gloves – proof of his innocence, her father as a boy, just about to go hunting with his Papi. She wonders why he's so bitter, but he won't say anymore. He looks tired and she can see he's struggling to breathe. He'll want a nap soon, but before she goes she wants to take a photo of him, that she can keep with the one of him when he was ten. She takes her camera out and to her surprise he doesn't resist. He asks her to pass him his comb and starts straightening his pyjama shirt, doing up the buttons. She takes a few pictures then sets the camera on remote so she can have one of them both together. After her third attempt it works.

※

The next day Dominique doesn't have to be there until two, so she decides to go to the Boulevard de Grenelle. She scans her map of Paris to see which métro she should get out at this time, but there are three on the boulevard – Bir-Hakeim, La Motte-Picquet – Grenelle and Dupleix. La Motte is the middle one so that's the one she chooses. The station is near the market and under the *métro aérien* – the overhead line along the centre of the boulevard, and as soon as she gets out she recognises it. She didn't last time, because it wasn't market day. And then she remembers market days were Wednesdays and Sundays. Here is where Maman used to buy their food. The food stalls still have green-and-white striped awnings. When she spots an onion stall, with its colourful wares laid out, it all comes back. She can smell the ham Maman used to buy, and the varieties of haricots – yellow, green, purple, ultra-fine. The scent of carnations mixed with more olives than she's ever seen. A giant rotisserie with a piglet turning gold. A mushroom stall with wild cèpes and chanterelles. Cheeses, dried-fruit stalls packed with dried ginger, apricots.

And here, next to the third métro station, Dupleix, is a stall that catches her eye. It has skinned rabbits laid out on ice, sliced from head to tail, the left side of their bodies facing the right, their eyes intact and staring at each other. There is a glass cover to the stall-top, and over it a window reflection. Dominique looks over to the right side of the boulevard and sees that the number is 77.

It's a pharmacy. She steps back and looks up at the windows on the second and third floors, with white shutters and small iron balconies filled with pot plants. The *métro aérien* trundles past – the sad whistling sound of her childhood.

The pharmacy confuses her because she doesn't remember it being there before, but the pharmacist insists it was and even describes how different it was then, with a stove in the centre of the room, and dark grey shelves. She buys shampoo as he tells her how there was once a long table down the centre. She mentions that her mother used to have small medical glass vials that had to have their necks sawn through with a mini saw, and wonders if he knows what they might have been for. He doesn't, but says it must have been something serious.

It half comes back to her, this shadowy pharmacy that wouldn't have meant much to a child in a world of her own, who might have glimpsed skinned rabbits from her bedroom window. A child who would certainly have been fascinated by the bunnies, and the suckling piglet swinging above them from a hook, wrapped in polythene – a cocooned *cochon-au-lait*.

On the right of the pharmacy window is a black iron gate, which she recognises. Perhaps the rest of the apartment block is residential? It's the same ironwork gate she used to pause at as a child before reaching up on tiptoe to press the release button. Dominique presses the Porte button and passes through. She peers through the inner glass door and can see the caretaker's room opposite the hallway flagstones. And there, by the lift at the back is the door to the cellar.

A man opens the door to exit and holds the glass door open for her. She catches her breath and steps in, feeling like a trespasser. Onto the cream and brown tiles. Looking up at the old post boxes and scanning their names. Can this be the same lift? She opens the door to a red interior. There's barely room for one. She remembers an old-style iron lift she went in with her mother, though mostly they climbed the stairs.

Stained wooden stairs with whirlpool grains she would almost drown in as she climbed to their apartment, its wooden floorboards drawing her further down – she could make herself vanish while Maman told her to close her mouth and stop catching flies. These stairs are the same, except there's a red carpet down the centre, but either side the wood is still grained.

Dominique reaches the first floor. The second. Where she stops at the door on the left. Their door. Painted in fresh grey gloss. She stares at the buzzer and starts rehearsing her spiel in French. What if they aren't in? She presses and a loud buzz makes her jump. Footsteps.

A young woman opens the door, holding a baby. 'Madame,' Dominique begins, 'I'm so sorry to disturb you. I've come from London and I know this may sound crazy, but I used to live in your apartment thirty-one years ago when I was little. I've come to Paris to visit my dying father and this is where we lived when I knew him.' She pauses, wondering if she should say more, but the woman motions for her to stay out, so she continues: 'I didn't know where my father was for thirty years. He vanished and now that's he's dying he's made contact.'

The woman looks her up and down suspiciously and Dominique's so frightened she'll not let her in that she bursts into tears. And the woman softens. 'The poor man, what's the matter with him?' she asks.

'He has emphysema, the last stages. He won't live much longer and I'm trying to get to know him again.'

She motions for her to enter, leading her down the corridor into the main room. Dominique falls silent, looking around.

'Please excuse the mess,' the woman says, putting her sleeping baby into a cot and moving a pile of clothes so Dominique can sit. Dominique takes it all in – the window, the once-bare floorboards which have been polished and covered with rugs, the door to the bedroom.

She glances at the far corner of the living room where Maman and Papa used to sleep. 'Would you mind if I looked around?' she asks, but the woman's relaxed now, sure Dominique is no threat, and curious about her story.

'Please do. Would you like a coffee?'

Dominique accepts, relieved she's so friendly, and goes back out to the corridor. It's smaller than she remembers, but there's the built-in cupboard where Maman used to keep her stilettos, and there's the space where they had a dresser where the sugared almonds were kept. She turns to her right and surveys the four other doors. She opens the one nearest the front door first, which is the toilet, no longer a squat in the floor. At the second door on the right, she hesitates. It used to be the storeroom where Vero and she slept opposite ends of a camp bed the first year they were there. The tall window is the same but curtained. She looks down to the courtyard. At night, long shadows loomed up from people emptying rubbish in the metal bins, though at the time she didn't know that's what the shadows were, thrown against the white wall, talking in echoey tones. The room's a nursery now, with blue and white gingham curtains and a carpet. It seems strange that a baby sleeps here. Do the sounds from the courtyard give him nightmares too?

Next, she explores the bedroom where Vero and she slept later on, in proper beds. The wall of beer crates covered in white sheets gone. The window's been mended. But the floorboards aren't polished. Surely they can't be the same ones? She kneels to look at the knots and remembers the stories she used to make up about them, the woods she crept into. How cross it made Maman, that her eldest could do that, just stare at the floorboards for hours in her own world. No wonder she preferred Vero, who responded to her. Dominique can remember the exact moment she told herself she was unhappy. She sat on the floor and spoke it out loud: *I'm unhappy.* She didn't know what it meant, or why she said it. She just knew something was wrong.

Was it something Papa had done? She could barely remember him here. Except the times he made her wait for him with her pyjamas pulled down for him to smack her on the bottom. And she could remember when they announced they were going to Wales, how she and Vero had to learn English every mealtime. Knife, fork, spoon, plate, pass the milk please. Papa was there then, reading his paper at the table.

She goes back into the living room and gulps her coffee. The woman is ironing and looks up as she enters. 'Did you find what you were looking for?' she asks.

Dominique smiles. 'Thank you so much, you've been very kind. I'll let myself out.' And she closes the door behind her, out into that corridor where they used to race their scooters back and forth. Past the kitchen where lunch is already cooking. And out of the door, down the stairs. Into the ground floor hallway where she stops and turns around. To look at the caretaker's door where a sign gives the times he's in – nine till one. She glances at her watch. It's 12.30. Knock now or he'll be gone. And she does. Then pushes the door open, calling out if she can come in. A man jumps up from the table.

'Hello,' she starts, 'I hope I'm not disturbing you?'

'Not at all,' he says. 'How can I help?'

'I know it sounds silly, but I used to live here thirty-one years ago when I was little and I've come back to have a look.'

'Please, have a look around,' he says.

'What I'd really like,' she says, 'is to look at the cellar.'

'The cellar? It's locked. I'm not sure I have the key.'

'When I was a child, my parents used to lock me in there.'

'You mean for punishment?'

'Yes,' she answers.

'You must have been very naughty,' he says. 'It's not good down there. It's locked because of the rats.' And he holds out his hands to show her how big they are. 'There's poison down there, which is why it must be locked.' Then he searches his keys and thinks he might have it after all, just as she's giving up. He tries it and she holds her breath. The door opens and he presses the light switch. He tries to discourage her, again mentioning the rats, that the musty smell is poison. She peers down the rough curved stone staircase, the flaked stone walls.

'I'll only go down a little way,' she says, inching down the steps. She takes a deep breath and forces herself, glancing back to see if he's still there. 'Is it okay if I take photos?' she asks.

'Of course,' he says.

Then the light suddenly goes. It's on a timer switch. He flicks it back on, laughing but reassuring her that he'll stay and switch it back on if it does it again. She goes down the steps faster this time, into what seems to be a fork. There's a low tunnel to her left and she takes it, passing doors with apartment numbers on them, electric cables sticking out from under them and along the walls.

The floor is beaten earth. The wood of the doors is worn, like driftwood. She takes a quick snap and rushes back up. 'What are those doors?' she asks him.

'They're electric meter cupboards. I'm just looking after the place for a few days. The real caretaker is on holiday,' he says.

The light goes out again and he presses it back on. Dominique rushes back down, and takes the right turning, down the gloomier fork, and like the first it's a dead end, an old brick wall at the back of the arched tunnel. Where is the window? She panics and dashes back up. Then stops.

There is her window, at the top of the stairs, just by the entrance. It's smaller than she remembers. She wouldn't have been able to reach it.

It isn't warped and wavy like in her dreams, but it's the right window, with panes onto the once cobbled and now concreted over courtyard and the now green plastic bins.

She tries not to think of her dreams, the two hooded figures against the window. What if there was only one man and it was night time and the other was his reflection? Why did he wear a cloth over his face? Something tells her to look to her left, but there's only a bucket and mop and cleaning things, not the mattress she was expecting, the mattress she used to stare and stare at until maps appeared on the ticking. She always had a crayon hidden in her hand. As she lay on the mattress and faced the wall, she drew until the man went away, until his shadow went away, the one that did the things that hurt.

Count to a hundred, he used to say afterwards, then come upstairs and go straight to bed. Don't disturb Maman.

The mattress was a child's, and lay at the beginning of the right tunnel, next to a cardboard box of toys. The cellar must have been kept open then. She must have stared at that window for the light. Must have stood looking up and out, not daring to turn around and go down the steps into the tunnel. It looks a thousand years old and hasn't changed, but she never looked at it properly, only through half-closed eyes. The tunnel was bigger then, but now it's barely high enough for her to walk through. Her child-self would keep her gaze on the two-paned window with its oval knob until the face would appear beyond it in the courtyard. Then two faces inside with her, one on the windowpane, and one between her and the window.

# 32

# KING VULTURE DAUGHTER

*IN THE BEGINNING, in the darkest part of the forest, my face floats up, a prism of colours. I hover under the lightbulb of a moon and look down at the carcass of my child self, can barely see what's left – vultures writhe over every inch of her. They spread their wings, thrust their necks out at each other and hiss.*

*The river loops in on itself and leaves oxbows where a spectacled caiman swims between lily pads. The wavering screams of giant river otters warn trespassers away from their den in the bank. Even jaguars are chased away by these water wolves. I'm homing in on the central scene, set like a puppet theatre on a pile of sun-bleached logs. I pass night hawks asleep on driftwood, their eyelids raised to check who's there. They close their eyes like Maman in the sleep room of the psychiatric ward. No human should see the spectacle that's unfolding.*

*But I'm not human. I'm the king vulture daughter. I perch on the totem pole of a tree struck by lightning and it all happens beneath me.*

*I see her first – the giant golden catfish, her whiskers like arrows and her white eye with its black pupil. I see the spectacled caiman. He looks like Papa with his glasses on, his snout buried in the catfish's hindquarters. She has no tail, this catfish; he has eaten it.*

*Below me on the blanched pole, a black vulture and five black hawks wait – one for each year of my childhood. But the king's daughter must feed first.*

*I wait for the caiman to gorge until he can barely stay afloat, his eyes crazed with zigzags and sipped by horseflies. He stalls, because he also wants to eat the hawks.*

*I have been waiting thirty years for this scene to unfold in the forest theatre. The river wolves bare their fangs, in their jaws are fish from sludge. They shake them to knock them out, then dive back down, emerging again to restart their wavering screams. I have been listening to that scream for thirty years. It's harsh but beautiful.*

*Now I descend. My wings make a whirring sound, like wind in the treetops. The caiman slinks away; he's eaten all he can, his belly swollen. He will climb onto a sandbank to sleep all morning. Maman the catfish will have to work even without her tail, parts of her rear missing. She is old as the earth and used to dredging the river bottom for scraps.*

*Now the caiman is too close to the otters' den, their father goes for his tail and the river froths with white scales. More and more otters attack and the caiman thrashes until the river is red. Wave upon wave of screams fade like a siren speeding down the road. The pups emit triumphant snorts and squeaks as the caiman floats belly up.*

*I pass the night hawks on my way back; they are fast asleep now, no longer concerned with me. They know it's all over as their driftwood roost floats on, along with uprooted trees and the detritus of storms.*

*It is over, my wings say, as I return to my nest. I glide through the hours that whirlpool through trees. I dive through the annual rings of my life. I wheel through knotholes in the wooden stairs, their grains are whirlwinds I have mastery over. My apricot wattle melts away. My wings float off to their origins – my primaries of elliptical galaxies, the downy hairs on my breast flickering like solar flares.*

# 33

# SIGHT

DOMINIQUE RUSHES UP the steps and out of the cellar. The caretaker locks the door behind her. She asks if she can go through into the courtyard that's been repainted dove grey and brightened by plants. She looks up at their storeroom window on the second floor, and the tall stained-glass windows of the stairways. She looks down to the small cellar window with its umbrella plant on the outside sill.

She thanks the caretaker and rushes out onto the boulevard. She needs to go back home and paint everything better.

How can she visit Papa now?

But she must. The pavement keeps distorting, the paving stones grow large then shrink, and there's a delta in her left eye. She's getting a migraine. She stops at a café called Grenella and orders a coffee to take painkillers. Passing voices are too loud. It's already one thirty and Papa will be starving. She must bear this. She will be with him but not with him. When she gets out, she will draw how she feels, in her hotel room. But there's something else she must do first.

She walks back towards their old apartment block, cuts down the side road beside it and makes a note of it: rue Dupleix. She comes to a park in the Square du Place Dupleix. It's like walking back into her childhood, except it's smaller. Here is where she used to play in the sandpit with her bucket and spade. She knew it was somewhere behind their block but not where, as she always used to get lost on her way back from school. She'd get as far as the park and lose herself in the sand. Then the park guard would sit her on his stool in his hut and phone Maman to collect her. She doesn't want to be disappointed, so as she passes the bandstand where she used to shelter when it rained, she tells herself the sandpit can't still be here, and as she walks along the path past the flowerbeds of fragrant lantana, she glimpses it in a low fenced-off area for children. One woman is sitting on a bench facing the sandpit. At first Dominique thinks only residents can go in through the shin-high gate, but it's open.

The sandpit is large and square, sunk into the ground. If the woman wasn't there she'd go in, but she just stares at it and sees herself playing, lost in her own world, rose-gold just like the sand on top of Auyán-tepui.

Walking back up the side of the square is like time travel. Here she is small again, lost. Next to her on the left is a wall she recognises from years of remembering. This is how her school was – surrounded by a grey concrete wall that curved up to her neck, but is now up to her waist, and continued in grey brick. This is her school! Just at the side of the park. No wonder Maman got cross with her for not being able to find her way home – it's just behind their block. She walks up tiled steps to a glass door protected by ironwork and peers in. Through the high windows opposite she can see the courtyard where she was bullied. There is the same grey concrete surround and the low circular concrete wall where girls circled her. She wants to get closer, but the school is locked.

⁂

She doesn't tell Papa she's been to the Boulevard de Grenelle. She smiles at him and picks at the food, guzzles the champagne to make time pass. She pretends she's spent the morning in the Jardin des Plantes, and chats about the animals and the rose garden. Does he sense her distance? She doesn't think so; she's a good actress and even manages a joke. She wants him to enjoy her visit. She isn't sure she'll come back. He likes the silk roses she's bought him to cheer up his room. When she apologises that they don't have a scent, he laughs. With the tubes in his nostrils, he can't smell anything, hasn't for years. The oxygen machine seems louder than usual, but she puts that down to the remains of her migraine. At least the lightning jags have subsided, leaving oxbows flickering over his room. Soon she will be in her hotel room where she can draw everything better – sketches towards a painting she'll call *The Sandbank*.

Papa is looking over her head at the television, which is so loud Dominique thinks her head will burst.

Then it does.

She's standing in his kitchenette with a knife in her hand, zigzags everywhere. When she looks down she sees cutlery strewn on the floor and all over the draining board. She looks up at the window – there's a big crack right across it like a sky river.

She holds onto the sink and sees the mirror is also cracked. Behind the crack her face has split in two and is the colour of quicksilver.

She remembers starting to dry the dishes, picking up a fork in one hand and a knife in the other, when the white humming started. She remembers throwing the first knife and how she whited out, but the rest is blank. She's outside herself. Then inside, but her head is too heavy for her neck. Then it's too light, as if her neck is made of water and only her mouth stays afloat.

Papa has switched the TV off.

Dominique waits for her head to stop reeling around the whirl-pool of her neck.

She's drowning inside her body.

'Domino . . .' he says quietly, 'sit down, you look pale. Don't worry. Lucienne will come soon.'

She realises he knows something's happened, but isn't going to mention it.

'Lucienne will see to everything. Now come and sit down like a good girl, just like you used to.'

## 34

# RUE ORTOLAN

T HE NEXT DAY Dominique exits the métro at Place Monge
and stops at rue Ortolan on her way to Papa's.

'Is it someone's name?' she asks him.

'No *chérie*, it's a songbird, the greatest delicacy in France.'

'What kind of songbird?'

'A bunting,' he says, 'very small. I've eaten one.'

'You've eaten a little bird?'

'Don't be so shocked, you're French, you should taste one, then
you'll see.'

'So, what does birdsong taste like?' she asks. He frowns at her.

'The chef brings it in a cage which has been covered. The bones
are exquisite, like hazelnuts. It's blinded for a month, fattened on
maize.'

'Blinded?' she echoes.

'It's done so quickly, hot needles poked in fast, it doesn't feel
them! It's to fatten it up.'

'And you eat the whole bird?'

'Everything, *chérie*. The chef brings the little bird and drowns
it in Armagnac.'

'Alive?' she asks.

'Yes,' he says. 'That way it's fresh. Let me see, there's a special
way of enjoying them, it's a long time since I was in a gourmet
restaurant. The taste is divine, I can taste it now,' he says, licking
his lips, speaking freely for once. 'After soaking it in Armagnac,
they roast it for eight minutes exactly.'

'Then I had to drape a white napkin over my head,' he says, picking up his napkin to show her. 'Whether it's to keep the flavours in, or to hide my face from God because of my shame, I don't know. I ate it feet-first, holding the head.'

Dominique drops her knife and it clatters on the floor. She looks at Papa with his head covered by the large white napkin, and the window behind him, where his head is reflected. In the semi-dark the napkin looks black. But it was white.

# 35

# SMELL

*H*E TELLS ME *to turn around and fastens a scarf over my eyes. He's calling me his little bird. That's when I send my bird heart up to keep watch. If he eats her there'll be no feeling left in my body, none at all.*

*The surprise is how full of flavour it is. I could smell my whole life in that bird – Marseille's sea-air, the lavender fields of Provence, heather from the Kabylie Mountains in Algeria where I was happy. Papa sighs.*

*I think that the bird's song is in his stomach, making his lungs and his heart vibrate, every bronchiole and artery flying. My father, an aeolian harp!*

*Didn't Juan call the wind music up on Auyán iroma? It feels so long ago now, so far away – that time when I could fly. I am Papa's caged bird and he keeps me in his right lung, inside the bars of his ribs. My song is sunlight on icicles – sweet and sharp and sad.*

*My father, hiding his face from God under a large white napkin, as the aromas waft into his nostrils and he remembers my scent, even now when he can't smell a thing because of the cannula. He remembers tiny bones crushed against his palate, the crunch of my beak, my song that he can smell thirty years later.*

# 36

# SAINTE-CHAPELLE

WILL SHE EVER be able to pass rue Ortolan without being flung back into the cellar? She makes for the Jardin, for light, and her friends the animals. The Alpine Garden has just opened for spring, so she wanders inside it next to the zoo, because if she climbs to the top south terrace she can get to the deer. She hand-feeds them grass through the wire mesh, their wet tongues on her fingers.

And today their keeper is entering the enclosure. He leads them with his wheelbarrow of hay and they all follow – the stags, the does and their fawns, their spotted coats are like shafts of light through rainforest canopy. She forgets the ortolan and the cellar. She is in the City of Light.

It surprises her how little she knows. That when she was a child, she only saw the Eiffel Tower, the Champ-de-Mars, the Jardin de Luxembourg and the zoo. Paris looks grey when she thinks back, not even black and white, just grey. The grey school and the grey apartment. The only colour she can remember is the orange Papa showed her once on New Year's Eve, explaining about its navel.

She longs for light, so she makes for Notre-Dame and crosses the parvis where she spies the spire of Sainte-Chapelle. She makes her way across the square and along the quai du Marché Neuf and joins a queue outside the Conciergerie.

It's one o'clock, and the sun is sparkling through the stained-glass windows of the oldest palace chapel in France. She's bathed in lozenges of colour, everywhere she walks the marble floor shimmers.

Fifteen fifty-foot-high stained-glass windows surround her; there is hardly any wall. She stares up at the western rose window over the entrance door, each pane telling the story of St John's apocalypse. All the other windows tell the story of Christ's Passion. The whole chapel is illuminated to bring heaven down to earth. It's an oblong, as if she is standing inside one of Papa's lungs, each bronchiole illustrating an episode in his life. Three windows are dimmer, made opaque by scaffolding outside, where men are busy renovating the glass where he's had surgery.

Dominique looks down again, at the marble floor, inlaid with lions and vultures. Even the windows are studded with creatures: a golden calf, fire horses, snow hares. She makes her way slowly around, reading the Passion through burnished scenes until her neck hurts.

All that day the colours pour through her.

The next morning, she sketches swathes of washes, thinks of the glass frog she saw by the river one day up on Auyán-tepui, its tiny heart pumping. She sketches in the panes of two stained-glass windows with a heart between, two tall lungs she can walk inside, bathed in summer colour. Papa's breath is all around her. A stream trickles between the gardens. His breath is the colour of health. She is walking under a lattice of bronchioles. She crouches on a rock hanging over the stream and gathers moss, places it inside his left lung. She is making a bed inside his body.

It's progress, she thinks, as she works.

Dominique lies on the moss bed inside his chest. Lozenges of light flicker over her face as she paints, casting scenes from his life. She paints Garrap, his German Shepherd, and the horned lambs he has learnt not to chase. The cows in the field are gold. The warhorses have shucked off their bridles. They roll on the grass, kick the air. They drink from the stream, the mare wades in cooling herself, while the stallion stands watch on the bank.

# SQUARE DE LA
# PLACE DUPLEIX

D ESPITE SAINTE-CHAPELLE, WHEN she gets home to London, all Dominique can think about is the cellar. She must paint it. By painting it she can change it.

She paints the bulging ceiling. The stairs are meat-coloured. It's like going down a throat. The floor at the bottom is beaten earth – dirty, like rat-fur. She looks ahead and there's a fork.

She paints the left tunnel first, with its doors either side with numbers on. She swirls her brush until the wood is like the wood of shipwrecks. She can hear the meters for each apartment inside. She wants to open one, but the cellar is so narrow the rats must be close. She can smell them. It's like the smell of the métro – almonds and coal dust and something else. She thinks of the cupboard upstairs, and how Papa unlocked it when she used to return from the cellar, and gave her sugared almonds.

The cellar is a dead-end. The wall curves round and stops. She paints the window at the top of the cellar, the window she recreated as her first installation on her foundation course at art school. The window with two hooded heads in front of it. The window that looked out onto the courtyard that reminds her of places on Auyán-tepui. She goes back down the spiral stairs and paints the right fork.

It's worse than the first. More of a dead-end. Just the doors and a last door – number 33. The wall curves and meets the opposite wall. It's hard to show how horrible it is. The silence. The airlessness. The electric meters ticking like a hundred hearts.

It was in the right-hand tunnel that she hid some of her soft toys in the last meter cupboard, to keep them safe. They came from the box where the cellar forks. And next to the box, a child's mattress. She draws the mattress and herself lying face down on it, when the ticking sounds slow to a halt. But that's all she can remember of what she did – drawing hard with her crayon, making maps of places where no one lives except her.

She draws the contour lines around holes she stabs into the material. It was down these holes that she once escaped. Down paths through a park where she finds a sunlit clearing that glows like Sainte-Chapelle. What's in the clearing inside the mattress? Dominique thinks for a moment. Then draws the sandpit in the Square de la Place Dupleix.

Dominique pauses. She scratches at the paint until a nest appears, hidden in the sand, excavates it, as if it's been buried. There is one small sky-blue egg inside.

As she steps back, surveying her painting, she sees that the sandpit is sunlit. It glows in the dark of her studio like Sainte-Chapelle at night, when there's a concert inside, a choir singing.

She has been painting all night. Dawn filters through the skylight as she spreads a wash of watercolour over the sandpit, then sits watching it dry. She daubs in the buttons of a child's mattress, paints a pattern of teddy bears on the ticking. They are coatis and tamanduas, woolly monkeys and sloths. There are hills and valleys. Soon she's pencilling in gorges, dark green shrubs of a park. There, where her head would rest, is a clearing of blazing sunlight where a child is playing in the sand.

The cellar has vanished.

# PART THREE

## 38

# RUE ABEL

DOMINIQUE PAINTS A series of children's mattresses. She props the seventh against the wall and sketches herself onto it, sleeping face down. She places a second canvas next to it and draws Papa on it, shrunk and emaciated, asleep on his left side – his good side, the right lung free, the thin sheet pulled back so she can see his ribs. She mixes ochres, hunter green, sand yellow. For months she's been studying her sketches of Auyán-tepui, researching the insects that she drew, endemic to the surface, staring at her notes until she remembers details of the valleys Juan and she rested in on their way up. She draws creeks with quartz columns draped with orchids that grow nowhere else on earth. She draws them on her father's bed. There are lumps on the mattress, cracks, and the sheer cliff-edge of the mattresses hemming them both in as if they're titans on two table-mountains – her and Papa, and sometimes she sees that it's her, and Juan on Papa's mattress.

She draws leaves of unknown plants, shiny to deflect the sun, fronds unfurling like things she's said to no one, as she sat in her room staring at the wallpaper. The vegetation climbs over Father's skin, roots in his flesh. Carnivorous carpets of sundews, rotting pitcher plants.

Then she turns to the first mattress, where she is lying face down, eyes too close to the fabric to see that she is surrounded by a valley no one else has discovered.

When Juan and she entered it, they lay down on the pink sand and gazed at each other, too tired to move. They fell asleep and dreamt of each other. She remembers waking with her eyes close to the ground, near a tussock of sundews, a hummingbird buzzing nearby, how it darted in front of her face and pointed its needle bill at her, its wings a blur. Then it was gone, and there was Juan again, his eyes open. She'd got up and started climbing up the slope towards the top of the cliff, holding the quartz valley in her mind like a geode, its miniature rock garden, which she carried all the way back to her studio in London.

That six-year-old girl is no longer alone, she's got her adult self to look after her. She can go back and help her, guide her drawing hand.

The crayon has dug so deep into Dominique's palm it's drawn blood. Her legs ache as if she's been climbing all night. Papa looks as if he's been climbing too. If a hummingbird buzzed in front of his face, he wouldn't wake. She's drawn him sleeping without his teeth in, so his mouth is puckered. He's snoring hard.

When is she going to visit him? Five months have passed since she last went to Paris. After seeing the cellar, she couldn't bring herself to go back. Even after painting it. But when she'd remembered the confession Papa'd made about the blood on his underwear, and Mamie Chérie laughing at him, her heart softened.

She knows that abusers are often abused themselves, that they do it as a way to reclaim power.

The expression on Papa's face haunts her, the bitterness when-ever he mentioned his mother. What had he endured to hate her so much? Dominique looks at her diary and sees that his birthday is coming up. She wanders around Oxford Street searching for a present, buys him a tartan cushioned tray that he can balance on his bed to eat his meals.

She phones the Hôtel St Jacques to ask if her attic room is free, and after she reserves her Eurostar seats feels less guilty. She will visit him for his birthday. Tonight, she'll phone and let him know she's coming. She makes herself breakfast then goes back up to her studio. The sun pours through the skylight, so she wrenches it open. She can paint for hours, imagining she's in the Lost World, leaping from rock to rock or over pink sand to avoid the hummocks of unclassified plants. There are shadows in Papa's mattress where a black toad can shelter, a horizon with a stone howler silhouette. His snoring has changed into a deep roar, as if there's a cataract in his throat, and out of his mouth the howler monkeys come bounding.

### TUESDAY 26TH OCTOBER

At first, she doesn't hear the phone. Her brush hovers over Papa's lips as she wonders whether opening them further will ease the sound that keeps deepening. As when she approached the base of Angel Falls, surprised that it wasn't the falls themselves that made that rumble, the water having evaporated before reaching the canyon floor, blown into gusts of bullet fine spray. Underneath the falls, that's where the sound originates, where the river re-assembles, tumbles down a chute of waterfalls, dwarfed by the giant above them.

The phone persists and now her painting hushes so she can snap out of its spell. The voice on the other end is French. 'This is the lieutenant inspector from the Prefecture of Police,' she says. 'I'm sorry to tell you I've bad news.'

Why are the police phoning her? She pictures Papa in hospital. 'Is your father called Abel Emmanuel Grandin?' the inspector asks.

'Yes,' Dominique answers.

'I'm sorry to say, he died last night,' the voice says. 'My condolences. You must come to the police station straightaway.'

'He's dead . . . ?' Dominique drops her brush and stares at her painting. Did she make him die?

'Yes, I'm sorry,' the inspector says.

'How?' Dominique asks.

'The doctor thinks he had a heart attack while he slept. The home help found him early this morning.'

Dominique tries to take it in. This wasn't supposed to happen yet. She hasn't given him his birthday present! And he was in bed, just like her painting! 'How did you find my number?' she asks.

'We had to search through his things,' the inspector says, 'and we found your letters to him. I'm sorry, we had to read them to search for his next of kin.'

Dominique winces at the thought of them riffling through those lines that took her so long to write, that were never meant to be read by anyone else. But she's just got to know him. She hasn't even given him the tray she was going to fill with photos and chocolates!

She makes a note of the address of the police headquarters, puts the phone down then quickly checks whether there's a Eurostar seat that evening. She has no idea how to arrange a funeral. She'll have to do everything herself. Shall she tell Vero? She has to know. Dominique decides to tell her what the inspector told her, but will phone her back when she gets to Paris and knows more. She can't bear to look at her painting. The howlers are hunched on his shoulders, their hands over their heads against the downpour.

⁂

By the time Dominique reaches the Gare-du-Nord it's already eight. She takes a taxi to the police headquarters, which is at the bottom of the rue de la Montagne Sainte-Geneviève, by Place Maubert. She stands below the imposing white building, wondering how to get in, until a gendarme stops her. She stammers the inspector's name and he ushers her up a flight of stairs into a tiny office. The inspector is an attractive dark-haired woman who points at a chair for her to sit. She's not eaten and the room is spinning. The inspector offers her a glass of water and her condolences again. Dominique explains that she only met her father two years ago, but hasn't seen him for five months.

'We had a difficult relationship, it was hard for me to see him,' she adds.

'I know,' the inspector says, 'I had to read your letters. I'm sorry,

'I realise they were private, but we had to find his next of kin. I understand your situation. There are papers you have to sign. Do you have your passport?'

'Yes. Do you need me to identify him?'

'No, the home help did that. We just need you to sign these forms to say you're his daughter and you'll arrange the funeral and his effects. Sign this as well, to release his body for an autopsy.'

'I've never arranged a funeral before.'

'Don't worry, it will be straightforward,' the inspector reassures her. 'Tomorrow, first thing, you should go to the Institut médico-légal and make arrangements there, then find a funeral director to sort everything out. You should also phone your father's lawyer and have him come to deal with his estate. Here's a list of funeral directors in this area.'

Dominique jots her instructions down then asks, 'Was he in pain?'

'No, the police surgeon says he died in his sleep, probably a heart attack. There will be a post-mortem to check.'

'A post-mortem?' she says. 'They're going to cut him?'

'We always do those when people die on their own with no witnesses,' the inspector says.

He was on his own.

'I should have been there,' she tells her.

'I don't think you should worry about that,' the inspector says. 'You can't be blamed. Why don't you go to your hotel and rest now?'

Dominique looks at her blankly and gets up to leave, but the inspector presses a polythene bag into her hand. 'I've gathered some of his things,' she says. 'You might like to have them. This old ID Card, which has a photo of him I thought you might like. I also found this photo of what I guessed was you next to him, and your letters.'

Dominique opens the bag and looks at the identity card photo, but doesn't recognise him; she catches a glimpse of her letter and thrusts it back inside. The inspector gives her the address of the *mairie* of the fifth arrondissement, where she must speak to the clerk in the Court of the First Instance and get the keys to his flat. She stumbles downstairs and out into the steep street, up towards her hotel.

## WEDNESDAY 27TH OCTOBER

She wakes at four, only having slept two hours. She's in a period room on the second floor overlooking the rue des Écoles this time, not in her usual cheap attic three more flights up. There are cracked gold mouldings around a circular blue sky on the ceiling above the king-sized bed. A red bird is flying across the sky with a twig in its mouth.

She reaches for her journal and tries to describe what's happened. It's the first time she's written in the Father Journal for a while. At the top of her entry she writes:

*Didn't keep a diary when I visited him last April. Too angry.*

Then she writes yesterday's date: 26 October 1999

I want someone else to organise his funeral and I'll tag along. But I do want to experience this closure with my father. It'll be the closest experience of him I've had, the most involvement, not in his life, but his death. Did my mattress painting cause his death? I was trying to capture the sounds I could hear in his throat, his struggle to breathe, the surfacing of one long rasp. Was that his death rattle?

She swings out of bed onto the plush carpet.

The bath is huge and she gets in and lies in the steam. It's too early to phone the lawyer. Where will she find a funeral director? Then she remembers the list the inspector gave her. How does she choose, by the nearest? Last night she was intimidated by the police. She was always frightened of them as a child, when they used to point their rifles at her, pretending to shoot. They thought it was a game, but she ran away crying. Now it comes back to her, how silent tears ran down her face as the inspector told her how her father died. The inspector softened then, spoke to her as a bereaved daughter, not just as someone who'd arrived late in her shift to sign the forms.

Then, when Dominique arrived at the hotel, Milène at reception asked her would her father be paying as usual and she had to tell her he'd just died. Milène was sympathetic. Telling her made it all the more real – he really was dead. It was eleven by then, and only the expensive noisy rooms were left, overlooking the street, where she knew she wouldn't be able to sleep. But the luxury was welcome.

She gets out of the bath and dries her hair. There is a long day ahead. She doesn't know how she'll cope.

As soon as it's nine, she rings Monsieur Roussel the lawyer, and tells him what's happened. He is very kind, tells her it's like a fairytale how she was reunited with her father. He's sorry they didn't have longer with each other. He is going to catch the train first thing in the morning from Tours and meet her at Papa's flat at two-thirty tomorrow to sign all the documents.

She peers at the list of undertakers the inspector gave her and at Papa's little map of the arrondissement, the map she's used each time she visited. She locates the funeral directors nearest to the Forensic Institute on the opposite bank of the Seine, two métro stops away, and phones them to make an appointment for this afternoon.

Dominique crosses the Seine from Gare d'Austerlitz, and gets off at quai de la Rapée, trying not to think about that name Rapée with its English connotations. Even in French it means 'grated'. The Forensic Institute is a raw red brick building just by the Seine, overlooking the busy road along the riverside. There's a small lawn and trees to the left of the main door, and on the right are steps down to the basement where the morgue must be. She steps over a grate and catches a powerful whiff of the sewers.

At first she goes up to one of the main reception desks, which are quite friendly looking, but is directed to a side door where she has to queue up at one of three booths. After half an hour she gets to speak to someone through a glass barrier, stammering with fatigue. A man passes behind him, dressed in white overalls and green latex gloves. Her father is inside somewhere, out of the flat he hasn't left for years. The official explains he's had his post-mortem and that it was just a formality. Everything is in order. They're sure he had a heart attack brought on by a crisis in his breathing. She tells him she wants to see her father and signs a form, then is told to wait in an anteroom while someone prepares him in the cold-room. 'Cold-room?' she asks. 'Will it be cold in there?'

'No,' he assures her. 'It's just cold in the cold-room where he's kept to stop the decay until the funeral. You'll be in the Viewing Room.'

She waits. More men pass in white overalls and green gloves. She smiles at one and he doesn't smile back. Then a young man comes to fetch her. She can go in now, and she follows him, steeling herself. She's never seen a dead body before.

When they reach the room at the end of the corridor she looks around but can't see Papa. The man waves at a glass partition and she sees him. It's as if the glass magnifies him because he looks huge. 'I'll leave you alone with him for a moment,' the attendant says and leaves.

Papa's covered with a white sheet but Dominique can only see his left side. His head is face upwards so she can see up his nostrils. She realises it's the first time she's seen them without the cannula. His eyes are closed, deep-lidded, a pained expression in the furrow above. His eyelashes are thick and black. His ears are large. His skin is waxy – cream-yellowish. There's stubble on his chin and tufts of silver and black hairs on his cheeks, even a tuft on the end of his nose. She doesn't think she resembles him at all. Is he really her father? He is not inside his head.

She is not inside her head. She is going through the motions. She thinks that this is the most powerful sculpture she's ever seen.

There's a red burn on his left temple and she wonders what it is. She can't see an inch of his body or hands as the sheet is pleated tightly around his neck. She asks him if he really raped Maman, but the young man comes back in. She doesn't dare ask if she can go in to touch him.

'Can I take a lock of his hair?' she asks, showing him her nail scissors. He goes and fetches a polythene bag, goes out again and reappears in Papa's room, walks up to his head and cuts on the right side. The head wobbles; she can tell Papa's dead as it moves without any response. The man holds up Papa's curl and she nods. He comes back in and she asks for a few moments more alone, but when he leaves her, all she does is say goodbye and stare at him so as to remember. As she leaves the morgue she retches into the verge. But now she must find the funeral directors, a few blocks away, in nearby rue Abel.

She soon locates the Pompes Funèbres sign. She's never been inside a funeral parlour before and has no idea what to do. But there are papers to sign and somehow the man makes it easy for her. Except that she's had no time to consider whether Papa wanted to be buried or cremated. Monsieur Roussel has told her there's no Will. Why didn't she ask Papa what he wanted when she could? She did think about it and perhaps she even asked him once, but all he had said was that he didn't want a church service or any fuss. She can't make this decision without Vero though, so she asks the funeral director if she can phone her. He tells her to go ahead and she tells Vero that she thinks he should be buried, not cremated. With the things he's done she doesn't want him burnt. It would be too much like going to hell. Vero agrees. They settle on the 29th for the funeral. Vero's going to come over with Jack tomorrow.

There are other decisions to be made. What type of coffin? What wreath? What hearse? Although his estate will cover the costs, she decides on a basic coffin, though the wreath should be a shrub. Will she water it? She foolishly asks if he can be buried in the Latin Quarter and the man tells her the only Parisian cemetery is in Thiais, in the suburbs. She has to hire the plot for twenty years. If she doesn't renew in twenty years he will be exhumed and placed in a common grave. Dominique calculates that she'll be too poor to deal with that then, but waves this thought aside. She's making decisions fast, she who is usually so indecisive. She can see that the man is getting impatient with her, and she's still feeling sick. They set the burial for 9:15 on Friday morning and agree that the hearse will be at the Institute at 8:30. As she gets up, he shakes her hand.

'It's strange that your father's name is Abel and we're in rue Abel,' he says, allowing himself a little smile at the coincidence. 'And also that he will be buried on his birthday.'

'Yes,' Dominique agrees,' but he uses – used – his middle name, was known as Manu.'

The *métro aérien* swings around the Forensic Institute and as it passes the back of it to cross the Seine, she can see a hearse parked by the back door. She looks back at the red brick building and notices that it's on three floors, with the basement much older. The basement bricks are the colour of the cellar. There are explosions in front of her eyes.

### THURSDAY 28TH OCTOBER

The next morning when she wakes they are still there – diamonds and stars expanding. Every spot inside her eyelids grows into kalei-doscopic patterns. It's beautiful but terrifying. Is this what it's like taking ayahuasca? As long as she keeps her eyes closed they continue. She doesn't have to collect Papa's keys until eleven, so she's allowed herself a lie-in.

The *mairie* of the fifth arrondissement is at the Place du Panthéon and is a vast municipal building. Papa said he'd worked for the mayor who was a friend of his. 'I was in with him, so that's how I got this little flat in my favourite quartier,' he'd said.

She can still hear his voice. But he didn't let her record it. She should have got him to leave a message on her answer machine. She sits in l'Autre Bistro on the rue des Écoles, eating her first proper meal for two days, composing her questions for her meeting with the lawyer, questions she must ask while she can.

When she reaches the flat, the door is open. Monsieur Roussel introduces himself and Madame Babin, the registrar from the *mairie*, who has come to officially seal the furnishings. Monsieur Roussel is younger than she expected. Ever since she received that letter summoning her to meet her father, she's imagined him as old-fashioned and formal. He apologises for keeping the door and window open and tells her he made sure he got there before her, to air the room a little, as they can smell after someone has died in them.

And there is a smell, which she tries to ignore. The bed is unmade, the sheet pulled back from the narrow single mattress, which has faint stains on it like islands on an old map. The mattress has maroon and cream stripes, just like her painting. She must have registered that before, she tells herself, but there's no time to look at everything now. Papa's pyjama bottoms are tangled up in the sheet and she catches sight of a still-full urine bottle under the bed and looks quickly away, hoping they haven't spotted it.

Monsieur Roussel shows her papers she has to sign to allow him to sell the contents of the flat for her. He again assures her there is no Will, though there is a small estate in various bank accounts, and according to French law, this will be shared between Veronique and herself as the only children.

Papa had always talked about that, how he wanted his money to be shared out equally, even though he would prefer to give her more.

'May I ask some questions?' she asks, pulling out the list she wrote at the bistro.

'Of course. Anything,' he says, smiling.

'Are we his only children? Did the genealogist he hired to find us discover anymore?'

'No, you're the only children,' he says.

'Can I keep the keys for now?' she asks. 'And can I sort through his things?'

'Yes, you keep the keys. Sort through anything you like. Take anything you want, and whatever you leave we will sell for you. When you've finished, return the keys to the caretaker. If he's not in, just post them through his door.'

He asks her to sign an inventory of the flat contents and again tells her it's like a fairytale, how they found each other after thirty years. He was so glad he could send her that letter when her father rang him to arrange a meeting two years ago. He looks genuinely touched by the whole thing and shakes her hand hard before leaving, saying how pleased he is to have met her, and sorry for such sad circumstances. Then he and Madame Babin go, leaving the door open.

Dominique stands staring at the mattress, suddenly realising the flat is silent. The oxygen machine has been switched off.

# 39

# HUMMINGBIRD HEARTS

S HE EMPTIES THE urine bottle and washes it in the kitchen-ette. Potatoes are growing shoots in a saucepan and two apples lie rotting in a bowl. The windowpane has been replaced, but his mirror is still cracked. There's a whole crate of champagne left in the narrow hallway, next to the silent oxygen-recycling machine.

She surveys Papa's bed-sitting room and tries a cupboard door. Inside there's a balsawood box containing spices in small, stoppered vials, and a note that says they're a gift from Lufthansa Airways. The box reminds her of one of those boxes from Susan Hiller's cabinet *From the Freud Museum*, with their glass vials, titles like 'Unheimlich' – unhomely. There are two intertwined stems of vanilla in Papa's spice box, and aniseeds, cardamoms, cinnamon sticks, three nuggets of ginger like uncut crystals. Each delicate vial is closed with a tiny cork. Also included in the box is a recipe for biscuits. Did he used to bake before he became too ill?

There she is again in the long mirror on the wardrobe door. She creaks it open wide. The inside is crammed with suits, jack-ets, trousers, linen and silk shirts with designer labels. How long since he wore them? They are his days. They too remind her of an installation – *The Story of Dresses* by Annette Messager, where the artist had placed dresses from a woman's life inside glass coffins, along with photos and words such as 'promesse' and 'innocence'.

Dominique tries on a pinstriped navy jacket, but it won't button up. Underneath the trouser legs are his shoes, shiny, as if they've just been polished, the shoetrees still in them. They are fawns nestling at the roots of trees, smelling of leather and mothballs. The wood of the wardrobe echoes with footsteps. She starts counting to a hundred and he finds her. He's whirling her in his arms, showing her off to dinner guests. But her nightie has got rucked up and she's trying to pull it down as he hoists her on his shoulder.

She pulls out the chair she used to sit on, *her* chair, and stands on it to reach the boxes on his shelves and bring them down. She opens each envelope and pores over the contents. When it gets dark she flicks the light on, pausing at the switches to try out his ceiling fan and play with the other cord dangling over his bed. Why didn't she visit in the summer? They could have thrown the windows open and listened to the birds foraging in the cypress outside his window over the medieval wall. He loved to tell her about that wall and the history of the area, but she didn't really listen.

She listened when he spoke about the last job he'd had, in charge of the quai Saint-Michel. And there it is written on an envelope with his address:

Monsieur Manu Grandin
Secrétaire general de l'association de défense des riverains
du quai Saint-Michel
Le Notre-Dame Hôtel
1, quai Saint-Michel
75005 PARIS

And the date: *29th April 1986*. The letter is from Léon Dupont, mayor of the 5th arrondissement. So it was true, and only thirteen years ago. She thinks back to what she was doing then. All that time he was here living in a hotel in Paris, advising jazz café owners with problems. Then she remembers that he'd told her the name of the hotel before. Why didn't she go inside the Notre-Dame? She'd gone inside the Argonautes, at least as far as the lobby above the café. The Notre-Dame had a busy café on the ground floor and that had put her off.

'They all came to me to talk about their problems,' he'd told her.'
I would sort them out. If someone couldn't pay their rent . . . if
neighbours complained about the noise from the clubs. There were
still jazz musicians playing then – Claude Luter, Claude Bolling,
Count Basie – they all played in the cafés under my hotel.'

He had a good life then, before the lungectomy. 1986? That was
when she could have done with a father. After the funeral she'll go
into the Notre-Dame Hôtel and ask to see one of the rooms. She
opens another bill, which is also addressed to him at the Notre-
Dame, and this one is dated August 1983.

He was at the Notre-Dame for three years? So that's where he
was when she had her breakdown and living in a squat on Income
Support. That's where he was the day she got married and she almost
ruined the day crying because he should have been there to give her
away. If she'd gone to Paris she might have bumped into him. Would
she have recognised him? Vero once said she thought she saw him
on the métro. It must have been him! She said that he stared at her
as if he recognised her. She has Maman's flaming hair and features.
Perhaps he just looked at her and thought of his ex-wife.

Dominique discovers that the wardrobe drawer is full of post-
cards and photos of fairgrounds in Marseille, strange large photos
of merry-go-round horses and antiquated stalls. She stuffs these in
a carrier bag to study when she returns to London. Her throat is
parched from all the dust.

It's time she left, but a small suitcase on the top shelf above his
bed catches her eye. How could she have not noticed it before?
Dominique balances on the bed to bring it down and unzips it.
It contains small glass jars holding cloth bundles. She opens one.

Inside is a sticky pink rag which she unravels. It smells of honey
and hydrogen peroxide and is wrapped around a photo. Dominique
unrolls the photo – it's of a little boy. Could it be him? She prises two
feather corpses rolled inside and knows immediately what they are,
these tiny angels with fiery throats – a male and female hummingbird
huddled in a last embrace.

Underneath the small glass jars with their mummified occupants, she finds more hummingbirds, a dozen piled on top of each other, their chests slit open. She peers inside one cavity and feels with her little finger.

Did Papa cut out their beating hearts and eat them as an aphrodisiac? She sees his cold face in the Viewing Room, the closed mouth with a heart smaller than her little fingernail placed on his tongue like a communion wafer, feels the last throb of breath on her own tongue.

Her father as a boy hunting in the forest with his slingshot. Pinning the bird down on a low branch, slitting the chest open with his penknife, tearing the still-beating heart out and chewing it. Papa the hummingbird catcher, keeping some of his quarries to sell as love charms.

As far as she knows, he's never travelled to South America. So where did he get hold of hummingbirds? At the bird market?

What hasn't he told her? Has he travelled to the Amazon as well? Or Mexico? She's heard of *chuparosas*, the love charms they sell there. Or did he just collect these hummer carcasses without hearts? And, why? From poachers? So many questions. Dominique thinks of her photo of Ruschi's suitcase containing thirty-seven hummingbirds. But they were alive when they were photographed, lovingly cared for by the hummingbird whisperer. Yet, she realises, they are long dead, these amulets she keeps hidden in her pocket, rolled up in the photo. What if she'd shown them to Papa? Would he have asked her to fetch his suitcase from the top shelf, confided in her about his treasures? She unwraps his birds from more glass jars. Some are wrapped in lace bras, others in panties. Each has a photo of a small child inside, wrapped around the embracing bird couples. Two are photos that look like him as a little boy.

One has a letter wrapped around the birds. She unrolls it. It's addressed to his friend Pierre Oudin.

My dear Pierre,

I want you to know what I've been running from. As you
know, I hate my mother with a vengeance. She hates me,
always has. She hates men and took every opportunity to
ridicule me. I've never told anyone what happened at that
Jesuit boarding school. No wonder I'm not a believer. But
never mind all that, I can't bring myself to write what the
Jesuits did to me, but perhaps you can imagine? No, no one
could. What matters is what my mother did when I got home.
It took me much courage, but eventually I asked if I could see
a doctor and she asked me why. I told her I was bleeding. She
said I was no longer a virgin. Then she laughed. I begged her
not to send me back, and she laughed again. That laugh – I
can always hear it. Every time the priest took me into the
cellar, I heard her. Even now when I can't sleep . . .

And there the letter stops. He didn't send it. He wrapped it around
his birds and stashed it away.

Her hummingbird father, his heart bitten out and eaten by his
mother, his missing heart between charred lungs. No wonder he
died of a heart attack. Dominique closes the suitcase and its contents
and takes it with her.

She thinks of a forest of hummingbirds without hearts. How they
are still able to fly backwards, forwards, sideways, upside-down, for
milliseconds after their hearts have been torn out.

## 40

# THIAIS

T HE ALARM JOLTS her awake and she forces herself out of bed into the shower. Vero turned up at midnight last night with Jack, just as Dominique was nodding off, so she's only had four hours sleep. By seven she's out, heading for the métro at Place Maubert, stumbling through the twilight. She changes at Gare d'Austerlitz for line 5. The train lurches around the back of the Forensic Institute and she gets out at quai de la Rapée. The Seine is wrapped in thick fog. She's too early. She goes up to the main reception this time, but is told to go round to the back entrance where the hearses arrive. She avoids the drain grating, but can still smell its sickly scent as she climbs down steps along the Seine side of the building, along the dirty arched windows sandblasted with grit from the road. The traffic and trains are constant.

She's still too early and wonders if she should sit on a bench until 8:30, but decides to go in. A man introduces himself and asks her if she's seen her father in his coffin yet. He leads her to a darkened side room, the third along the corridor. Relatives cluster in the other side rooms. Papa's room is empty. The coffin is basic and open to his chest. Papa's wrapped in a white nylon body bag up to his neck. He's greyer, smaller than in the viewing room. His name is on a plaque on the lid.

Dominique peers into him. Wants to open his eyes. She tells him she's loved him as much as she could. She walks around to his left side – the side she saw in the Viewing Room. The red bruise has crept further up the side of his face, it's purple now. She can't stand looking at it and walks back round to his right. She touches his forehead, expecting it to be cool but it's burning cold. The bristles on his chin have grown. He needs a shave.

Vero arrives and Dominique sits with Jack while she goes in. Hours seem to pass. Eventually Dominique goes up to the man in charge and he says the hearse is delayed because of the fog and an accident on the périphérique. When it finally arrives it's time to close the coffin and they go in for a last look. Jack wants to see him as well and Vero decides that it's better that he does, even though he's only six, rather than hiding it all from him.

When he sees Papa, he says, 'Hasn't Manu got a big head!' and Vero stops the man covering him up for a few minutes more so Jack can see his grandfather for the first and last time. 'Sweet dreams, Manu. Sleep well. Bye-bye,' he says.

Dominique takes a last look herself and notices that Vero has placed a photo inside with him. The man unzips the top of the body bag and slips the photo on his heart. Then they close the lid and screw it down. She asks her sister what the photo was and Vero says it's of him and Maman when they were young, walking down a boulevard, hand in hand. So he'll remember the good times. Why didn't she place something in with him? Vero is like that, thoughtful. They sit in the waiting room again, where one of the strip lights is flickering above them, and when Dominique goes back in to check what's happening, they are still screwing the lid down.

Eventually they are called and the coffin is carried into the hearse with the wreath Dominique had ordered. She gets into the front and Vero and Jack sit behind. The fog still clings to everything, thick as embalming fluid.

Three quarters of an hour later they arrive at Thiais cemetery. It's big as a town. They pass through a high stone arch, where someone signs some papers and they drive around formal avenues. They drive and drive. The graves are surrounded by hedges, so with the fog, it's hard to see. They get lost, double back, then stop at section 6 where six gravediggers are waiting for them. The coffin is lowered into a hole on rope pulleys. 'Isn't it a deep hole,' Jack says.

There is no ceremony. Dominique wonders if she should have paid for one. She can see white roots sticking out of the sides of the hole. They stand in silence for about ten minutes and she tries to concentrate, but the gravediggers are watching, so she tells them they can get going and they immediately start shovelling in earth. The coffin shakes as they throw more and more in. As they leave, they are emptying whole barrow loads into the grave.

# 41

# HÔTEL NOTRE-DAME

T HEY EMERGE FROM the métro at Place Maubert, ravenous, and go into the bistro Village Ronsard for an early lunch. Jack has been waiting about too long and throws his cutlery around, pretending to shoot a machine gun. 'I can't take him anywhere,' Vero says, grinning.

'How is your hotel?' Dominique asks, trying not to be embarrassed by Jack's antics.

'It's fine,' Vero says. 'I found it online, it's just by the Panthéon.'

'Is it noisy?' Dominique asks. 'The St Jacques is. It's hard to sleep. They put me in a room over the street this time. I prefer the ones over the courtyard.'

'Ours is quiet,' Vero says, 'and not too expensive. More than I'd usually pay, but it's not every day you bury your father, is it? By the way, Sis, thank you for arranging everything. Amazing how you did all that.'

'It had to be done,' Dominique replies.

'It would've been cheaper to cremate him,' Vero says.

'Would it? I didn't want to do that. Something told me not to.'

'You have to trust your instincts, don't you?' Vero agrees.

'I hope you don't mind?' Dominique says.

'No, we agreed on the phone,' Vero says. 'You were there dealing with it all and I see what you mean about the fire! Jack, try to sit still!'

'Yes! It would have been like he was in hell, considering what he did . . . Vero, aren't you sorry you didn't get to see him again?'

'When's my chips coming?' Jack shouts at the waiter, who smiles wryly at them.

'No, Domino, I'm not,' Vero says, then looks away, frowning. 'I get very little time with Jack now his father has custody and what with my work, it was either go and visit Papa or see my son. And as I said before, I won't take – I wouldn't take – Jack with me to that flat. Children sense things. The way Papa looked at me sometimes . . . I didn't know where to look. I didn't want Jack to see that. It might have haunted him as it's haunted me all my life. Do you remember when I dropped out of uni?'

'Yes, that was such a shame,' Dominique says.

'It was because I remembered what he did to me then,' Vero says. 'I saw the university counsellor and she's the only person I've told, apart from you. I took a lot of drugs. I was depressed.'

Dominique looks at Vero. She was such an extroverted child. She made friends easily, while Dominique was withdrawn to the point of muteness. While Dominique sat sulking, Vero would make jokes that made Maman laugh, and Maman loved her for it. It pains Dominique to see how she's lost some of her vivacity. She looks at her beautiful red hair and sees that it's starting to grey early, which is never how she thinks of her.

'I just didn't know how to *be*,' Vero says. It was like everyone else knew what to do and I didn't. No one told us how to behave with people, how to be normal, but when we were kids we didn't know home was crazy!'

'I felt the same,' Dominique says, 'but because I went to art school, it didn't matter so much, not to have social skills. People there expected you to be strange and we were! I could make my own world in the studio and that's what I live for.'

'You're lucky,' Vero says as the food arrives. 'I wish I was artistic sometimes and could deal with it through my art.' Jack tries throwing some chips at his aunt but Vero talks to him gently and he stops.

'What you going to do this afternoon?' Dominique asks.

'I think I'll take Jack to Disneyland. After what he's seen today, it's important he has some fun.'

Dominique hasn't thought about the rest of the day and tells her she'll probably just wander around the bookshops. 'When are you going home, Vero?'

'I have to get back tomorrow morning, drive Jack back to his dad, then go to work for the night shift.'

'It's funny,' Dominique says, 'I was going to come and visit Papa on Monday, the day before he died. I would have seen him die. I would have been with him. The only reason I was going to come later was because my hotel didn't have my usual attic room.'

'I wouldn't worry about it,' Vero says. 'He would have died anyway!'

'But I hadn't seen him for five months. I visited him four times then couldn't go. I was too angry.'

Jack is looking bored again, so they agree to meet up at nine that evening to say their goodbyes, then they leave. As Dominique leaves the bistro, she thinks of Papa under the earth, locked in his coffin, so far away from his beloved arrondissement.

She's too tired to do much so she veers towards the Seine, down the familiar cobbled alleys, and soon finds herself in the rue de la Huchette milling with tourists. The Caveau de la Huchette is open and she goes in to explore one of Paris's famous jazz clubs, which opened in 1946, according to the plaque on the door. She sits on one of the red velvet chairs in the brick-vaulted cavern, sipping a Pastis and gazing up at the old photos of jazz greats on the walls. Papa would have sat here, back in the late forties before he met Maman, then later on when he lived in the Argonautes and Notre-Dame hotels. The Argonautes is a few doors down and she decides to go in this time to see where her argonaut of a father lived.

She finishes her Pastis, head spinning a little, and goes down another flight of stone steps, to the under-cellar, and peers down a deep well the Rosicrucians used as an oubliette. And again the image of Papa screwed down in his coffin flashes into her head. She feels cold at the thought of him spending the night in the ground, the clay soil packed in above him, and wishes she had come earlier, to say goodbye to him. She thinks of that photo Vero placed on his heart. She has a copy, which she found in Maman's black trunk. Maman is baby-faced, her red corkscrew curls haloed around her. He looks like a man about town, with his black moustache and glasses. They are strolling down the Boulevard Saint-Michel hand in hand. Everything is yet to happen. Tonight, he'll take her back to her hotel and lead her to a vacant room. She is still heady with the promise of jazz and Django Reinhardt, whom he claims to know.

Dominique goes out and searches for the Argonautes. It's just next to the rue du Chat-qui-Pêche, so she darts into the narrowest street in Paris, barely two metres wide. The smell of urine is overpowering. There's only one small window above her. She runs down to the Seine end, in the quai Saint-Michel, then walks back around to the beginning of the rue de la Huchette, too scared to go back down the alley.

The entrance to the Argonautes is up a rickety staircase lined with oak beams and posters. When she reaches the glass door at the top, she rings the buzzer and the receptionist lets her in. She has a sense of déja vu, and realises she must have got this far before because she recognises the safari-style furnishings, only there seem to be more of them now: more animal prints, jungle hens and giraffes stuffed everywhere, even along the stairs. She can hear water trickling and wanders into the tiny atrium at the base of the deep courtyard, where there's a small fountain behind a table and two chairs, surrounded by tiers of ferns and bamboo.

She summonses up the courage to speak to the receptionist. 'Hello,' she says, 'I wonder if you can help me? My father used to live here, about twenty years ago.'

'Twenty years ago?' the receptionist repeats, 'that's a long time.'

She looks barely twenty herself, but Dominique continues: 'Yes, he lived here and then at the Notre-Dame. Is it at all possible that I could look at one of the rooms?'

'There's only a courtyard room empty at the moment,' she replies, 'but I suppose you could look inside. What did your father do?'

'He worked for the *mairie*, he was secretary for the quai Saint-Michel. He used to help the residents and café owners here. His name was Manu Grandin.'

'The owner will be back Monday,' the young woman says. 'She's been here twenty years. Perhaps she'll remember him? Why don't you come back then?'

'I have to go back to London this weekend. It would really help to see the room,' Dominique insists.

The receptionist passes her the key to Number 304 and Dominique climbs up. It's a 50s-style narrow room with a single bed, a desk, and a blue-tiled floor. The wallpaper is also faded blue, and the bedspread orange candlewick. It looks just like Papa's flat – a dingy, bachelor pad. The window looks out onto the small courtyard and into other apartment windows. She doubts the room has changed in twenty years. There's a sink near the door and a shower cubicle, but no toilet. Papa must have stayed here or in a room just like it. She could be him standing here. She takes a photo then leaves, first checking the rickety corridor for the toilet. She goes in and uses it, imagining him shuffling along in his paisley dressing gown each morning.

Emboldened by this success, she makes for the Notre-Dame Hôtel around the corner, at 1, quai Saint-Michel. The café on the ground floor is bustling, but she's not going to be put off this time, so she walks past it, hunting for a door. And there is a discreet entrance. She climbs up the stairs into a spacious lobby with a less friendly looking receptionist who stops her. Dominique tells her story, and she shakes her head. There are no rooms vacant at the moment so she can't see one. But she does tell her about the hotel, how the building is four hundred years old. Dominique goes up to the windows and gazes out at the Seine and the vast hulk of Notre-Dame.

'What a view!' Dominique says. 'Can I just sit here and look at it for a while?'

The receptionist shrugs her shoulders and gestures at the seats facing the windows. Dominique sits, wondering what to do. Tears have started rolling down her cheeks and she gets out a tissue. After several minutes, the receptionist says, 'Madame, a room has just become available. You can go and see it now if you like, before the maid cleans it.'

Dominique leaps up and gratefully takes the key. It's on the seventh floor, under the eaves, just where Papa would have lived. As she takes the lift, her spirits soar. The door springs open. There's an unmade double bed below the original beams. She lies on it and can see the towers of Notre-Dame through the window. The gargoyles are staring down at her.

# 42

# GALLERY OF CHIMERAS

S HE'S SET HER alarm to go off early and lies there resist-ing the thought of Papa under the ground, worms nudging his coffin. Yesterday he would have been seventy-two. She could have carried his lunch into him on her quilted tray with its polystyrene bubbles to keep the surface level – a tray of frozen songbirds!

She hums the tune he once loved to sing to her: *Alouette, gentille alouette, alouette, je te plumerai.* He's plucked his skylark to the skin. She shivers as she soars, singing a waterfall of song. She's out of reach of the poacher and the kestrel, but the air is thin and her wings are naked. Has she spent her life in his freezer, waiting for him to eat her?

She thinks of him up in the Notre-Dame Hôtel, having a lie-in and looking up at the gargoyles. That's what she's going to do today, go up the towers. Lucienne once told her she must go up to see them spouting rainwater during a storm. Climbing the stairs will be good for her. She can take her sketchpad.

Even though the door doesn't open until ten, there's already a long queue. She stands staring up at the gargoyles along the east-ern side of Notre-Dame, elongated necks all jutting out above her, their mouths open, as if the whole cathedral is howling. The queue grows and she's handed an information sheet. Although there are gargoyles around the towers, the stone creatures she's about to view are chimeras, not gargoyles, they don't drain water. But first, there are four hundred spiral stone steps to climb, an ascent that reminds her of the Lost World. Notre-Dame is the Auyán-tepui of Paris, and she's about to meet its spirits.

Dominique steps out onto the narrow balcony of a gallery and stops to catch her breath again. The Stryga – the first chimera – is perched on the stone balustrade, horned, winged, face resting on his hands, tongue lolling. He is staring down over the Latin Quarter, directly at the Notre-Dame Hôtel. As she inches along the gallery, clinging to the tower wall, it seems that all the chimeras are staring down at the streets. Some with their mouths open, howling, others lost in thought: fauns, devils, dragons, basilisks – goat-like, with rodent, canine or feline features. Their granular limestone skins flecked with traces of fossils. They have prey trapped under their claws, or gnaw a mauled victim. And there are beasts: a pelican, an elephant, puma, vulture – it's a petrified menagerie. If she cranes her neck down, she can see gargoyles with bat wings, crouched on corbels, more dog-faced howlers with long necks jutting out and over the Seine glinting below them, a passing bateau-mouche gliding under their chins. The Eiffel Tower dwarfed in the distance. She inches back round to pass onto the back gallery and is startled as a bell peals, the deep sound vibrating right through her and almost shattering her eardrums. Verdigris apostles rise either side of the steeple and a shivering stone angel with shrivelled wings tries to blow a trumpet. The expression on his face is terror as he faces the pelican, the elephant, the eagle, and one chimera that has been so eroded by rain its face is blank, but somehow more sinister for being featureless.

Back to the front, past the rodent with a puma face, gnawing what could be a man, but the flesh of his prey is so mauled it's hard to tell. Yet these chimeras are exhilarating. They are having fun, watching Paris unfold through the centuries from their eyries. Most of them face the Notre-Dame Hôtel and the rue de la Huchette just behind. Dominique has seen them looking down on her, and here's the proof. Paris is watched by a zoo of limestone monsters, all five hundred of them jutting from the cathedral walls.

Gargoyle from the old French for throat – *gargouille*, the gurgling sound made as water gushes through hundreds of them around the cathedral, waiting for her father's death rattle, the drawn-out painful breaths of his emphysema, the last few years when he'd clutch his chest and struggle to inhale, the exhalation with all its catarrh and coughing.

# 43

# RENÉ-VIVIANI SQUARE

I T'S A RELIEF to walk back over the Petit Pont into the garden of St Julien-le-Pauvre in the René-Viviani Square. To look at the new bronze fountain in the centre and the oldest tree in Paris at the back – a false acacia, imported from Guyana by Jean Robin in 1602, its deeply fissured trunk held up by two concrete columns. To sit on the very bench Papa would have sat on, just outside his hotel. From here the view of Notre-Dame is clear, and although the garden is overlooked by the gargoyles, they are somehow tamed by the flowers, and their power is reduced when the sun is out.

She can imagine Papa sitting next to her, reading *Le Monde* and admiring the roses after breakfast in his room in the Notre-Dame, the whole side elevation of the cathedral out of focus with his reading glasses on. But even here there are blocks of leftover stone carved by Viollet-le-Duc, the architect who designed the gargoyles, though these are offset by the new fountain with its stucco of stags that spout water in honour of St Julien, who murdered his parents.

Dominique's read Flaubert's story of St Julien, how disturbing his sadism was in killing animals, that pigeon he watched convulse when he tightened a coil around its neck. The talking stags on the fountain told him he would murder his parents after he killed one of their kind. When St Julien did accidentally murder his parents and realised what he'd done, he decided to take care of the poor and redeemed himself.

She has killed her father.

She should have visited Papa every fortnight as he asked, so he always had that to look forward to during the two lonely weeks between her visits.

Now the dainty bronze stag-heads spout water from the river that St Julien used to ferry travellers across after he built a hospital on the bank to help the sick. Looking at her father sitting on his bench, is it possible that he was both cruel and kind? Did he enjoy watching her frightened face in the cellar? Or did he shut that away from himself and just concentrate on his pleasure? And those thirty years afterwards, how did he shut it away all that time? What did he do to carry on living with himself? Was he kind to children? Did he watch her sitting opposite him in his tiny flat and see a talking stag that he had killed? Is that why he used to switch the TV on loud? Or did he not see the stag at all? Is it possible that he could have forgotten what he did to her?

'They built a new fountain in my favourite square,' Papa had said, 'and when I could still go out as far as the quai Saint-Michel, with my small oxygen tank in tow, I used to sit on a bench to recover, and watch the stags on the new bronze fountain spout a trickle of water.' His face lit up as he described it. 'There's a museum at 16 rue St Julien-le-Pauvre, which has a cellar that dates back to the fifth century!' He'd puffed for breath, then added, 'There used to be a torture chamber in it too.'

She visualises him sitting on the bench only four years ago, admiring the new fountain with its triangular sides, each decorated with a relief of waterdrops, a stag's head in the centre, and at the sides the infants the sculptor depicted, waiting for a better world – so the plaque says. Her father, in front of a monument to water, the very first year she went to see Angel Falls! Maybe he sat there catching his breath as she sat on the lookout point catching hers after the ascent through cloud forest? She takes out her sketchpad and draws him by the fountain.

She investigates the street to look for the museum, but it's gone. What is there is a nightclub, just behind the church, in rue Galante, called Caveau des Oubliettes, just like the one in the rue de la

Huchette, riddled with subterranean passages that once had port-holes to drown prisoners in the Seine. So the barman tells her, as he opens up the ground floor bar, pointing to skulls on the walls, and photos of the cellars that don't open till ten.

She thinks of how the network of cellars and vaults extend under the Seine as far as the Conciergerie opposite the parvis of Notre-Dame on the île de la Cité. There are no instruments of torture from her childhood here. No proof that it happened, that what Vero and she patchily remember is the truth. They have admitted that their memories are just memories of memories, and not the memories themselves, but they promised each other when they were children that they would not forget them as long as they lived.

The false acacia knows, its black trunk propped by cement. Every year, ivy grows into it, and every year the good gardeners of Paris cut the ivy back before it asphyxiates its host.

## 44

# THE LETTER

WHEN DOMINIQUE GETS back to London, it starts to sink in that Papa is dead. If only she'd gone earlier. And if she'd visited more often, as he'd asked, he might have opened up to her, told her more about his mother, and that school where he had to turn himself into a gargoyle to survive. There was always something cold about Mamie Chérie - Dominique had been wary of her ever since she'd insisted her granddaughter should become a secretary and stay at home to look after Maman instead of going to art school.

But she still hasn't gone through those letters she found in the wardrobe drawer, and perhaps there's some information there – letters from his mother? She empties them out onto the studio floor. But there's nothing from her, they're just like the other letters she found on his shelves - bills and memos from the *mairie*, or notices to tenants in the rue de la Huchette, pleas for more time to pay rents, or building permissions, problems of the bookstall sellers along the quai Saint-Michel and Portobello. It's hard to read them and see his handwriting that he withheld from her. None are personal. Obviously, he wasn't one to express his feelings. She makes herself another tea and scans each business note for the smallest clue about his life. Then, as she opens a faded envelope, she realises it looks more promising: it's another letter to his old friend, Pierre Oudin:

My dear Pierre,

I trust you are well and that pretty wife of yours is behaving. I'm not so good. I could get out and about by taking an oxygen cylinder with me. You would have laughed to see your pal on the street trailing his trolley like a dog! But now it's too hard to climb the stairs, even though I'm on the ground floor there's that flight up from the courtyard. Impossible to drag the cylinder up. Hell, it's too hard doing anything. Please don't come to visit me anymore. My place is a mess and I can't even share a cognac with you.

Yesterday I visited my doctor at the hospital. It's bad news. I have to set my affairs in order. I'm not afraid of dying as such. What terrifies me is the idea of being buried, because some days when I can't breathe, I'm buried alive in this hovel of a flat. Thank goodness they cremate people these days. But that's enough of such talk, please throw this letter away when you get it, and forget about your old pal, who's just feeling sorry for himself.

Your friend, Manu

He didn't want to be buried!

He didn't post this letter either. Why didn't he tell her he didn't want to be buried? He would never broach the subject and she was too wary to bring it up. And now he's under the ground!

She wants to pretend she hasn't read it. Each time she picks it up, she hopes it's changed. No one else has seen it, not even Pierre Oudin. She thinks back to the burial and the brutal way the grave-diggers tipped barrows of soil into the hole that foggy morning the moment her back was turned.

There's only one thing to do. But will French law allow her to have him dug up and cremated? Monsieur Roussel will know. She must phone him, and Vero, to see what she thinks.

She explains to Monsieur Roussel about the letter and he assures her that it's not legal so she needn't worry about it. Nonetheless, even he admits to feeling uncomfortable that Papa has been buried against his wishes. If she wants to dig him up and cremate him, it will be a lot of trouble. She has to get a court order and the sooner the better. She has to get Vero's permission. And Dominique has to be present at the exhumation, which must take place before 8.30am by law. It will cost money. Is she sure she wants to do this? No, she doesn't want to, she *has* to do this. Can he get the ball rolling?

Next, she phones Vero, but she's at work. She tries her mobile number. She answers and Dominique says it's urgent. Vero goes out into the corridor and listens.

'I think that's ridiculous, Domino,' she says, 'we've buried him and that's that. Can't you let it go?'

'No, I can't,' she says. 'I wish I'd cremated him now. That's typical of him not to have told me. But I can't bear to think of him underground. I have to do this, Vero.'

'You don't! He doesn't deserve it,' Vero says firmly.

'I've no choice. I need your permission. The lawyer will send you a document to sign. You will sign it, won't you? And post it back straightaway.'

Vero goes quiet and she waits. 'As long as I don't have to do anything else,' she says, 'except sign this document. You'll have to do the rest. And, sis, lighten up! He was never a father, don't worry about him.'

'Of course,' Dominique assures her, 'you won't have to do anything else.'

'What do you have to do?' Vero asks.

'There's a lot of paperwork. And I have to be present at the exhumation.'

'Oh God! Will they open the coffin?'

'The lawyer said they have to open it as soon as it's exhumed, to let out any gases. But I don't think I have to witness that, just the digging part,' Dominique says.

'Sounds ghoulish, and I thought I was the crazy one! What about the cremation?' Vero asks.

'I don't know, Vero. I've never been to a cremation. I don't know what happens, do you?'

'No idea,' Vero says, getting impatient. Dominique can hear someone shouting for her.

'He won't want a ceremony,' she says, 'so I expect it will be as basic as the French burial. He won't want his ashes buried, so I'll have to think of what to do with them.'

'I'll leave that up to you, Domino. As far as I'm concerned, I've said good riddance to him. I can't bear how he got in touch just to say bye-bye. He could have contacted us earlier; we could've had a father for a while.'

Dominique puts the phone down and wonders what to do while she's waiting for the lawyer to contact the authorities. What if they say no? But he assured her it would be okay, though not without a hassle. All she can do now is paint.

She pulls out the mattress painting and stares at Papa's unfinished bed. She thinks of his hotel bed and the gargoyles glaring down at him. What was so exciting about the chimeras? They have such energy. They lean down craning their sinewy necks. It's a whole zoo up there, mirroring the Ménagerie in the Jardin des Plantes below. She gets busy stretching a canvas, which gives her time to dream. Her photos will be back from the chemist by now, all those chimeras poised on the parapet, their horned heads silhouetted against the Paris skyline.

# 45

# THE NOTRE-DAME ANGEL

THE BEST PHOTO is of a devil. His limestone skin is flecked with white grains like worm casts. His eyes are reptilian, yet his features are half-goat, half-wolf, his muzzle open as if rapt in looking, his fangs bared, each one larger than a door in the buildings below him, silhouetted as he is against the seven-storeyed apartment blocks of the quai Saint-Michel. He arches his back and peers down through the garret skylights of the Notre-Dame Hôtel. Below him stretches all of Paris – ivory and cream coloured, like a decaying bride in the autumn sunlight. The Seine is dove-grey. Ant-like tourists amble over the cathedral forecourt, idly chatting. The devil's uni-horn is bigger than the Eiffel Tower on the horizon.

How Dominique hated Paris when she was a child, playing in the Champ-de-Mars or under the Eiffel Tower. She should hate it now, with everything she's seen – those visits to her father's dingy room, the cellar, the cemetery. Her photos of the cellar are splayed on the floor, but she keeps them face down.

The devil is alive. Yet he's not frightening. He is evil, but only in the way that a predatory animal is innocently cruel. There's something endearing about him. He's stuck in this pose, forever surveying the streets and boats passing below, though only through the corner of his eye, his attention caught by that hotel where Papa lived. He seems perpetually excited, like a cat watching a vole. And although he's stuck here on the balustrade of the Chimera Gallery below the south tower, he appears to have just landed. Perhaps time is different for him. A century is dust floating through the air on a downdraft. It will land soon. There's an illuminated countdown to the millennium on the Eiffel Tower, but it's puny as a souvenir.

Beside him all fifty-five chimeras watch and wait. Below and above them, five hundred gargoyles open their throats ready to howl. She can still feel the vertigo as she leant over the balustrade jutting out from the walls. She has buried her father. Now she will own his ashes.

Behind the south and north towers, the chimeras are more sinister, more eroded, so their heads are almost featureless, distorted pinhole eyes, a smear for a muzzle. Who is the shivering stone angel standing on the pinnacle of the nave roof? The verdigris apostles are too engrossed in their proselytising to help. She thinks the angel is her father's soul about to blow into a trumpet, but he hasn't yet dared release a note.

Georges Roussel told her it will take at least a week to rush through the paperwork for the exhumation. She will pass the time by painting the angel surrounded by stone ghouls. The tips of his wings have long ago dropped off and his features are blunted by the elements. Eight hundred years he has been standing on the tip of the nave. Perhaps his music is ultrasonic and these beasts have come to its high clarion – the pelican, the elephant, the leopard who has a lump for a face, the bear who could once have been in the bear-pit of the Jardin des Plantes. The angel tilts his face towards the south balustrade, where the chimeras are more human but no less threatening: a dog-headed woman with a rubbery neck, a gnarled wizard.

Fog swirls around the parapets. More chimeras crowd round: hydras, salamanders, a horse-faced stryga, men with shrouded crow faces. The rodent has bitten his prey's head off. He has a rat face but human hands. He is the father who crept down the cellar steps and locked the door behind him. The angel shakes in the wind. He wishes it would blow him over. He is tired of trying to control his ghouls. Yet more crowd around, on cornices, corbels, quoins. Even bat gargoyles crouch near, straining to hear his stone song.

She's trying not to think about the opening of Papa's coffin.

Monsieur Roussel assured her that this is usually done out of sight of the relatives, but it won't stop her imagining it. These eroded faces are preparing her. The limestone is cracking and blistering. Time has eaten away faces with worms of rain.

There are days when she doesn't have a face. When her life is small as Papa's kitchenette, its window to the outside cracked, her face drowned in the silvering of his shaving mirror. There is a fridge and before it a small bench where they sit, his cheek touching hers, as they peer into the Mer de Glace, and watch it melt.

They crawl over the blue glacier that creaks and groans. France has everything, he's saying, even icefalls for you to scale with your crampons.

She brings him his birthday tray, with its meal of frozen song-birds, crystals thawing on their tongues. She's laid them on a bed of ice with photos of herself as a child, her infant faces embalmed in frost. If she breaks this frozen sea with her ice pick, she'll find corpses in the ice – her young selves waiting to be kissed back to life. Each in its glass coffin, bearing captions such as 'promesse', 'innocence', 'jeunesse'. The deeper she hacks, the younger the child, until she reaches the incubator where she lay premature, while Maman was packed in ice to lower her fever.

Dominique has never painted her birth before, the narrow canyon she inched through, long as Kavac where she almost drowned. A vine snake swims alongside her. Ice floes bob to the canvas surface.

If she axes its frozen sea she'll find her father, his arms crossed in prayer, his sheets ruched around his neck, his wings unfolding like a king vulture as he launches into mountain air. She decides to write him a letter:

Papa, keep blowing your stone trumpet. Blow as hard as your lungs allow, blow your last breath in one howl. Whatever good is in you, I'm listening. My brushes are listening as I create more monsters for your soul to calm.

All the time you lay in your narrow bed in too much pain to get up, to eat even, this angel stood through driving sleet and heatwaves. You would have remembered him. You nodded when Lucienne said she'd seen the gargoyles spouting during a rainstorm. Deprived of human company, you may have chatted to them from your bed. Perhaps they descended in the early hours, crouched around, bringing the scents of Paris with them. Perhaps there were times the pain was so intense you sent yourself up onto the gallery, high out of reach of your body, to enter the stone angel or the devil. It hardly mattered which, as long as you could survey your quartier, and beyond, to the boulevard near the Eiffel Tower, where you once lived, though perhaps you draw a veil over those years.

And perhaps you still send your soul up here from your underground pit, to join the stained and pockmarked denizens of these galleries. To breathe one more breath from your stone mouth, pursed-lip breathing into the long stone flute.

# 46

# RETURN TO THIAIS

DOMINIQUE FINDS HERSELF back in Thiais cemetery at seven-thirty on a crisp autumn morning, in the semi-dark. The gravediggers have already dug out most of the hole and are waiting for her to arrive with the undertakers before they pull out the coffin. They wheel away barrows of soil, these men who stood impatiently watching as Vero, Jack and she tried to gather their thoughts ten days ago, wondering if they should at least try to pray, or say a few words, but had just stood there, each wrapped in their own thoughts.

She approaches one of the undertakers to ask if the body will have decayed and he assures her it won't be too bad because he was embalmed. He suggests she looks away as they unscrew the lid. He repeats that they have to open it here while it's outside so any gases that have accumulated will be released before he's brought to the funeral parlour. She watches as the men unscrew the lid, and starts pacing as it takes so long. Then suddenly it's off and she catches Papa's face – and it's the same ashen grey as the chimeras. Then they screw back the lid and she goes and sits in the front of the hearse to wait for them, wondering what will happen next. The driver tells her to sit in another car in case the deceased smells.

En route, they tell her they have arranged for him to be cremated at 2:30 this afternoon.

'Where?' she asks.

'There's only one crematorium in Paris – the Père Lachaise. We'll go there at two. Have you decided what kind of service you would like?'

'No, I haven't thought about it. Can I do that now?'

She wonders what she wants, now that she has a second chance. The driver reassures her the funeral director will deal with it when they get to the parlour.

Back at rue Abel, the director lists her options. Does she want a service? She can't really as Papa was not religious; it would be hypocritical.

'But you could read a poem, say a few words if you like. What music would you like? They have a wide selection. Here are some suggestions . . .'

She looks at the list and decides on the contemporary option as it includes Gershwin's 'Summertime' and Jeff Buckley's 'Hallelujah' recorded at his concert in France. But she asks to change the last track, as she doesn't want 'Amazing Grace'. Do they have some Django Rheinhardt? Then she foolishly tells them that her father knew him and the director smiles politely.

'Do you want to be present when the casket is placed in the furnace?' he asks, 'or would you prefer not to see that? You don't even have to come to the crematorium. We can arrange for it all to be done for you.'

'Yes,' she says, 'I do want to be there, and I want to see him entering the furnace. Will he still be inside the coffin?'

'Yes, he goes in inside it and it's sealed. Is anyone else going to be present?' he asks.

'No, just me,' she says, looking away, embarrassed that her father was so alone. 'My sister lives in England and couldn't come,' she explains.

'Rest assured,' the director says, 'Monsieur Roussel has faxed me the document with her permission to go ahead. Would you like another wreath? Perhaps the same as before?'

'Does it go in with him?'

'No. You're only allowed to place one or two flowers on top of the casket. The wreath is just there for the ceremony, then removed and placed at the back of the crematorium.'

'No thank you. I'll bring a few flowers,' she says, deciding to bring some scented roses, Papa's favourite. 'Where's the crematorium?'

'It's in the 20th district,' he says. 'It was the first one in all of France. You'll see – it's quite something. Now we must decide what you'd like done with the ashes.'

'I've already arranged with the lawyer that I want to take the ashes back to England. He has the authorisation from the *mairie*. Here it is –' And she shows him the document Georges Roussel has obtained from the police, hoping he won't ask her what she plans to do with them as she hasn't yet decided. Though she does know that she wants to take them to Venezuela, so pretends she'll be flying back home.

'Okay,' he says. 'Luckily, your father was buried in a poplar coffin, which can go in the furnace, not a harder wood, so you don't have to buy a new one. All that remains is for you to choose the urn, but since you're taking the ashes overseas, you will have to place them in a plastic screw-top container. The crematorium will provide that and seal it for air travel. You'll have to carry it on board as hand luggage and lock it in a box or suitcase. I'll get you the *laissez-passer* document you'll have to show at customs, and you must also take a copy of the death certificate and certificate of cremation.'

He points for her to sign the papers and assures her Monsieur Roussel has already arranged for payment from Papa's estate, then shakes her hand and ushers her out, asking her to return at two.

# 47

# PÈRE LACHAISE

THEY DRAW UP through the entrance of Père Lachaise Cemetery and Dominique immediately spots the gold dome of the crematorium building from the picture the funeral director showed her, with its two imposing chimneys. The building is flanked by four huge columbaria, one on each corner. The sun is out. She's pleased Papa didn't have to stay at Thiais cemetery, this is a much better place.

The funeral director leads her to reception through a door on the left of the building, then leaves, saying his goodbyes. She asks the receptionist how long the cremation takes and when can she have the ashes? They go through her requirements, then she's led into a waiting room with Vivaldi playing softly on the tannoy. Someone enters and takes her into the Room of Last Respects.

Papa is already there in his coffin.

'We must keep the ceremony short,' the cremator tells her, 'because the deceased has been exhumed. The body is refrigerated so there won't be an odour, but we must hurry.' A new plaque bearing his name has been placed on top of the coffin.

'Is it possible for me to be alone with him?' she asks.

'I don't see why not, just for a few minutes,' he says, then exits. As soon as Ray Charles' version of 'Summertime' starts playing, with the mention of 'your daddy', tears trickle down her cheeks.

Dominique hears the phrase 'spread your wings' and thinks of Papa rising to the sky in the smoke; this isn't a bad place for his fumes to swirl. She tells him about the new zoo she's found, up on Notre-Dame, just over the hotel where he lived, and about the eight-hundred-year-old angel standing on the pinnacle of the nave, surrounded by chimeras and gargoyles, how he can charm the stone beasts with his trumpet, even though he looks scared. Then she places her two roses on the coffin, and whispers that the white one is from Vero.

The music switches to Jeff Buckley's 'Hallelujah' and when the lyrics get to the first cold and broken hallelujah, the cremator comes back in. Then Buckley is singing about every breath we drew, and she doesn't hear anything else, just her father's breath amplified by the oxygenator, the angel's eight-hundred-year-old breath stuck inside that stone trumpet.

'Are you ready to pay your final respects,' the man asks. She nods, not understanding. He opens a door and wheels the coffin into another room, which she hasn't noticed before, but now realises she can see through a glazed panel. She follows him but he gestures that she's not allowed in. He places the coffin on the retort and closes the door behind him. She rushes up to the glass and watches as he removes Papa's name plaque and stamps the coffin with a wax seal.

Django Reinhardt's 'Twilight Melody' starts as the man turns towards her and asks if she's ready. He presses a switch and the furnace hatch rises. The coffin slides in and the metal door descends then locks. He switches the burner on and she can hear a roar, like all five hundred gargoyles making howler monkey reveilles – the sound she heard when she first rang two years ago and waited for her father to come to the phone.

The man comes back in and asks if she wants to wait in the waiting room or come back later for the ashes, adding that it's much better if she waits somewhere else. 'Can I walk around the cemetery and come back when they're ready?' she asks. 'How long does it take?'

'Ninety minutes for the incineration, then we have to let the furnace cool before we collect the ashes, and then they must be pulverised. You're welcome to take a walk – the cemetery is very beautiful, but don't get lost. Here's a map so you can find the famous graves. But do have a wander around the columbaria first; there are niches for Maria Callas, Max Ophuls, Stéphane Grapelli, Max Ernst and many more. Come back in two to three hours' time. You can come back later if you like, there's no hurry.'

She walks down the crematorium steps towards the crescent columbaria and makes for the front one on the right. Ashes are stored in pigeonholes with black plaques and gold inscriptions, in banks of sixty, six deep, ten across, many bearing posies. A stone staircase leads up to a narrow balcony to view the second level, but she hesitates to climb, going towards the darker far end, passing pillars swathed in the stink of piss mixed with carnations. She sits outside on a semi-circular marble bench.

Papa is burning.

She tries not to think about it and focuses on the flowerbeds, formal but naturalistically arranged like meadow flowers. In front of the crematorium there's a steep arc of steps descending to what she thinks must be the furnace bases but turns out to be more columbaria, two floors of them reaching down under the main building. It's dim down here, like all Paris cellars. It makes her feel that she's trespassing, aware that she is the only person alive here.

Then she strolls along the tree-lined cobbled avenues of the cemetery, pausing at a monument to the Spiritist Allan Kardec, with the inscription: *Naître, mourir, renaître encore et progresser sans cesse, telle est la loi*, which she translates as: *To be born, die, be reborn again, and so progress unceasingly, such is the law*. A cluster of people is at his sepulchre, and in front of it, to the side and at the back are tiers of potted begonias, gardenias and miniature roses. The scent is overpowering. A young blonde woman darts up, urged on by her friend, and holds Kardec's shiny black marble shoulder in the shrine. Dominique sits on a nearby tomb and watches as she stands there with her eyes closed in intense concentration. She clasps the statuette for a long time and when she finally re-joins the group, her friend takes her place. Perhaps they are trying to reach a dead friend, to will his rebirth?

What if Papa is reborn? Will he be any better? Will he progress?

Dominique explores the narrow path of the Chemin du Quinconce, which leads from the side of Kardec's grave, searching for Sarah Bernhardt's tombstone, but can't find it. She glimpses the white crematorium chimneys through the branches of chestnut trees. Smoke is pouring out of one.

She thinks of Papa in his fireproof brick bulkhead of a cellar, the white bees of fire humming around him, lifting his flesh, his bones exploding. How did 'Hallelujah' go? That bit about moving in you. It's as if Papa is speaking in the rising fumes.

With every billow she feels lighter. His stone body, which pinned her to the mattress for thirty years, is vaporising, turning into a fire angel above the tall black-capped chimney. And he is getting lighter, cleansed by fire. He is young again, dancing. He has not yet done anything to hide away from in the hotels of Paris.

The crooked Chemin du Quinconce becomes the Chemin des Anglais, which slopes uphill towards Chemin Molière et La Fontaine, who lie side by side behind iron railings. Then the paths become wilder, the graves more overgrown; some even pushed up by tree roots. A stripy grey cat is asleep on one, enjoying the weak November sun. Dominique peers into the sepulchres, most of them abandoned, one with a disintegrated chair, as if once someone used to come and sit in there to talk to the dead in the dark. The newer, more ostentatious monuments look owned by the rich, with their ornate statuary and inscriptions, their angels, owls and eagles. One small white plaque in the shape of a book says: *Fauvette, si tu vole autour de cette tombe, chante lui ta plus douce chanson* – Warbler, if you fly around this tomb, sing him your sweetest song. On the opposite page is a painted warbler on a twig of blossom and underneath the marble book is a portrait of a young man. Tears pour down Dominique's face as she realises that Papa is almost ash.

At the top of the hill she finds a green bench and sits. She can see down over the cemetery, sepulchres crowded like narrow houses, and beyond, the living city of Paris. What a city of the dead there is here for Papa to fall on; his ghost is setting its grey cloak down, caressing the skeletal copper treetops, leaping towards the stratosphere. A chestnut leaf flutters towards her, like that hand he extended over his little table during their first meeting. It lands on the ground beside her feet, flickers, then is still.

I'm not mourning him, she tells herself – I'm mourning his second departure. He only got in touch to leave us. He has vanished again – the bastard. She sits there staring at the orange leaf glowing in the increasing dark until it's time to collect the ashes.

# 48

# TOUCH

DOMINIQUE DECIDES TO have the next morning off from anything to do with Papa. She takes the métro to the Palais de la Porte Dorée, near the Bois de Vincennes. It's an Art Deco building with ornate reliefs of animals all over the exterior, and an aquarium in the basement.

She strolls in to watch the Nile crocodiles and alligators in their sunken pit in the main hall, and the glass dome on the bank, with two newly-hatched albino babies under a heat-lamp. Behind them a passage leads around to river species of the Americas, to the electric eel in his small tank, floating in seaweed. She loves his French name, *Anguille électrique*, and the Latin, *Electrophorus electricus*, which makes her laugh. She has seen one in an oxbow lake, hidden among fronds in the shallow bank, its blunt head and minuscule eyes nudging upwards as if to sense her, its long ochre-grey body encased in a charged halo. Juan told her it was always there, skulking in the shallows.

Dominique fumbles in her pocket for the letter she still carries, unfolds it and reads it by the dim light of the aquarium twilight.

Yesterday I went to meet your father, Abel Emmanuel Grandin, in his home. Despite the many years of his disappearance, he asked me to come to Paris urgently to see him so he can make contact with you.

He made contact alright. She thinks how Alexander von Humboldt called electric eels numb-fish. How he drove horses into an infested Amazonian river. How the horses' eyes almost popped out as they reared up trying to escape, their legs thrashing, their manes standing on end – how some of them died from the shock. How one eight-foot electric eel is not enough to kill, but clamped against a horse's belly can cause seizures that drown.

Her father has just pressed his entire body against her, hugging her in his bronze dressing-gown.

Dominique runs out of the aquarium, out of the Palais basement, onto the pavement, and takes deep breaths. She's back in Papa's room and cannot escape.

After that first hug on the evening they met, he never clamped his body so tight against her again. She would pull away when he tried. But whenever she left his room, she had to shock herself back into the world, the steep route that led out from his apartment, down the eel-like rue de la Montagne Sainte-Geneviève, as if she was emerging from a murky tank.

# 49

# À MON SEUL DÉSIR

*I* THINK THE *Amazon basin is my childhood. In the darkest part, where the backwater is turgid, Papa clamped his hand over my mouth. My eyes went wild like a foal first lassoed. Did I kick? Is that why the electric eels surfaced? They were always floating inside the mattress, waiting to coil their whips around my body.*

*Is that why a red flower is blooming on my sheet? I know it shouldn't be there because Papa has long vanished. But when I tell Gran about it, she says, 'Now that you're eleven, this means you're becoming a woman.' I shake my head, tell her the roses first appeared when I was six. She says that's not possible. But that now there are things I must know. She gives me two paracetamols and a hot water bottle, lets me stay in bed all morning.*

*Maman says I'm precocious, that I already know what desire is. I say yes to sound grownup, feel ashamed for not knowing and for knowing. It sounds important this word with its slippery Z and an R at the end like a trapdoor.*

*À mon seul désir, the lady says to the unicorn, and she hides Papa's soul in her jewel box for safekeeping. I decide to hide the new word away, it's as dangerous as an electric eel.*

*The numbness in my belly is dragging me down into leech-infested water. I float there all day, my nerves firing. The eels surface like drowned lightning bolts – even one touch can send a volt up my spine.*

# 50

# HOWLER CHIMERA

AFTER THE CREMATION Dominique feels restless, so when Juan phones and invites her back to Venezuela, she accepts his offer. She'll use Papa's money to go back to Auyán-tepui. Juan says he's sorry when she tells him her father's died, but suggests that perhaps she should do what the Yanomami do, and drink his ashes in a plantain broth to give his soul a good home.

'No, Juan, I don't want that man in my body!' she yells.

'I'm sorry, I didn't mean to upset you,' he says. 'That was a stupid thing for me to say.'

'I'm sorry I snapped,' she says.

'But will you come?'

'You try stopping me,' she says. I've just got one painting to do first. I'll come in two weeks. That'll give you enough time to arrange everything, won't it?'

'Yes, I think so,' he says. 'Whatever you want, let me know. It'll still be the rainy season so the falls will be full.'

'I want to climb Auyán-tepui again,' she says. 'But this time I must reach the top of Angel Falls. You will stay with me this time, won't you?'

'I promised you I would and I will. You'll never reach it on your own and I won't leave you up there with the Mawari spirits again.'

Once she's decided to go back to Venezuela, Dominique feels better. The canvas is ready for her. The sooner she works the sooner she can start planning her trip.

The surface is oblong with a deep frame of brick shapes. Inside lies her father's body. The coffin vaporises. Flames shoot out from the cremator roof onto his chest. His bones glow in the fire. The combustion chamber emits a roar, like howler monkeys just before dawn, or Notre-Dame's trumpeting angel on the peak of the nave roof.

At points in the afternoon, when she's been working since the early hours, she can hear that roar. She can hear it change from a deep furnace blast into a shriek. Flesh lifts up and floats. Islands of pelvic skin hover, before whooshing out into the room as smoke. Papa's face vibrates in the heat-shimmer. His mouth opens like the howler chimera's. A rain of sparks smooths his features, erasing his eyes, leaving a blunt under-face, which shrivels and coils upwards. In the rising coils she scrawls lines from 'Hallelujah'. And fainter now, barely visible, in the last coil of whirlpooling flesh, the words 'holy' and 'breath', then 'sorry'.

At times she paints so quickly her hand goes numb. She withdraws it and it's ice-cold. The studio becomes the cemetery – everywhere she looks there are tombstones, angels, withering flowers.

She touches her own face. She is so alive. She breathes in and feels oxygen reach the smallest bronchioles of her lungs. She breathes out and feels powerful. Often, she thinks herself back to her seat in the Père Lachaise and watches the smoke billowing out of the chimney like a waterfall in reverse, studying how it rose and fell in curls, dissipating then reforming higher up. She traces its progress – *and so progress unceasingly, such is the law,* she writes on the brick frame, and *be born, die, be reborn, then die again. Be buried, exhumed, cremated, buried.*

*I won't let you rest, my tormentor.*

As she paints, Dominique thinks about her recurring dream of the cellar. And it occurs to her that the dream isn't about the cellar in the Boulevard de Grenelle. It's his room – the books, the piled-up furniture, the window at the end, those dusty empty boxes she had to squeeze through every time she visited him. She dreamt about it before it existed, when she was a child entering the tunnels hidden in her bedroom wall. That's why she felt uncomfortable with him, always wanting to leave as soon as she could. But why would she dream about him hurting her then, when he was too ill to do anything? *Because her six-year-old self was there with her.* Every time she visited him, she was back in that cellar. It was brave to go as often as she did. She went because she wanted to try and redeem him. Not everyone would have done that. Instinct would have driven them away, as it drove away Vero.

With this thought, she feels better about painting him burning, but it's not the subject that's exhilarating. It's that she's painting in a way she hasn't tried before. She's decided to paint what hasn't been painted, but because it's taboo, it's not going to be easy to live with. Rituals with ashes have been done before, by other cultures. Juan joked that she should drink her father's ashes in a plantain soup like the Yanomami.

She's never painted what was fashionable, ignored Systems painting and the tutors' efforts to get her to be a formalist, make her paintings about edges, form and paint. Her new painting of the combustion chamber is the insides of things, not edges.

# 51

# BREATH

'WHAT HAVE YOU got in your backpack that's so heavy?' Juan asks. 'Let me carry it on my basket.'

'No thank you, I have to carry it myself,' Dominique insists, securing the straps, as they set off from Guyaraca Camp. She's surprised at how happy she is to see him again and how much he's trying to be helpful, as if he too is happy to be with her. She looks at his face decorated with urucu dye, the white feathers stuck in his black hair, and he smiles self-consciously and strokes them.

'Harpy eagle down will protect me from the Mawari in the sky-world,' he says.

He's walking beside her instead of ahead as he used to do. Despite the huge basket on his back, his steps are light and soundless. Every now and again he offers his hand to help her through the tall grass. Then the morning fog swallows him and all she can hear is his machete slicing through vegetation. She treks alone with her thoughts and the high-pitched chiming notes of a flock of tepui parrotlets, which fly past to land on trees.

'I can breathe easily now,' she tells Papa's ashes. 'Your bones aren't so heavy. We won't need that extra oxygen. Can you hear the parrotlets?'

By the time the sun has burnt through the fog, they've reached the shelter of the middle rainforest and trudge upwards, every now and again catching sight of the second escarpment wall. They have to focus, stepping over the tangle of slippery roots as they enter the upper cloud forest with its electric blue ferns and stunted bushes loaded with epiphytes.

As they climb, Dominique asks Juan how he got the harpy eagle feathers for his hair. 'We captured a chick,' he says, 'and raised her in a large cage, lined the bottom with branches.'

'How did you catch it?' she asks.

'I climbed up a huge kapok tree to get her. The mother attacked me and almost knocked me out, dive-bombing me, so my brother José also climbed up to distract her. I hand-reared the chick, fed her slivers of monkey.'

'And you killed her?'

'No!' he says, 'I love my eagle. Her name is Adelsa. We only take down feathers from her chest when we need her help. I've brought some for you if you like.'

'Didn't you wear king vulture feathers last time?' she asks.

'Yes,' he says, 'but this is stronger. The harpy eagle is a more powerful helper.' He stops to take Adelsa's photo out of his pocket. Dominique smiles because she too has a photo in her pocket and she thinks that they make a fine pair, her father and a female harpy. Adelsa's face is owl-like, her huge amber eyes look out at them, her beak is open with a pink tongue. 'She's hungry,' Juan says, 'waiting for me to feed her.'

They sit on a rock and he brings out a small tin of tree resin, daubs it on to the underside of each feather and sticks them in her hair. 'You'll be safe now,' he says.

'Could I have some for my father?' she asks, unfastening her backpack.

'Your father's in there? You've shrunk him?'

Dominique explains she is carrying his ashes. She tells him because of the emphysema how hard it was for him to talk between each gasp for breath. How the only way she can reconcile herself to him is to imagine him climbing: he had to conserve his every breath and not waste any in talking.

'We'll have to do that when we reach the last wall,' Juan says.

'I thought if I carry him and breathe for him,' she says, 'as hard as he breathed, then I'd understand.'

She takes a deep breath and wrenches the lid off the urn. Juan watches her as she thrusts her hand in and runs her fingers through the ashes. They feel like talc mixed with sand, but there's a surprising amount of grey-white chips, which she realises must be his bones. She quickly withdraws her hand and Juan passes her a few snowy feathers. She drops them in and closes the lid, then sits staring down into the forest far below. The calls of fiery-shouldered parakeets break the silence. The flock lands on an emergent tree below them as Dominique sees that her hand is covered in a glove of white powder. They set off again, over the trip-roots.

When they reach their rock overhang at El Peñon, Juan goes in search of firewood and Dominique is left alone, gazing down into the evening fog. She thinks of Papa in the combustion chamber and of Juan with Adelsa, feeding her monkey flesh, and somehow the two images merge into a double exposure. She can see the furnace jets firing gas at Papa's chest and his shoulders bursting into flames.

The drawing draws itself in her sketchbook, the harpy juvenile taking her maiden flight, his shoulders that are flame-wings. Her father, shaking the blizzards of his wizard-wings, unsteady in his hot nest. His coverts grey as ash, his primaries shooting into violet air. Her father with a double halo of white heat, sprouting his harpy crest. Lifting off through the furnace chimney and over the trees.

She looks up and Juan is there, watching her as she finishes the last line of smoke. He lights a fire and places a treat of two chicken legs on a frying pan for their supper.

'Can I draw you?' she asks.

He looks pleased, pours them a Polar each and runs a hand through his hair. She works quickly in the fading light, using smoky strokes. His eyes are large as Adelsa's and have the same fierce depth. She draws the campfire reflected in his pupils, his hair afloat in the evening breeze, the white feathers fluttering. Any moment now he also will take off.

That's what she wants to capture. How *there* he is and how *not* there, his dyed skin a smudge, about to fly off with the smoke from the fire. She's feeling light-headed herself, hungry and tired; she can smell the chicken frying. Not yet, she tells her stomach. And loses herself once again in Juan's face - umbers and russets of burning wood smouldering just under the urucu streaks. Only a face as real as his can distract her from Papa's ashes.

As they sit there, with her concentrating on her drawing, Juan lost in thought, a tepui tinamou calls - a long, high, tremulous whistle. 'That bird lives only here,' he says. 'Nowhere else on earth. Just here on the slope of the Devil's House and one or two other tepuis.'

If she could draw its wail she would, so as to remember it. Perhaps one day she will look back on this journey and think of Juan, not her father. Her obsession will pass and she will learn to love a man again. Like learning a new language, it will be hard.

# 52

# BLACK JAGUAR

'WILL YOU TEACH me some Pemón?' Dominique asks. 'Only if you help me with my English,' he says. 'I hate it when I make mistakes and sound stupid.'

'Your English is excellent,' she reassures him. 'It's me that's stupid, not knowing your language. How do you say I want a beer?'

'*Wanok anempai édai*,' he says.

'*Wan ok an em pai édai*,' she repeats slowly, several times, as he passes her another warm Polar and laughs. They tuck into their chicken legs. 'Do you mind if I ask how your wife died, Juan?'

'Okay,' he says. 'As I said, it was a Kanaima death. She was attacked by a *kaikuse* – black jaguar. It was my fault.'

'Why your fault?'

'She was working in the garden,' he begins. 'Our *conuco*, which is far from the house. Our youngest son was sick and the *capitán* told me that if I could get some black jaguar blood to pour over his head he would get better. I went on a hunt with five friends. We prepared for it well – fasted, bathed all night in special herbs to cleanse us so he wouldn't be able to smell us. I didn't go near my wife, did everything right.'

'So, what went wrong?'

'We set out before dawn and soon picked up a trail in the forest, where he'd been spotted before. The dawn light was misty; there was dew on all the leaves and I could hear it drip. I could even hear the ants walking on the forest floor, I was so clean. We selected our hunting ground, cut down a few bushes so it was clear. Soon we heard him! He wailed. *Graauu! Graaauuu!* The jaguar's wail makes the hairs on your arms stand upright. A flock of partridges flew up and we knew the beast was close.'

'Was he stalking you?' she asks.

'I was up a tree,' he explains. 'My job was to call to the other men in bird whistles. I called the tiger song again to tell them he was close. It was then the branch broke and I fell.'

'Oh god! What did you do?'

'I climbed quickly back up the tree. But it was too late. The cat had seen me and ran off. The men followed him and shot some arrows into his backside.' He stops to wipe a tear from his eye and she knows what's coming.

'That jaguar ran and ran. He was so angry. He ran into the plot where my wife was working, our garden in the forest. It's very dangerous to be near a wounded jaguar. That brute ripped my wife's scalp off and mauled her shoulders. The flesh was hanging off when we got there. The men managed to kill him quickly with a knife in his heart. But it was too late. Blood was pouring down her face and we knew he'd bitten into her brain.'

'And you couldn't save her?'

'No,' he says. 'We couldn't do anything. We carried her back to the village and applied leaves, sewed the rips up. She lay for seven days before she died. We saw the marks of Kanaima on her – a V cut into the sides of her lips. And knew it was the work of a devil who had taken a jaguar shape.'

Dominique hugs him and they stay there holding each other. 'I'm sorry,' she says. 'I shouldn't have asked.'

# 53

# A MOUNTAIN GATE

I T'S COLD, SO they sit sipping rum, huddled around the fire. 'Now you tell me about your father,' Juan asks. 'Why have you brought his ashes here?'

And it all comes out: two years of having a father.

'You told me how you made him appear with your painting of Salto Ángel,' Juan says. 'I've often thought about what you said, how you made a spell with paint, just as I do with urucu paint.'

'And some of your marks are like mine,' she says.

'Are they?' he says. 'I've always liked painting people's faces. I practise the designs on bark first.'

'Sometimes,' Dominique says, looking into the darkening forest, 'bad things happen, as they did to your wife. You falling out of the tree – it wasn't your fault, perhaps the tree was rotten.'

'I wouldn't climb a rotten tree,' he protests.

'But sometimes,' she continues, 'good things happen like magic. I painted my father's portrait and afterwards realised it looked just like him! A few days later, I saw the letter from the lawyer and wondered why he was writing to me. I never expected to see my father again.'

'I said you're a sorceress.'

'Yes, I may be,' she says. 'He vanished when I was a child. He'd forgotten me and I didn't think about him. He was dying. That's why he wrote. His lungs were rotten as your tree. He wanted comfort from me. He said he wanted to make amends.'

'Did he make things better?' Juan asks.

'No.' She shakes her head. 'He wanted to – I think. I reckon he couldn't live with himself if he admitted what he'd done. He raped my mother and that's how I was born.'

'That's terrible, I'm sorry,' Juan says.

'She hated me because I reminded her of him. And how he forced her to marry him.'

'No one could hate you, you're beautiful,' Juan says. Dominique blushes.

'My mother was engaged to someone she was in love with at the time. I can't talk about what he did to my sister and me.'

'He was your father. He should have protected you,' he says, looking angry.

Dominique feels upset even mentioning it. But it's such an old wound she can barely touch it.

'I visited him in Paris four times,' she says.' My sister Vero went once.'

'Perhaps she was right to keep away.'

'Perhaps bad people can't be changed, but I wanted to believe he was good. My mother was mad, so there was also the chance that she'd made it all up, but when she died she left so many letters, and after reading them, that seems less and less likely to be the case.' She steals a look at Juan; he looks lost in thought. 'Do you think people are good?' she asks him.

He looks at her and shakes his head. 'That jaguar who killed my wife was an evil spirit. People are good. The forest is good. But there are devils that take the shape of people and animals. That's why it's so dangerous to be here, at the gate of the devil's house, this *tepui* is where the mountain devils live. They live on top, far from people. They imprison our spirits inside the rock. It's old rock, older than the moon.'

They both look up to the summit.

'It's certainly haunted,' Dominique says.

'Our people have learnt to live in harmony with each other by living apart,' he says. 'So, if a man has two wives, they will live far from each other and the husband will visit each one and they won't quarrel. We are a good people. We have learnt how to be good from plants and the stories of our grandparents, which we still tell the children, even though we go to church and pray to your white god.' As he's talking, a mouse opossum climbs down the hurricane lamp and dangles over the fire.

'He's after our scraps!' Juan laughs and she starts giggling. The rum and tiredness get the better of her and there's a curtain of drizzle beyond the overhang.

'*Katurui,*' Juan says. 'That's what we call that kind of rain – saliva of the stars.' The rain stops and starts. One minute they're pelted, then it vanishes only to start again from a different direction.

'The stars are arguing,' she laughs. 'I'd better go to bed; we'll need an early start tomorrow.'

Juan has propped her tent next to the fire under the rock roof. She hovers by the flap, wondering where he's going to sleep as it's too wet and cold to put up a hammock, but he retreats further under the overhang and curls up beneath his blanket. She lies listening to the thunder getting louder. Every now and again her tent lights up with blue light. She opens the flap and looks out at bolts of lightning thick as tree trunks, dancing around them, enclosing El Peñon in a spectral forest.

One bolt lights up their recess and she sees that Juan is sitting up watching her. His face is luminous in the ghost light, and she can see the shadows of his long lashes. 'You can't sleep either?' she asks.

He comes towards her, puts his arm around her waist. She huddles against him – for warmth, she tells herself. How long since she's been this close to anyone? She thinks of her father's hug, that first time she entered his room. She ought to hold back now, but it's too late because suddenly he's kissing her, and this time she doesn't stop him. He pauses and she pulls him back to her.

ॐ

Even though she wakes up before dawn, Juan has already left her tent.

She peeps out to see him crouching over the fire, heating water for coffee and instant porridge. He smiles at her. 'Today is going to be a good day,' he says. 'Listen, I can hear *iroma* – the tepui's breath.'

He hands her a coffee and she warms her hands around the tin mug, realising how comfortable she is around him. She remembers noticing how quiet his voice was when she first met him and how attractive she found that. It seems to come naturally to Pemón to speak quietly.

Before the sun's first rays appear, the howler monkeys start their unearthly roar. Waves of sound go right through her, up out of the fog. She remembers that first phone call, before she heard her father's voice, before he said *I have thought of you every day of my life*, how the howlers preceded him. She believed him then. Now, she's not sure, but then she was willing to think the best of him. And now Juan is speaking. His voice doesn't slice through her out of the past. It's the voice of the future.

A morpho butterfly glides past, lazily flapping its metallic blue wings, like lightning flashes in slow motion. 'Careful!' Juan says, watching it land on Dominique's arm. 'Morphos are sometimes a Kanaima too, when they get drunk on rotting fruit. Then we call them *avakaparu*.'

'It's getting drunk on me. Perhaps it's my father's soul,' Dominique says. 'It's tickling!'

'It's a *tigre mariposa*, but we can't see the jaguar. He's invisible.'

The morpho closes its wings, its under-wings dark brown with eyespots, like a black jaguar flashing his eyes. It opens its wings again as the sun comes out. Dominique has never seen such a blue. 'I wish I had a colour like that,' she says. 'Then I could paint the blue shadows in your hair.'

'My shadows are blue?'

'Heavenly,' she says.

Juan strokes her hair as a musician-wren starts its dawn song. 'Your hair is the notes of that musician-wren's song,' he says. 'It's a sad song full of longing. When she sings, all the other birds in the forest stop to listen. She's built her nest in your hair.' Dominique listens to the mournful flute-like notes. And it's true, all the animals in the forest have gone quiet.

'I'm sure there's a pygmy marmoset in there too!' she says, laughing, and she tries to tame the strands, pulling them up into a ponytail.

'I have a macaw at home,' Juan says, 'as well as my harpy Adelsa, but the macaw is free, not in a cage.'

'What other animals do you have?'

'Two dogs, a tamandua, one toucan, an agouti and an ocelot,' he replies.

'An ocelot? Wow an ocelot!'

'I rescued her when her mother abandoned her. She comes and goes, always returns to lick my face when I'm asleep.'

'Who's looking after them now?' she asks.

'My parents. But the ocelot looks after herself, she's wild. She only comes to me.'

Dominique will look back on this morning as the moment she fell in love. When Juan talks about his animals, she forgets the ashes, and for the duration she feels free. And he seems to feel the same way, she's almost sure of it now.

So that when he says *Apötöpö eday*, she knows what it means. There he is in his I *love* NY T-shirt, stirring the porridge and looking at her. '*Apötöpö eday*,' he repeats. 'I loved you when I first saw you at Kavac, when you climbed out of the plane and looked up at the tepui as if it was home.'

'And I love you too,' she responds before thinking. Does she? She's almost sure.

'When I've scattered my father's ashes, I'll be free. He's still in the way. I have to breathe with him right to the top. I have to understand what it's like finding it so hard to catch your breath. I have to place my soul inside his throat.'

Then it hits her again that she said she loves him back. How is that possible? She thinks back to her arrival at Kavac, how dreamlike it was to see the cliffs of Auyán-tepui again, Juan standing there to welcome her like a guardian of the wild. She'd been instantly attracted to him, but shrugged it off. She had come to be in her painting where Papa first appeared to her. She had urgent business to attend to and a guide was just a guide. Even though his voice made her feel as if she was home.

And he has an ocelot!

They climb in silence up the cleft that splits the top cliff of Auyán, the only gateway to its summit. Juan goes up ahead and throws her down the rope. She heaves herself up the pink slabs, too high to offer hand or foot holds. Papa is on her back, in the plastic urn.

'We're here!' Juan says through the fog as she picks her way up the last rock.

At the top, the air is drier and the fog has gone. It's as if she's climbed up the back of her painting, passed through the swirls into its world. She thinks back to Père Lachaise, the smoke coiling out of the crematorium that day as she sat watching the leaf fall out of the autumn sky. But you'd need to be an angel to cross these crevasses.

'We need wings,' she tells Juan.

'Vulture wings?' he asks.

'No, angel wings,' she laughs, happy to be back on the top, approaching El Oso Camp.

'But you're the king vulture's daughter,' Juan replies, 'and they have stronger wings than your angels.' And just as he says it, they come across a crevasse two metres wide. She braces herself to leap across, refusing to take her backpack off. That's the deal – it has to stay on. This is how Papa felt when she asked him a question he didn't have the strength to answer, that he couldn't answer without falling in. She peers down and can't see the bottom.

'Here we go!' she says to Papa. 'Brace yourself, we're going to fly across and when we reach the other side, I'll know the answer.' She walks backwards and takes a run-up then leaps into the air. And lands safely, next to an orchid. Is that her answer? She thinks how the root of orchid is orchis – the Greek for testicle, because the bulb looks like one. The mountain has spoken for Papa. 'All that is over now,' he'd said, when she accused him of being a playboy. And here are his sex organs, harmless as a flower.

It's progress.

'Did you rape Maman?' she asked the air before she leapt. And Papa took a deep breath from the swamp of his lungs and whispered, 'Perhaps you'd call it that, but it wasn't to me.'

With each crack in the rock, and each cliff they encounter, she asks more questions. 'Why did you hurt me?' But she answers it herself. 'Those priests were your parents in the boarding school. Did you think that's what parents do?'

Juan has his invocations and she has her conversation with the backpack. Every now and again they come across a bizarre insect – a red and yellow spider, a giant blue centipede, a scorpion, a black prehistoric toad. These are the inhabitants of the house of spirits. And they might as well carry scripts on their backs, because they appear each time Dominique asks another question. The closer they get to El Oso, the lighter her pack becomes. El Oso, where the sun is beating down at midday, and where they can bathe under a waterfall.

'Can you see this view?' she asks Papa. 'Isn't it beautiful? There are no other people up here, no one to hurt you ever again.'

Juan leads them on towards Campo Lecho and the second 'wall' on the surface, behind a bend in a fork of the Churún-Vená River, downhill over black slabs punctuated with islands of bromeliads. The river is gold. They stare at the rocks that emerge from its orange waters, their flat tops a sandy pink. Juan is transfixed.

'It's three years since I've seen that,' he says. 'Three years of dreaming of this moment.' And he strips off his jeans and T-shirt and jumps in, so that he too is gilded.

'*El dorado!*' she says, stripping off and following suit. The water is icy and instantly refreshes her. She climbs up onto a slab and lies there, sunning herself. Juan sits on the rectangular slab next to her and looks lost in thought. She thinks of him up here with his wife and feels jealous. Then she remembers that Pemón women don't go trekking, they stay home and work in the gardens, make manioc bread and cachiri beer, and care for the children.

'Would you like to have had a girl?' she asks.

'A daughter? She would have looked like her mother. Tomasa could have lived on in her.'

'How long were you married?'

'Twelve years. I didn't want to remarry, and I didn't take a second wife while she was alive. I loved her very much.' He looks at Dominique, then away into the water, bends down and cups some in his hand to drink. 'I think I could love you as much, if you'll let me.'

Before Papa's reappearance, Dominique could only love someone unavailable like her father. Now, here he is in her backpack, weighing her down. And then she realises she doesn't have it on. He's on the riverbank. So she turns her thoughts back to Juan. 'How long have you worked as a guide?'

'I've had many other jobs,' he says. 'Before Tomasa died, a sting-ray in the Carrao River got me. I was ill a long time. While I was ill, the stingray spirit visited and told me to become a *pia'san* – a shaman, so I could cure the sick. I trained and worked hard. I could make people well.'

'You're not wearing the urucu or eagle down anymore,' she says.

'No. The spirits were here, but they've already seen us and been frightened off by our masks.'

'Is that why I feel safe?'

'Yes, there's no devil here,' he says.

'And I'm with a healer,' she replies.

'No, I don't practise anymore. I went to Caracas University when I was a boy, and studied natural science. But I hated the city. I couldn't stay there. And my family needed looking after – my parents and sisters. I studied for a few years then returned home.'

'So that's when you started guiding?'

'Tourists were just starting to come to Canaima, and as I spoke English I was popular. I did that for a while, and worked in Canaima Hotel when business was bad. Just before Tomasa died I became a shaman, but it didn't make enough money. No one wants a shaman anymore, so I returned to guiding, but I still know my *taren* – my spells.'

One of the black rocks on the bank looks just like the Stryga on the Notre-Dame chimera gallery, his chin resting on his hands, watching them. Others are like the eroded leopard. They are up on the towering cathedral of this country, among its gargoyles. Dominique climbs out onto the bank and starts drawing the forms, and the orange-gold river water, gurgling around rock pedestals, Juan sitting on one, his legs in the water. Below him the shallow riverbed slopes down to a deep pool. The water is clear as amber.

'What's that hummingbird?' she asks, as it flies past with a buzz.

Juan turns towards the pitcher plants on the bank. 'It's Aruka! He's saying an incantation.'

She scans the pitcher plants for the source of the high-pitched calls and spots a shining green hummingbird.

'He's one of my helper spirits,' Juan tells her. 'When I was a shaman, he would accompany me on journeys to the sky-world. He lives on the tepui, with Tukui the goldenthroat. They work together. We're going to need their help if we're to reach Angel Falls in time. Let's go.'

They dress and Juan packs up her tent then they set off upriver, following the Churún-Vená in a north-easterly direction, across the plateau. Sometimes they find themselves among skyscrapers, crawling along boulevards between towering striated rocks. Then they reach a swamp and it starts to rain hard so that she's wading through thigh-deep mud, Papa balanced on her back, Juan pulling her along. The rain encloses them, shuts them off from each other. She can barely see Juan's hand through the sheet of water.

## 54

# ANGEL FALLS

THEY REACH THE Dragon's Mouth, where Churún-Vená river plunges underground. Juan beckons Dominique on, over a rocky maze that takes them hours to cross, to where it reappears, gushing out of the fissure. The rain lasts all day and all night. They camp under another overhang, and Dominique wonders how she can fulfil her dream with visibility down to nil, but Juan stays positive.

'It's almost the dry season. The rain won't last. And the good thing is that the falls will be full. You'll see, it'll work out,' he says, kissing her. She snuggles up to him and thinks about her good fortune in meeting him, a gift from the sky.

Despite the storm that night, she manages to get some sleep. Every time the thunder wakes her, she's flying through the air of her painting – that painting that drew her here through her father. She floats through his body and it's made of light. She floats through droplets of jasper, through feathers of his ashes.

She wakes with a jolt at 3 a.m. and listens for the rain, but there's no sound. Juan is asleep in his blanket. She marvels at his patience, letting her get slowly used to him so that she can trust him. It's always been like this. She remembers her first time with her first boyfriend, how she slept with him for months before having sex, how she hallucinated he was the devil when they finally tried. She didn't know then why this happened. She thinks of the mattress in the cellar, the crayon in her hand. Draw, it told her. Draw what is happening when you are older and can bear to remember it.

Drawing became the only way she could let the cellar into her mind. She became a child when she was painting her world, a world that terrified and enthralled her.

She rises now, out of the tent, and starts making coffee and porridge by the light of the hurricane lamp. Adrenaline is coursing through her. The time is approaching.

Juan joins her and they eat then wash up in silence, preparing for their last trek along the Río Churún-Vená. By first light they have already set out towards the northwest cliff, trudging along the swampy ground between rocks eroded into half-formed creatures of a sky zoo that she recognises from the Chimera Gallery at Notre-Dame, across the streets and alleys of Paris – ancient city of childhood. Dawn illuminating cobbled playgrounds. The silver-pink sands of a sandpit where a girl once played so deep into her world that a fog enclosed her and the exterior world vanished. From then on, she could make her parents' world vanish. The park keeper would find her singing quietly to herself, playing with the sandcastle at twilight. Then Maman would be summoned and she'd be dragged home. She'd sit at the kitchen table and draw the sand world, so that it would surround her with ramparts.

Much of the surface of Auyán-tepui is black, but here and there, outcrops of pink quartz glow. After a brief lunch, they walk faster, climbing over walls of a cityscape planted with sky gardens of shrubs that only grow on this tepui, sundews glistening around swampy pools, their red dew-traps refracting rainbows.

Juan also stays silent, as if he's entering a dream he's not dared dream again. He's been here before, with Tomasa. She is the only woman to have walked in the house of evil spirits, that first year he'd decided to become a shaman. Later, when they return to Guyaraca Camp, he will tell Dominique this, how brave his wife was, how he never hoped to find another woman like Tomasa.

This is where he had walked after fasting for four days, so light-headed a cloud clung to his face, and in that cloud Anwoná the king vulture father beat his wings against his cheeks, giving him more and more impossible tasks to fulfil. He remembers leaning over the precipice and almost falling into the mists that blew up from Churún-Vená, his name for Angel Falls, Tukui and Aruka humming to keep him steady while his spirit jumped. He remembers the rush of air almost knocking him out, how the falls seemed to stand stock still while he floated among arrows of spray, as if the bag of the sun had ripped and showered him with darts.

His skin was pierced all over. He had trembled with heat and cold, then came to in their hut, Tomasa bathing his fever. When he'd asked her where she had just been, she gave the right answer. He had not dreamt it. They had climbed the sky ladder together. She was stronger than him because she had not fasted or drunk *cachiri* until she was sick. She pulled a leaf out of her pouch and said it came from the lip of the waterfall and grew only there.

When he and Dominique reach the edge of the plateau it is still drizzling. They set up camp in silence, worried that their plans will fall through. There is no visibility across the canyon, just a bank of dark grey clouds. Juan whistles to himself as he works, and smiles each time she looks at him. 'You'll see,' he reassures. 'It will be fine,' and he taps his nose. They huddle in the tent.

She wakes at 4 a.m., listens for rain, but all she can hear is the wind whistling through the rock formations and out over the canyon, and a deep roar shaking the mountain. They eat in the dark, waiting for sunrise. Everything is neatly packed away in Juan's basket and her rucksack, ready to give them maximum time on the edge.

# 55

# THE FACE IN THE FALLS

I T I S I M P O S S I B L E to reach the rim. The Churún-Vená river has gone underground again and now resurfaces in a boiling fountain, only to plunge back into the rocks. They are close to the edge of the plateau, scrambling around to try to get a view of the mammoth, which gushes out of fissures several metres beneath them and almost fills the amphitheatre. They sit on the edge of the escarpment, staring open-mouthed. The view of Devil's Canyon, almost one mile below, gives Dominique vertigo.

She removes her backpack, takes out the plastic screw-top urn and ties it around her neck. Juan swings a knotted rope round a rock column and fastens it to his waist and around her. The only way to reach the falls is for her to dangle over the rim.

Juan will hold her as she climbs down over the precipice. She will have to have complete trust in him.

'Adarö e'marikmapai,' he says, as she climbs over the edge. 'I'll tell you what it means later.' She can't hear anymore because the falls are deafening, like a continuous thunder roll.

So here she is dangling over thin air, her waist tied to the rope around a man. She could plunge to her death, down the cliff. The gusts that blast out from the cataract are blinding. She waits for a lull.

She is opening the letter from the lawyer, reading the first line. But she is no longer full of hope. Her father will never apologise and now she knows why, and she's starting to come to terms with that – a new hope.

The letter is in her pocket and she's in his bazaar of a room, with its prehistoric furniture and stone boxes piled high. The room is exploding, then re-assembling. She glances down, expecting a plunge pool, but all she glimpses is a jumble of rocks.

Vero is down there, she thinks. After Papa's funeral, Vero found some letters in Maman's trunk that Dominique had missed. She wouldn't tell her what they contained, but she had another breakdown, which culminated in a suicide attempt. She had always been too unstable to look after Jack and this was further proof for the child-welfare people. For a while she was not allowed to have her son stay with her, and this made her worse.

Dominique remembers her own suicide attempt when she was twenty. She was staying in a squat due for demolition. That day, the police had come to evict her. Her boyfriend had left her in the middle of the night while she was asleep. She'd woken and glanced out of the window to see him carrying a suitcase to his red jalopy. He'd just left. No note. Nothing.

She took twelve sleeping pills. The painter who lived downstairs had said, 'No one loves anyone else. We are all alone. All lovers will eventually leave you, that's how it is.'

And that was it. She would always be abandoned. She drank half a bottle of vodka, took one more sleeper and sat and waited.

At 3 a.m. she had scrambled through her emergency address book and found Vero's number. It took Vero a while to answer and when she did she sounded sleepy. Dominique told her about the sleeping pills, but Vero said, 'I think you should do it. It's a good idea.'

Dominique pleaded with her, telling her how abandoned she felt. That it was like floating in outer space, no tether tying her to earth. But all Vero said was that Dominique had woken her up and she wanted to go back to sleep. She had work in the morning.

It took them years to get over that conversation, and the postcard that followed, where she'd scrawled, *I think you should do it, Sis.* Years later, Vero apologised, said she'd taken too many drugs and couldn't think straight.

As for Dominique, she didn't even fall asleep. She stayed there, rocking herself until dawn.

That was her first suicide attempt, if she doesn't count sitting on the ground behind a shed when she was at school, trying to cut her wrists with broken glass. Those were only half-hearted attempts she told no one about. She was thirteen then. But all through her twenties she made several other attempts – lying on the kitchen floor next to an open oven with the gas on.

This wouldn't be a bad way to go, she thinks now, not daring to look down again.

But she has no intention of killing herself. Juan is waiting for her, holding her safe and she's tethered this time. There are paintings to make, she's determined to get better; to paint what hurts until it's better. She can change the past with art. What would she do without art? She can't imagine what it's like for people who aren't creative. What do they live for? But her art is a kind of love and that's what they live for, she decides: love. Despite all the cruelty in the world, there is love and it redeems us. There is mother-love, and okay, she's not a mother, and didn't have her mother's love, but she pours her love into art. This, she now realises, is precious. She will do anything for her art.

She is not dangling over Angel Falls for her father. She is doing it for her art. She will paint it, over and over, until she gets it right. Critics will accuse her of repeating herself, but she doesn't care. She must get it right, even if they don't get it.

What is a waterfall? Is it just a river coursing over a plateau, sometimes over and sometimes underground, until it gets to the rim, then leaping almost one mile to disintegrate, only to re-assemble further down in minor falls, to join the steep Churún river? She wants her paintings to make that leap. To be life force.

Dominique tips the urn over and Papa slides out to join the needle-fine spray, which has lifted far above the rim of the waterfall and back down to slap her. She doesn't think Papa wants to be released here in this hostile place where humans shouldn't be.

The remoteness is what drew her here that first time, when she walked into a travel agent and asked if there was any way she could get to Angel Falls. She was lucky, because Canaima National Park had just opened to tourists, helicoptering the rich onto the top of the plateau, flying chartered Cessnas into Devil's Canyon, to fly by the falls for the view of a lifetime. They'd even started river tours to the base in the rainy season, using Pemón navigators and motorised dugout canoes to reach the under-falls and lookout point. She remembers her first sight of them from the boat, how everyone stood up, and the canoe almost capsized as they stared open-mouthed at the white giant against the red sandstone amphitheatre, the waters swollen by recent rains. Then the storm when they hiked to the lookout point near the base, how dark clouds obscured the top and thunder ricocheted back and forth in the semi-circular cliff enclosing the spectacle. How they scrambled back uphill as the river rose.

She knew then she had entered a non-human place. It was a risk she took again, when she asked Juan to guide her here. Juan, who knows all about the Mawari spirits, who thinks that the souls of eaten animals live in the mountain, that the gaps in the rock are their windows.

A sudden blast pushes her over and her hand slips. She's dangling upside down.

The water forces her further down and she can't see anything, spray pummels her like a punchbag. She somersaults several metres.

She is hanging upside down in the white storm of Papa's kitchenette, knives flying around, her face pierced by icy pins. She's staring at her silver skin in his shaving mirror, her face cracked in two, splitting her lips so she has two mouths. She can't right herself. She can see slivers of Papa's face stretched out, flickering and shattering like glass in the descending plumes. He's pulling her down with him. The water holds his face steady then pulverises him, grains of his cheekbones hurled down into the river.

But Juan must be pulling her rope. She swings herself back and forth, like on Papa's knees, grasping for a firm handhold, past the crumbly wet sandstone into the drier heart rock, then heaves herself up onto a ledge beside the falls. Where does her strength come from?

Her shoulder feels stabbed, but she'll wait for Papa to be swept down-current, along the rocks and whirlpools of the turbulent Churún, until it meets the Carrao, then joins the Caroní with its expanse of ferocious rapids. She waits in the water-smoke until he's joined the Orinoco Delta and is washed out to sea.

She believes that his soul lifted out of his body before it fell, to settle in the cliff. She can feel his eyes on her. There he is waving at her from a quartz pane, no longer held back by the oxygen lead like a dog. He's come to his window to say goodbye, to thank her for being brave enough to visit him.

# 56

# BULLET ANTS

DOMINIQUE WIPES THE spray from her cheeks and finds they are gritty where the ash flew back in her face. She is wearing a mask of her father's ashes. She doesn't know how she descended the plateau, but here they are back down on the lower slope, on terra firma.

'Ow!' she cries, as something stabs her finger.

'Bullet ant!' Juan shouts. 'I've also been stung.'

Dominique rubs her hand. They both examine the vine they held onto to climb down the bank. Juan says they must hurry now and put antihistamine cream on. He's amazed at how quiet she is; a bullet ant is the worst sting in the world and he's having trouble not crying out with the pain.

'You're very brave,' he says, 'but if you have antihistamine pills you should take them too; anything to get through tonight. By tomorrow morning it will throb less, and be fine by tomorrow evening.'

He tells her about the Wayana tribe and how they have an initiation rite for girls. Their boys wear ant gloves to become men, like other tribes, but their girls also have to do the ant test, only they press a mat woven with ants to their chests and must not cry out while the ants stab.

Dominique feels like she's been shot in the hand, but she's also excited, because she's been stung by the bullet ant of her painting.

*Imagine*, Papa says, *what it would be like if you'd grown up with me.*

She looks around, but no one's there. Juan is ahead, rushing to get back. Her whole arm is throbbing and she has to hold it out away from her, any contact and the pain is unbearable.

*Imagine*, Papa says. He reaches up to his shelf and pulls down a woven mat.

Juan turns round to check how she's bearing up, but Dominique just grimaces. Her hand has swollen.

'Imagine,' she says, 'I got stung by a 24-hour ant!'

'Domino,' Juan whispers, putting his arm around her waist, *'adarö e'marikmapai,'* and this time translates: 'I want to marry you.'

She must be hallucinating, and he must be delirious too, it's the bullet ants speaking. But when she looks at him, he looks serious. Her hand throbs as if she's been writing a letter to her father.

# 57

# THE ANT SHIELD

*D*EAR PAPA, TODAY *is my last day as a child. Maman says I can no longer wear just a vest. At bedtime I press it to my face, say goodbye to the white cotton that held me so cosily every day. Tomorrow I will have to wear a shield. Into my shield a hundred girl ants will be woven, their thoraxes strapped into the lace, heads out, jaws hissing, their stingers pointing inwards.*

*You are my tobacco shaman. You reach for a last cigar. You blow on the ants. You fan the fury of my warriors who defend the forest of girlhood. My soldier girls in armour that's clicking like your clock. It's time, they tick, for the brave ones who carried waterdrops without spilling, it's time for them to help me. But you blow smoke on them and enrage them.*

*If they could anchor their stings, they might be able to haul themselves out of the lace. And they do, Papa – a hundred stingers pierce in unison.*

*'Breast tissue is kind,' Nurse says. 'It heals with almost invisible scars.' O my bullet ants, I don't cry out.*

*Papa, are you listening? I've carried you over the mountain of my life like a waterdrop. I've released every atom of you. My breasts are swelling but my workers are victorious. At nightfall I release each from her bonds. Your daughter signs this letter with ant blood.*

# PART FOUR

# 58

# TASTE

FIVE YEARS LATER, 2005

DOMINIQUE RETURNED HOME to think about Juan's proposal and decided against it. He wouldn't be happy living in London, and she can't move to Venezuela. But they wrote to each other and once she'd bought a computer, they kept in touch through long emails, stories about Adelsa the harpy eagle and Coco the Ocelot, the puppies and tamandua – an ever-growing bestiary.

How could she forget the one who held onto her while she dangled over Angel Falls to scatter Papa's ashes?

Then the emails petered out and stopped. Tears would come to her eyes as she remembered their second expedition. It all felt dreamlike now – the musician-wren's song rising from the lower slopes at dawn, how he'd compared her hair to its sad notes filled with longing. She was lonely but used to her own company, relied on herself. Juan kept saying he'd come to visit her, but he hadn't, and she didn't go back to their Lost World.

The first year after Papa's death she couldn't go back to Paris. But then she started visiting, just a few days at first, in a hotel, then for months at a time. She rented an attic room in the narrow rue du Pot-de-Fer, which had a terrace overlooking the Panthéon dome, and doubled as a studio. Most days after working she strolled over the Pont-au-Double to the parvis, and gazed up at the Notre-Dame towers. Sparrows still haunt the low privet hedges in their concrete beds, just as they did when she used to visit Papa. She loves to stand there, holding out her hand for them to feed on seeds she buys from the bird market.

Often, she makes for the Fauverie, where she has discovered a new black jaguar called Adonis. He's only three, but already huge. She likes to watch him at feeding time. It's five o'clock; if she rushes, she'll get there in time.

And she does, because here is the young keeper with her keys, going into the interior of the octagonal Fauverie. Dominique follows her into the big-cat house and waits. The hatches are going up from the exterior cages! First in, as always, are the caracals, Sylvain and his mate, who can catch ten birds with one leap. The girl thrusts turkeys through their chutes at the back and waits, but they dawdle before feeding, and a small crowd has gathered so they are shy. It's the turn of the snow leopards now. Dominique moves around the concave set of plate windows to see Raj pause at the hatch high up on the back balcony, to land with a thud on the floor. *Oohs* emanate from the crowd. A hunk of horse is tipped into the feeding trough and he has it. Now it's the turn of his young cage-mate Zara, fed in a separate cell. But in the cage next door, Bébelle, the elderly North China leopard is beside herself, pawing at the mesh above her feeding chute. The keeper hesitates because Bébelle is swiping the chute, and she doesn't want to lose her fingers. Bébelle grabs her turkey as soon as it comes through, and shakes it at Dominique. She leaps back up to the relative privacy of the balcony and tucks in.

Dominique's torn. Watching Bébelle is gripping, but she knows whose turn it is next, and she must tear herself away and move into the centre of the house, lean over the rail guard, and poise her camera ready. But what's happening? Adonis is rubbing his cheek against the mesh at the back, and the young girl who's feeding them from the back corridor plants a kiss on his muzzle! Adonis the black jaguar, pride of the zoo, his fur more chocolate than black, the rosettes star clouds in a bronze dusk.

Dominique can feel her father's tongue on her neck. She grabs the guard rail to stop herself falling. She's not had this flashback for years; she thought she'd got over it. She must drag herself out of the gulch she's fallen into. She's here, with Adonis, who is so harmless the young girl has kissed him. Here is the rabbit thrust through, covered in white fur. Adonis carries it in his jaws, right to the front of the window, against the plate glass, and drops it. Dominique watches as he rips off mouthfuls of fur, spitting them out. The floor is covered in snow.

Snowflakes had clung to Dominique's hair like down as she'd climbed the stairs to Papa's flat, knocked, then inserted the key he'd given her. 'Is it snowing?' he'd asked. 'I hadn't noticed. You must be frozen. When did you get back from Venezuela? Come and kiss your old Papa and let me warm you.' He'd trapped her hand between his and rubbed it warm. She's not sure if she's the rabbit or the jaguar now.

It's the only time of day that Adonis springs into action and puts on a show, otherwise he sleeps at the back of the outdoor enclosure behind a stand of bamboo. Occasionally, he spots a green uniform passing in the distance, and springs up on his stocky legs, rubbing himself along the inside of the curved glass, hoping for a feed.

The spectacle is almost over. There is only the clouded leopard couple and they are sleepy, being nocturnal, not crepuscular. And the new North China leopard pair, Tao and Bao-Bao, won't come down from their respective balconies until the humans have left. Tao eventually peeps around a pillar, then retreats. Bao-Bao snarls at Dominique from the top, recoiling behind her pillar. Dominique snarls back.

'It's going to be a white Christmas,' Papa had said, and then laughed. When he released her hand, she felt as if her scalp had been ripped off. How could the hand of an old sick man have done that? She'd gone into the kitchenette and examined her head in his silver-crazed mirror on the wall, and seen marks like love bites, Vs cut into the sides of her lips. She'd looked away at the old wall outside the window, and when she looked in the mirror again, the marks had gone.

# 59

# SIGHT

A DONIS HAS BEEN moved from the Ménagerie in the Jardin des Plantes to a larger enclosure in Vincennes Zoo near the Bois de Vincennes. Dominique spends days there waiting for an appearance. He's lying behind a banana palm; she can just see him belly-up like a pet cat. She wanders about, visiting her other favourites – the wolverines, the puma the other end of the zoo, the fossa, and the wolves at feeding time, racing after frozen blood cubes thrown into their pool. But it's a no-jaguar day.

Sometimes she thinks she glimpses Juan through the other vitrine, searching for Adonis, or behind a crowd by the lemurs in the great glasshouse, when the black and white ruffed lemurs make the whole greenhouse throb with hair-raising calls, and she stands remembering the dawn howlers.

She is on Auyán then, waking up in her tent. Juan is still asleep. She has time to draw him – capture his likeness. When he wakes, he'll accuse her of stealing his soul, but it doesn't matter because he has a spare one. All she has of him is this sketch. She made others, but this is the one which changes every time she looks at it. His mouth slightly parted, his eyes flickering as if the lids are about to open. Then they do open and she can see herself in each pupil, two happy Dominiques in a fatherless world.

And today, she's sure. That's Juan by the woolly monkeys! When she goes up and touches his arm, a stranger turns round. Don't be silly, she tells herself – how could he be in Paris?

# 60

# EMMANUEL

ONE DAY, AS she's standing on the parvis, gazing up at Notre-Dame, the bourdon bell Emmanuel starts tolling. She looks up at the south tower, to the belfry above the Chimera Gallery, and lets the long note envelop her – a reverberating F sharp. As long as Emmanuel tolls, her father is alive again. Tears roll down her cheeks as she thinks of his ashes scattered on the rocks of the canyon, buffeted by gusts then washed downriver, as she hung like a bellringer over Angel Falls. Juan is pulling on the rope as she swings herself back and forth until she has the rock face in her grip again. Juan who's twice saved her life. She's crying for him now.

But Papa is calling her back. Just as she'd heard his voice approaching the cellar door, his footsteps echoing as he descended the spiral steps. As his shadow blocked the light from the cellar window, she summoned her black jaguar, her coatis, her weasels, where nothing was supposed to survive. Scientists had said that no big mammals lived on Auyán-tepui.

Yet she and Juan had heard a jaguar one night, and now, at last, there was proof from an expedition's camera traps, set just two kilometres from the top of Angel Falls, inside the gorges of the Churún-Véna where the riparian jungle was dense: a photo of the tree with its scratch-marks. She is back in her tent with Juan as it is lit up with lightning, and thunder rolls make the gully they'd camped in shake. It had been like standing inside the great bell Emmanuel as it rang.

And here is Paris without her father, as if he had never materialised out of the fog to beg her to visit each fortnight. How long the days are! She wakes at five and paints until lunchtime, showers, then heads for Notre-Dame, the Fauverie, or to Adonis at the Vincennes Zoo. Watching Adonis reminds her of the gully up on Auyán – the night Juan woke her and placed his finger on her lips to shush her. They lay in silence as they listened to the growls around their tent. Then, the unmistakable coughs of a jaguar, his breath penetrating through the thin canvas.

But it's no good, because she can't help thinking about Papa. And now, she's discovered that when a bourdon bell is installed it's blessed. A priest has chanted Emmanuel's blessing. The draught makes the clapper sway – a growl like the jaguar. She can feel the growl inside her, tickling the back of her throat. What did her father say? *At the bottom of the steps is a fire. You must not go through it.*

His iron tongue rests in the open bell of his mouth, the belfry of his face asleep. She must climb the tower, up his spine, to the bell cage. She thinks that the cathedral is on fire, that the flames in the cellar have crept through the locked door. Halfway up, she stops, checks the vials in her backpack. One contains water from Angel Falls, the other holds dew gathered in the jaguar's pawprint, the one she and Juan found just outside their tent, that last night by the falls. These are her waters – holier than the water she lay in inside her mother after Papa had raped her.

The cathedral is on fire, but she continues climbing up the narrowing spiral steps, through the wooden door, looking back across the nave roof once more to check if she has time to climb up the bell cage steps. Emmanuel is humming to her. She opens the first vial, anointing the outside of the great bell of Paris with spray from her kilometre-high god, the one that called every night after Papa's letter arrived. The hum is Papa's last breath. The smoke billowing is the smoke from all his cigarettes. It is his last cigarette, and she lets him finish it.

Dominique praises the child that he once was, before the priests got to him in the Jesuit school. She crosses herself, tells them not to hurt him anymore. *You don't know what those priests did!* he'd protested. She takes out the photo of him up a tree in his short trousers - Emmanuel when he was only ten. Had they got to him already then? His face with its smile for the camera his mother is holding. He's wearing white gloves for her and posing formally. Dominique realises his forced expression is because he's looking at his mother. She must be calling him her fallen angel.

Dominique wonders if she too is ruined. She thinks back to her twenties, how she'd let men treat her badly and had no idea how to protect herself. She should have gone around in an iron dress like this bell. She thinks about the priest marking where Emmanuel is to be anointed, white chalk crosses on the outside - east, west, north and south. And on the inside, where the holy oil must go. She thinks it must be like this for other young women, walking inside a sacred bell that says *I'm special and you must treat me right.* But Emmanuel is Papa's voice, and never protected her. And no one protected him.

Are people born bad? Dominique doesn't think so. She decides that they become unhappy when they are babies, or children, as she did. She remembers the children's home, the nurse telling her to stop crying because she'd get permanent furrows down her cheeks.

The spire of the cathedral topples over, creating a draught that slams all the doors and sends a fireball through the attic. The wooden roof is on fire! She can see black smoke billowing from the rafters.

She takes out her second vial, the one with the pawprint dew from the cathedral roof of the Lost World, the one that should not exist, the one she and Juan listened to after the storm, who had not yet seen a human. Who had sniffed them, and they had heard his breath. She thinks of Adonis in his cage, as she is now inside her cage, the bell surrounding her, the bronze weight of Paris - all thirteen tons of copper and tin, the clapper half a ton of exorcised iron. She is standing upright in him, surrounded by the stone zoo of chimeras.

Just what did Mamie Chérie do to him?

'When I came home for Christmas, I thought she would take me away from that school. All I had to do was tell her what the priest did. For a long time, I couldn't bring myself to tell. Then I made myself do it, I opened my mouth and out flew the hummingbird, to its nest in another country. And I could not un-tell her. I think that was when I lost my way.

'She made me strip out of my uniform and turn around. Her nails were sharp. She said I was no longer a virgin, that I had to grow up sometime. So you see, Domino, I did grow up, with a vengeance.'

He'd looked away then, ashamed. And Dominique knew that was as close to an apology that she would get. 'You see, *chérie*,' he'd added, 'it really wasn't my fault.'

But she hadn't been listening properly. She realises now the courage it must have taken to tell her his mother's response.

She keeps his strange suitcase with its bottled chuparosas in her studio, a found object she plans to one day exhibit. It took her months to make herself open all the glass jars, un-stoppering them to inhale their scent of honey and formaldehyde, of longing and betrayal, daring herself to read the notes wrapped around each hummer couple. She could only do it after a few drinks, wanting to know what they contained, and not wanting to know.

She has unwrapped all his love charms and read the notes he wrote, like letters launched in a bottle. Except, these didn't get launched into the sea, they flew through the breathless air of a suitcase. It was only when she unrolled the last note that she realised the extent of his suffering.

Every Saturday morning, before breakfast, Father Matthieu came. I was always awake, shivering in the cold dormitory. I followed him to the cellar and kneeled on the floor, praying as he told me to. At first, I cried. Later, I learnt to control myself by sending myself out of my body like a bird.

One day, Charles in the bed opposite me followed and watched through the keyhole – that's what he told his friends. I can still hear them laughing that they want to have a go. I was small, couldn't defend myself.

I waited until Christmas when I would be home. Maman would be able to help. This thought was all that kept me going. Otherwise, I would have hung myself that day in the woods by the playground.

Then, at last, school came to an end and I escaped, ran away to Paris. Oh, there were easy ways for me to make money, someone with no self-respect like me. One man grew fond of me, so it wasn't all bad.

Later on, I got a job in the bookshop and my misery came to an end. I wrap my last words on the subject around these hummingbirds and seal it in the bottle.

Dominique stands inside Emmanuel, protected by its iron armour, and vows to try harder to forgive him. From now on, whenever Emmanuel is rung, she will listen properly. She will let the bell ring its bass notes that echo over the bridal white buildings of Paris, and know it's mourning Papa's life, proclaiming peace after bloodshed.

❧

A fireball has just exploded through the forest of rafters, creating a draught that made all the doors slam in her attic apartment.

But why is she painting Notre-Dame on fire?

Dominique is back in Papa's room, taking two tape recorders out of her handbag. 'What have you got there?' he asks. She can already tell from his face that he's annoyed.

'I've brought tape recorders,' she stammers. 'I want to record your voice.'

'But why two?' he says. 'Do I have two tongues, like your double-headed vulture?'

She laughs again at his joke and puts one back in her bag. 'I brought two in case the first one breaks. I don't want to forget what you sound like . . .'

'Ah, you mean after I've gone? No, *chérie*, I can't talk into a recorder, it's not natural. If you come back every fortnight, then we'd relax and I'd be able to chat more easily into your contraption.'

Has she remembered right? She'd told him the vulture myth and then had thought it the right moment to bring out the recorders and ask. Then she'd felt ashamed. Of course he didn't want to have his voice recorded to be played when he was dead. How could she have asked?

Why can't she forget him? His ashes must have washed into the Atlantic long ago and reached other shores, pulverised by surf, fish swimming through his dust. Every time she passes rue Clovis, she goes up to the wide end of the old wall where it abuts the pavement and touches its bittersweet stone. She stands in air from seven years ago. She could go back up the outer stairs and through Papa's door that she's drawn, stuccoed with branches of a dense wood at night, every inch pulsing with life. There are nightjars pretending to be branches, and branches pretending to be nightjars. The chameleons move slowly as vines, changing their skin colours to match their background. Their eyes move separately like periscopes, watching her put his key in the lock, entering the night-forest, where now, the branches are emerald tree boas.

She has to pull herself back to the present. And now she feels guilty that she's painted Notre-Dame on fire – it's sacrilege! She decides to scrub out the flames and start again. She paints in the copper statues of the apostles on the spire, green from verdigris, and as she paints, Juan's face keeps appearing in the vanishing flames.

Papa's voice isn't Emmanuel, it wasn't deep and reverberating. It was a small voice, like the parrot that spoke to her in the Marché aux Oiseaux. 'Bonjour!' the parrot said, then whistled and spoke in a strange language.

'He's not for sale,' the man said. 'He's the last speaker of a vanished tribe.'

'Which tribe?' she'd asked, but the man shrugged.

And now, Dominique remembers her dream of Angel Falls. How she'd sat on a stool inside a cathedral and the falls were where the altar would be. Papa's face had appeared and she'd painted it. The falls were smoke, not spray. They were the god of the lost world's burning cathedral. The Amazon rainforest is on fire. It started with control burning, to get rid of brushwood in the understorey, and leapt up each tree like a fire jaguar.

She peers into the dream but can no longer see Papa's face, only Juan's as he fights the flames.

# 61

# RUE CLOVIS

DOMINIQUE HAS BEEN on her own a long time. She fills the solitude with work – she has almost enough new paintings for another solo show. Her jungle paintings grow larger and more detailed. If she's not careful, they'll label them raw art, or worse, her as an outsider artist, even though she spent seven years at art school.

In the late afternoons she wanders through the winding streets of the Latin Quarter, down to the parvis of Notre-Dame, along the gardens on the south side, talking to the feral cats in the cathedral grounds beside the flying buttresses. She brings scraps and hopes they won't fight over them. They have started to appear whenever she arrives, and, once, the battered tabby tom let her stroke him. Afterwards, she likes to sit on a bench and watch the sparrows sand bathing. Ever since she stood inside the bourdon bell, she hopes this will be the day she finally forgives her father and can forget him, but she still ends up talking to him like an imaginary friend.

But today, as she sees children playing in the sandpit, she becomes aware that someone is watching her. He approaches and she avoids him, not wanting to break her trance. 'Domino?' he says. She frowns his way, but that voice! 'Domino? It's me. I've found you!' he says.

It's really him, his serious eyes. 'Juan! What are you doing here?'

He sits beside her on the bench and takes her hand. 'I come here every day looking for you,' he says. 'I go to the parvis you told me about, and I search the crowds. Sometimes I go to the big zoo by the Porte Dorée and sit on the rock by Adonis's enclosure, like you said you do, remembering our time on Auyán, hoping you'll come to see him too.'

'We must have just missed each other,' she says. 'So often I thought I saw you. I did see you through the jaguar glass once. But you vanished when I approached.'

'I've missed you,' he says. 'I've never met another woman like you. So, I worked hard, guiding tourists. I learnt some French. Then, six months ago, flew to Paris.'

'Six months ago. You've been here that long?'

'Yes,' he says, squeezing her hand. 'I couldn't find you and I lost your email. Besides, if I'd warned you I was coming, you'd have told me not to.'

Dominique wonders if she would have put him off. 'I was feeding the cats,' she says.

'I know, I watched you.'

'Oh, you were watching me?' She hopes he didn't catch her talking to Papa like a crazy woman.

'They reminded me of Coco,' he says.

'How are you? And how's your beautiful ocelot?' Juan had taken Dominique back to the communal hut after their descent from Auyán and Coco was there waiting for him. She climbed up him then sat on his shoulder and purred, but Juan warned her not to touch as she was unpredictable with strangers.

'Coco died.'

'Oh no, how?'

'She brought her second litter to show me,' he says. 'Soon after, she died fighting a male who was trying to kill them so he could mate with her.'

Dominique remembers her floret markings like sunlight through flowers. 'And Adelsa?' she asks.

'Adelsa will live forever. We have a big cage for her now, but she still comes out to be handfed.'

Dominique will never forget when Adelsa's eyes met hers; it was like looking into two whirlpools, and when she looked away, the harpy's glare remained. Even now she can feel the irises pulling her in.

'And you?' she asks.

'I'm well. I'm so happy I've found you at last.'

'Six months!' she says. 'That's a long time to be here alone? Are you alone?'

'Yes. I never found anyone like you. You're right, parts of Paris are like my mountain. That's what I say when I get homesick. It makes me sad to see the jaguar in his tiny garden.'

'What do you do here?' she asks.

'I passed my French driving test,' he says, 'and I'm a taxi driver now. Are you on your own still?'

'Yes, same as always.' It must be hard work; his handsome face looks tired. 'Where are you living?' she asks.

'In a one-room apartment not far from here,' he says. 'I was lucky, the mayor's son liked me and set up a regular account, so I chauffeur him and his father around. He got me a *logement social*. Barely one room, but it's just by the old wall which reminds me of Auyán's cliffs.'

She thinks about him looking for her, leaving his people behind, so far from home. He did all this for her! This was how Vero once found her, coming to London and standing by the Whitechapel Gallery every day, until Dominique turned up. Vero knew Dominique went there to see every show, but she didn't have her address because Dominique had tried to lose contact with her mother and sister when she moved from Mile End to Muswell Hill.

Juan must have really wanted to see her again. The least she can do is buy him dinner. She's not sure how she feels yet. There's the instant attraction like before, but can she trust that? 'Are you hungry?' she asks. 'Let's have an early dinner.'

Juan gives her one of those warm smiles that used to encourage her, when they were up on the summit in fog and she got frightened they'd get lost. He made her feel safe then, but now it's the paintings that make her feel secure. It's taken her years to learn to rely on herself. She's reluctant to give that up.

She chooses L'Autre Bistro on the rue des Écoles where she used to sit before visiting Papa. She orders the house red and they drink, hoping to feel less nervous in each other's company. Juan slips his hand over the table and lays it on hers. 'I can't believe I've found you at last,' he says. 'It's taken me so long.'

How often did they miss each other weaving through the cobbled streets? Was he hidden behind a group as she walked along the Seine? Or at the bird market? She spent hours there every Sunday, listening to the captives, watching the ones sold. Often there'd be a tame parrot on a woman's shoulder that she could stroke.

'At first I just worked,' he explains. 'Long hours, so not much chance to look for you. But that's how I learnt to speak fluently. It was hard going, especially at night. I got attacked a few times.'

'Oh no!'

'Don't worry,' he says, 'I'm strong, I easily fought them off. And now here you are! I knew I'd find you one day.'

'I only live in Paris part of the year,' Dominique says. 'You could have come to London.'

'I thought of that,' he says. 'But you told me how big London was, and that I wouldn't like it. Though when you spoke of Paris, you seemed to love it.'

They sit there, chatting about their adventures, carefully avoiding mention of the nights in her tent and his marriage proposal. She loves how tactful he is. But does she still love him? She was in love then. He hasn't aged much either. But she has some grey hairs among the black. Has he noticed? He doesn't say so, though just before the dessert arrived, he leant over and stroked her hair, called her his little ocelot as he used to when he painted her face.

She glances at her watch and sees it's almost eleven. Juan offers to walk her home to her studio and she accepts, promising herself that she won't let him in. She leads him up the rue de la Montagne Sainte-Geneviève, wending her way towards the rue du Pot-de-Fer, when he stops her at the crossing with rue Clovis.

'I live here,' he says, waving at the building on the left.

'So, you meant this part of the wall?' she says. 'This is my father's street. Which building?'

And Juan leads her through the iron gates and across the courtyard, to the white building at the back, just by the wall. The flagstones gleam in the lamplight, and there's a new flowerbed along the side, under the wall.

And there is the fir tree that grew outside Papa's kitchen.

Juan points to Papa's window. 'I found the cheapest room to rent in the Latin Quarter, at a special rate from the mayor.'

Dominique glimpses Papa at the window, blowing her a kiss. Surely Juan doesn't mean his room? He must mean the one above, but how strange he's in the same building!

Everything is moving in dream time now. They go up the outside steps to the outer glass entry door, and Juan taps in the code, just as she had done all those times visiting Papa. Even after he died, Dominique had managed to get through the iron gate to the courtyard; she always carried the code in her bag. The glass door springs open and they go up the first flight of stairs that leads directly to Papa's door. Where Juan stops.

She stares at it and the wood panels grow branches and emerald tree boas that hiss at her. He unlocks the door and pushes it open for her. To the darkest part of the forest, where a bed is camouflaged by leaves. The doorframe writhes with scorpions and bullet ants. He flicks the switch and she still can't make her feet go in. He starts to hug her, but she pulls away. The air is turgid as a tank and she's drowning.

Then he's kissing her, telling her she almost drowned. The words float towards her in bubbles and burst. He helps her to a chair where she sits obediently. The room swirls with spray from Angel Falls, and she's tumbling downwards, a one-kilometre drop. 'I'm drowning,' Dominique says. But Juan looks puzzled.

'You're safe here,' he says. 'Look how I've turned this room into a garden.' She looks around and it's not Papa's room. It's clean, with mint walls and the shelves are filled with plants. The bed is the other side, by the window. Juan offers to make tea. 'I remember how much you love tea,' he says, 'and how I used to boil water for you up on the mountain. I've even got milk.'

Dominique wades towards the table in the centre. She is in her father's swamp. There are plants all around her - orchids, rubber plants, a fiddleleaf ficus. Their stems crawl with leaf insects. Vines trail down from the top shelves to the floor.

Juan comes back in with a mug of tea. Dominique remembers the first evening she visited Papa, how there were no rooms left in hotels because of the fashion fair. How scared she'd been that she'd have to sleep here with him.

'What's wrong?' Juan asks.

'I don't feel well,' she says. In fact, she can't stay one moment longer. She gulps some tea then says, 'I start work at five, I have to go.'

'That's the time we used to wake on Auyán,' he replies. 'Do you remember?'

He offers to walk her to her door, but she refuses. She's used to walking these streets on her own. He tries to hug her again, and she pulls away.

# 62

# TOUCH

DOMINIQUE REACHES HER studio and slumps on the floor. Why does he have to live there? All those times she managed to pass through the outer gate into the courtyard. Only a year ago, she'd got up the nerve to go up the outer steps and someone came out of Papa's building, so she was able to slip in and up the stairs to his door. She'd pressed the buzzer and heard someone moving around, but they hadn't come to open it. She'd called, explaining that her father lived there before he died, and could she come in? But the woman had refused, so Dominique had given up.

It wasn't that she wanted to be inside the room, it was the miracle of having a father for two years. Of having a fatherland. Because, she realises, that's how she feels about Paris, where the Parisians ask her where she's from, because of her English accent and her vaguely Nepalese face.

And now, she's been inside the room. And Juan lives there. The coincidence is bizarre. Did Juan conjure the room as well as her?

The world has shrunk to just one cell – even the Amazon jungle is inside it. And there's a double bed now, not the electric single of Papa's, which used to sit him up at the touch of a button. The bed she'd sat on long into the night, sorting through his bills after he died, trying to find clues about his life. The air Papa breathed through an oxygen recycling machine, as if it was the last air on earth, and he the last human. Dominique has never felt human. Then Juan appeared in the world's lungs, and she started to feel again. Now, Papa is Juan's shadow, and her source of light is spoilt.

The next morning she can't concentrate. But she must! She has another show to paint for. Even though she's been lonely, she relishes the solitude for work. She mustn't let Juan spoil that. She's arranged to meet him for lunch at Le Flore en l'Île, a café across the Seine on Île Saint-Louis. They'll meet on the benches behind Notre-Dame's flying buttresses and walk across together, as if flanked by giant buttresses of kapoks in the world's cathedral forest.

He's already there when she walks up, he's smiling at her in the way that always reassured her, even when it was raining on the mountain. They cross the bridge and choose an outdoor table. He holds out his hand. There are snowflakes in his palm. 'Look what I've brought you,' he says. 'Some down feathers from Adelsa. I brought some for myself too. I carry them in my pocket for luck. That's how I found you.'

'Thank you Adelsa,' she says, taking the feathers that are shining in the summer sun.

She orders salade niçoise for them both and they eat, catching each other's eyes and lowering them. Dominique tells him about her upcoming show, how important it is to her, that it's at a smart gallery in Cork Street.

'I tell you what,' he says, 'we'll take things slow, as if we've only just met for the first time.'

'Perhaps we could meet up every few days to explore Paris together?' she suggests. 'What about going up the Notre-Dame towers? Have you been up there?'

'No,' he says, 'but I've spent a lot of time walking inside the cathedral, hoping you'd come in. The flower windows are beautiful, like looking up a giant tree through the canopy.'

'Ah, the rose windows. I do go in sometimes to look at them. But the south tower has a chimera gallery on the outside and you'll love it. It'll be like being up on Auyán. We'll have to queue for ages to get in and start early in the morning.'

'I also love those small windows at the top of the walls,' he says, 'below the roof.'

'The clerestories?'

'Is that what they are?' he says. 'They beam down shafts of light like the last rays in the forest. It reminded me of how I once saw a deer lit up by rays, making it glow as if made of glass.'

'Shocked quartz like parts of Auyán?' she says.

'Yes, that's it,' he says.

Dominique suddenly feels homesick for their private world up on the surface. 'D'you remember our hummingbirds?' she says. 'I think the clerestories are like their throats!'

'What shall we do today? Can we go see Adonis?' he says.

'Yes, let's do that,' she replies. 'Have you seen his fiancée, Sin?'

'Is that the gold *tigre* in the back cage?' he asks.

'Last time I was there, Sin was in the main area and Adonis in the back,' she says. 'They alternate them. But they sniff each other through the mesh. Did you see her sister? They had two of them at first, to choose one for him.'

'Yes,' he says. 'They always played very rough! Why did they choose Sin?'

'I don't know. Perhaps Sin was more friendly to Adonis?' she suggests. 'The keeper told me girls are more aggressive than the males, that their growls were like thunder when they fed them indoors in the evening. But Adonis just rolls over and wants his belly rubbed.'

'The females are more aggressive,' Juan says, 'because they have to defend their young from males, and have to hunt as well as look after cubs.'

'Sin's still too young to mate, but they talk to each other through the wire.'

'Like us?' he says.

'Yes.' Dominique laughs. 'Like Romeo and Juliet.'

Dominique has an annual pass, which means they can skip the queue, and get Juan in free too. They make straight for the jaguars, passing the woolly monkeys on the way. There's a crowd around the viewing window, which means that Adonis is on his front rock.

And he is. But so is Sin! Three keepers are on walkie-talkies and a vet is in attendance with a dart gun.

'First contact is very dangerous,' a keeper tells her, 'but it's Sin who scratched Adonis's nose - see?' Adonis is lapping water from the trough. He has a red scratch down his broad black nose. He returns to the sunlit rock platform and Sin follows him, leaping onto his back and play-fighting. He is so much bigger than her, yet it's she who's tiring him. She bites his head and he pretends to bite her back. She nips his paw and they tussle playfully. 'He could kill her with one snap,' the vet says, 'but it's going well.'

Dominique thinks how badly it's going with Juan. She tries not to think that he's in Papa's room. She'll never go back. Has Papa put a curse on her? Perhaps he's getting revenge because she threw his ashes into the falls? Or found Juan? Maybe he's jealous!

Juan is quiet. 'Are you thinking of Tomasa?' Dominique asks.

'Yes,' he says. 'Though Adonis is gentle, not like the devil who killed my wife. I'm thinking how small their gardens are, but Adonis looks quite content.'

'They're happy to have each other's company,' Dominique says.

'Like us!' Juan replies, and he puts his arm round her waist and hugs her, and this time she lets him.

'D'you realise Sin is short for Sinoda, which is Adonis backwards?' Dominique says, basking in his closeness.

'From now on, everything will be reversed, we will cure ourselves,' he replies.

'With one of your *tarens?*' she asks.

'No, with the good jaguar spell!'

They stand watching Sin play with her mate, roughly, then head-butting him for a cuddle. How patient Adonis is. Every now and again he pads over to the water bowl, as if to replenish his powers. She straddles him and he looks perplexed.

'It's the wrong way round!' Juan laughs.

'I don't think Adonis knows what to do!' Dominique says.

'He still has contraceptive,' the vet explains. 'A pill, we give it him in his treat. We're just waiting for Sin to get a bit older and come into season, and for the go-ahead from the breeding logbook, then they can have cubs.'

'Imagine a baby Adonis!' Dominique says, as the jaguars are lured back into their separate indoor quarters with hunks of horsemeat. 'I love Paris in the summer.'

'I love winter too,' Juan says. 'At first, I was so cold. And people kept bumping into me because I walk with jaguar feet.'

Dominique remembers how soundless his bare footsteps were in the forest, how he didn't crack one twig. Even now he's wearing soft moccasins. 'Then, one day,' he says, 'I looked out my window and saw the sky was full of harpy feathers! I rushed out and danced.'

'In the courtyard?'

'Yes,' he says. 'The feathers melted on me! The neighbours stared. Afterwards they clapped. Children came out and threw snowballs.'

Dominique imagines him dancing in snow pure as a new canvas. In Papa's courtyard. Wiping it clean with white jaguar steps. It's hard to part that evening, but she's got an idea for a new painting.

# 63

# BLUE-AND-GOLD
# MACAW FEATHER

WHENEVER A TAXI passes, Dominique can't help checking to see if it's Juan driving. But she can't answer his texts. Is it because he's available? Not unavailable like Papa and those men she used to fall for when she was young? Or is it the room?

Then he stops texting her and she's left wondering.

A week goes by.

Surely it wouldn't hurt to meet in the Jardin des Plantes? There's a good restaurant there where they could have lunch. Take things slowly as planned. She texts him back and they arrange to meet at the rue Linné entrance. Dominique wears her rose sundress and spends time putting on makeup. She's never been in the Jardin with someone before.

Juan is already there, watching her approach. He's got a white T-shirt on and is holding an orchid. 'This is for your hair,' he says, kissing her on each cheek twice, French style. He pins it on her and they walk along the path that leads to the Alpine Garden, both feeling shy.

'I've something to tell you,' he says.

'Oh!'

'A confession,' he says. 'I didn't only come to Paris to find you.'

'Oh!' she repeats.

'I'm now the Pemón *cacique*,' he says. 'I came for a climate change conference last November, to talk about goldminers destroying our rivers. While I was here, I looked for you. When I didn't find you, I decided to stay longer – that's how it happened.'

Dominique isn't sure how she feels that he didn't make this journey just for her, but it does make her feel less pressured. They descend down the tunnel into the Alpine Garden and turn left, towards her favourite tree. She reaches for a spray of pine needles, crushes a few, then holds them up for him to smell.

'It's like lemons,' he says.

'Or lime zest?' she says.

'It smells like a forest no one has entered before,' he says, 'at dawn.'

'It's a dawn redwood,' Dominique says. 'I've seen them where they grow in China, and their cousins the coast redwoods in California.'

'We don't have this tree at home,' he says, feeling the soft red-brown bark. 'Trees are our teachers, but they're being murdered by ranchers and miners.'

'I remember looking down onto the forest from the plane, on my way to Kavac Camp,' Dominique says, 'and seeing bare earth cratered with burnt stumps.'

'Our land is dying,' Juan says. 'That's why I came here, I had to.'

'Yes, I've seen the damage,' she says. 'When I was driven down to El Dorado in the jeep, to the Brazilian border on my way to climb Mount Roraima, we got out and spoke to miners on barges at the river bank, saw how they dredge the riverbed and use mercury to pan for gold nuggets.'

'The *garimpeiros* poison our water,' he says. 'Even the giant catfish are floating belly up – if they can't survive with their prehistoric scales, how can we? It's hopeless fighting the miners, they're illegal but no one can stop them so far upriver from the park guards.'

'You must!' Dominique says. 'For all our sakes. I'll help you. Tell me what I can do.' She thinks that Papa is a goldminer, dredging through her pristine waters, that she's been poisoned and always has the taste of mercury in her mouth.

'The white fathers who came to bring us Jesus, their children are ruining our land,' Juan says, as if he's heard her thoughts.

She's read that deep in the Peruvian Amazon there are tribes that can communicate through telepathy. It wouldn't surprise her if Juan could. 'Perhaps I could paint posters for you?' she suggests.

'I'd love that,' he says.

'We'd make a good team,' she says. 'And you could paint your mask designs with your dyes.'

'I brought some urucu and genipap with me!' he says. 'In fact, a box crammed with spells.'

'I know,' she says 'we could work as an artist duo, as activists.'

They've wandered into the far end of the Alpine Garden, into the ravine guarded by a headless statue. 'This used to be an old bear pit,' Dominique says, 'but it didn't have vegetation then, just concrete.'

'Poor bears!' he says.

'Yes,' she agrees. 'They drowned during a flood.'

'This is like one of our valleys on Auyán,' he says, listening to the stream coil around their feet and plunge into the old pit which is now lush with ferns. 'Maybe I could try doing some painting? Designs of our animal helpers and plant teachers?'

'I think that's a great idea!' And Dominique can see them working side by side in her studio, two hermits not needing to speak. They get so engrossed in plans that they leave the Alpine Garden and meander towards the Ménagerie. After a while they walk in silence, listening to what the other is thinking.

And there, just at the edge of the blue-and-gold macaw cage is a large blue and yellow feather. A keeper is inside, cleaning, and Dominique asks if she can have it. 'No,' the girl answers. 'We can't give animal parts to visitors, not even feathers, they could have diseases we don't know about.'

'Never mind,' Juan says. 'I have one just like that in my box.'

'You do?' she says.

'Yes. I must have known you'd want one.'

Dominique sees that the morning is blue and gold, that there'll never be one like this again. The feather is celestial blue on one side of the shaft, ultramarine on the other, but the underside is acid yellow like a field of rape. The day is a knife that must cut her with barbs. It will take time for the yellow to transform from sulphur to sunlight. No one else can help her except Juan. And now that she knows she can be by herself, does it mean that she can be with another person again? And with that thought she relaxes more in his company, showing him the king vultures Margot and N'Golo, in their cage opposite the macaws.

'What if these are the last king vulture gods?' Juan says.

'They won't last much longer,' Dominique says. 'They're already over twenty years old.'

'And they've been here in this small cage all their lives?' he asks.

'Yes, the Ménagerie has a special breeding programme, and each year they lay chicks, which go to other zoos. Sometimes Margot takes care of her chick, but sometimes they have to hand raise one with a glove puppet so they don't bond with humans. I saw one in the nursery once.'

# 64

# HUMMINGBIRDS

A FTER LUNCH, DOMINIQUE invites Juan to her studio. 'If we stop on the way at my place,' he says, 'I can fetch my box of spells; all the *tarens* I brought from home.'

Dominique frowns. How can she face that room again after what happened last time? She takes a deep breath. Why should Papa spoil everything? If she was brave enough to visit it four times, and after he died, surely she can brave it now, with Juan, who's the opposite of Papa? If she gets scared, she thinks, as they go through the black gate into the courtyard, she doesn't have to actually go in, she can just wait at the door while he fetches the box.

They climb the stairs, her lagging behind. It's as if she's climbing sandstone blocks behind a waterfall that's pummelling her face. Perhaps she's drunk too much wine, because she can barely reach each slab. The water is icy and shocks her awake as they reach the hallway. There's the door; it springs open with the familiar creak.

She hovers at the entrance as Juan pulls out his box from under the bed. The room is different in the sunlight that's pouring in through the open window. There seem to be even more plants now; luxurious vines hanging down from every shelf.

'I can't resist the flower market,' Juan says, laughing, when she admires his indoor garden. 'But then I have to do more taxi work once I've spent all my money on plants.'

'Perhaps you could do less taxi-ing, if you work with me in my studio?' she says. 'I've been selling more paintings recently. I think the gallery would love your designs.'

'You do? I'd much prefer to paint,' he says.

'That's settled then,' she says. 'We could make temporary pieces with charms in tiny cages or glass boxes, like Joseph Cornell, or Joseph Beuys and Anselm Kiefer's small pieces – I'll show you their work, you'll like it. Let's just see what happens.'

'You'll paint some posters for me?'

'Yes,' she promises, 'and we could fly-post them at night, replace them when they're torn down.'

'Good idea,' he says. 'People who live in cities don't know what's happening – the fires, the rivers getting poisoned.'

'The world's lungs dying,' she adds, stepping in to the room.

'Let's not talk about such sad things now,' he says, and starts to tell her the Pemón names of his houseplants. He pulls her towards him but she steps back onto the threshold, starts jotting a few names in her notebook; wanting to incorporate them into the posters.

'Why don't you come in?' he says. 'Is something wrong?'

'This room . . . it's this room! It's where my father lived.'

'Oh!' Juan says. 'Are you sure?'

'Of course I'm sure! It's his room, where he died!' And as everything goes quiet, she hears the oxygen machine chugging in the corner of the toilet. The sound goes right through her.

Juan places his box in his back basket, which he's brought with him. 'Well, it's my room now,' he says. 'I've cured it with plants. Let's go.'

He's avoiding looking at her. For the first time, she feels unsure of him. Does he think she's obsessed? Doesn't he believe her? They are back on the mountain in driving rain, each lost in their own thoughts. And just as suddenly, the stars stop arguing and she takes his hand.

She leads him over to the rue du Pot-de-Fer. They pass the Place de la Contrescarpe, bustling with student cafés, and into the hush of her studio with its skylights, where he opens his spells for her.

There are chips of rose quartz from caves inside Auyán. A box of giant iridescent beetles. Dyes wrapped inside banana leaves. 'Here's your macaw feather,' he says, pulling it out from under bundles of other colourful feathers. She holds it up to the light, so the blue shines like a sapphire and the sulphur a sunray.

He plants it in her hair, next to the orchid, then kisses her, and she thinks everything will come right.

'I also have a suitcase of spells,' she says, breaking away from him with a laugh. 'In fact, I have two suitcases of spells. One is just a photo but it's my favourite thing in the whole world.' She reaches into her dress pocket and shows him Augusto Ruschi's photo of thirty-seven hummingbirds asleep in their suitcase, which she always keeps warm with her body. Although she thinks of it being the size of a suitcase, it shocks her how small the photo is, only five inches across.

Juan is transfixed. He reads out the caption: 'In Cloth Straitjackets.'

'It's my most treasured possession,' Dominique says. 'I found it after I showed my father a photo album of my childhood. There are thirty-seven hummers in there, and I was thirty-seven then.'

'But, are they hurt?' Juan asks. 'Are those bandages?'

'No, 'she explains. 'The hummingbird whisperer, Augusto Ruschi, used to wrap them in a cloth with a hole in the centre. He'd gently push their heads through the hole and tie the cloth around their wings and bodies. Then he'd feed them sugar water through a pipette, and when he'd collected enough birds, he'd lay them in this suitcase, so that the head and bill of one would rest on the body of another, rows of them.'

'I see, they're sleeping, though that one has his eyes open,' Juan says, still looking worried.

'This is how he travelled with them, storing them in the hold of a plane, even across the Atlantic,' she insists. He must understand.

'How did he catch them?' Juan asks.

'He used a tame pygmy owl decoy, and he'd whistle like the owl while waving a long pole covered in sticky oil. When the humming-birds flew up to attack their predator, they'd get stuck on the pole. Then he'd carefully wipe the oil off their feathers, dress them in their pyjamas and place them in a fridge for half an hour to lower their temperature so they went into torpor, to conserve energy.'

'Oh no! Not inside a fridge. He *was* cruel.'

'No, no, no,' she protests, 'he wasn't cruel! Hummingbirds fall into torpor when the temperature is lowered, that's what the article said, so he was just lowering it for them. He loved his birds, and they were wild, but he half-tamed them by attracting them with their red food flowers – hibiscus and so on. He loved his birds and they loved him.'

'I believe you,' Juan says. 'Don't worry. I can see why you love this photo so much.'

'When I first came across it in the bookshop, it was like opening a jewellery box. I knew there were colours under the cloths. That the birds were safe in their coma.'

'They look trusting,' Juan says.

'The picture gave me the same feeling I had when I watched my father turn the pages of my album.'

'Will you show me this album?' he says.

'Yes, I will,' she says. It's called "The Childhood".'

'The childhood?'

'Yes,' she says. 'I think of the Amazon as earth's childhood, a forest of sleeping birds.'

'It was once safe,' he says, 'when we looked after it, all the forest people. Then the Christian fathers came, and the miners and loggers.'

'Yes, the fathers should have kept away,' she agrees. 'My father even peeled back the cellophane sheets to get to the photos beneath, and picked them up as you would a baby. He turned them over to see the writing behind – the date, the name.'

Dominique thinks back to that evening, but she no longer sees the photos. All she can see are the hummingbirds in their swaddling clothes. How each was a year of her life, kept safe behind cellophane. She knows they weren't always kept in her album, that she stuck them in just before she came to Paris to meet her father.

But once she'd stuck them down, it was as if they'd always been there.

'Do you know what kind of hummingbirds they are?' Juan asks.

'Well,' she says, 'I guess they must be Brazilian, from the Santa Teresa Mountains where Ruschi lived and still has his reserve. But I always imagine they're Venezuelan, from our *tepui*.'

'They're Tukui and Aruka, our helpers on Auyán, and their families and friends!' Juan laughs.

'Would you like some tea?' she asks.

'I'd love a Cuba Libre,' he says.

She disappears into her kitchen and comes back with ice-cold drinks. 'They're hummingbirds that live only on the *tepuis*, like the tepui goldenthroat I saw when I went into the bushes. They beat their wings more than eighty times per second – but you know that.'

They sit there sipping rum, chatting about hummingbirds as the hours pass and Dominique relaxes, sure now she has him back. Festive coquette, sapphire-spangled emerald, jewelfront. It turns into a game: she says a name then he answers with another. The room glows with thornbills and racket-tails, woodnymphs, hermits and woodstars.

When the air shimmers with copper-green and ruby topaz, her head reels as if she's drunk a whole bottle of champagne. Her sketchbook is filled with new colours to paint with, colours only flowers have seen before, as the hermits and Incas drink their nectar, and the hummers' throats change colour with each sip. Juan laughs as she continues making names up, as if she's just painted her birds and they've sprung to life all around them.

He takes her hand in his and tells her how it's always the female who weaves the nest, how tiny it is, and how most nests are cups, but some have tails tapering down, woven with lichen and jaguar hairs, orchid rootlets and down from harpy chicks. How brave the fairy birds are, pointing their bills at predators. Dominique remembers the grunts as she squatted in the bushes on Auyán, thinking a jaguar had crept up on her, only to find the gold-green bullet buzzing in front of her face.

'I said I have another suitcase of hummingbirds,' Dominique says, feeling emboldened by the rum, 'but I hope you won't be upset by them.'

'Why would I be?'

'I found them in my father's flat,' she says. 'In your room! On the top shelf, where your vines grow.'

She goes to the table and unzips it.

'Oh! They're in bottles!' Juan says.

'Yes, and in jars,' she says, holding one up to the light. 'They're love charms – *chuparosas*. I don't know why my father had them, or where he got them from, perhaps the bird market. Have you been there yet? We must go.' She opens the jar and gently pulls out the mummy of rags wrapped around the birds and starts to unpeel them.

'They're bad spells,' Juan says.

'No, they're love charms,' she repeats.

He picks the bundle up and examines the two birds in their embrace.' Some of them don't have hearts,' Dominique says.

'They're bad spells,' Juan insists. 'Why did your father collect them?'

'I don't know,' she says, 'but he wrote little notes to wrap some of them in, and they're very sad.'

'Oh, he sounds like a very sad man.'

'He was,' she says, and feels like crying but won't. 'Don't you think it's best to wrap your secrets inside bottles and post them into a river?' she asks. 'Then they can float downriver and out into the sea, without harming anyone.'

'They look so old and dry,' Juan says, frowning.

'Yes, that's true,' she says. 'And someone cut out their hearts.'

'Who would do that to a bird?' he asks.

'Someone desperate for love perhaps?' she suggests. 'I read that there are spells where you have to eat a hummingbird's heart. In fact, there was an artist in Mexico who ate hummingbirds.'

'Who?'

'Diego Rivera, who married Frida Kahlo, who was also a painter.'

'And were they happy?'

'No! They divorced, but got remarried though.'

'So, there's hope?'

'Yes. They adored each other, but he loved other women too. He was cruel to her.'

'I'm not cruel,' Juan says abruptly. 'Not every man is cruel. And in my culture, it's easy for an unhappy wife to leave her husband.' He reaches into the bottom of his box of spells and pulls out a small box.

For a moment, Dominique thinks it's a ring, but as the tissue paper unwinds, she sees it's something better – a nest the size of an eggcup. It's built on a small twig, and above it a brown leaf is its roof. He places the hummingbird nest in her palm.

Dominique has never seen one before. He shows her how pliable and strong it is, woven with spiderwebs so it can stretch when the nestlings grow. 'I watched the mother making it in our garden,' he says, 'and saw the two eggs hatch. I saw the mother feeding the chicks mosquitoes, and when they fledged and flew away, I took the nest for you.'

# 65

# À MON SEUL DÉSIR

DOMINIQUE PLACES THE nest on her desk. It's the most beautiful thing she's ever seen, even better than Ruschi's photo.

He takes her hands in his. 'Come back with me. I promise to make your father's room so different that you'll be able to stay there with me.'

'But why don't you spend the night here?' she asks.

'I can't stay near those birds. I'd hear them singing what people did to them. I'd dream about having my heart torn out.'

'But can't you see, in my father's room I'd get bad dreams too,' Dominique replies, but as she says it, she knows she has to try. 'Okay, then I'll come to you, but perhaps you could move?'

'No! I can't. My room is so cheap and I have to send money back home for my parents.'

'I'll just get my toothbrush and drawing things,' she says. 'I'd like you to tell me the names of all your plants and I want to draw them tomorrow.'

They walk hand-in-hand down the crowded rue Mouffetard, up to rue Clovis, just like the lovers Dominique saw kissing after the first day she spent with Papa. She feels brave, confident Juan will make it work, just as she felt sure that he'd save her when she lost her foothold on the cliff, even when Angel Falls made her spin in freefall.

She knows that this time, at last, they'll make love.

They bound up the short flight of stairs, and she half shuts her eyes and glides until they're at the top. There's his door. It's just an ordinary wooden door. But as she waits for Juan to unlock it, it grows into a forest. When it opens, the Animal Master stands before her.

She can smell chlorophyl, the heady scent of stephanotis and gardenia. She sits at the table as she once sat on a rock in a cloud valley on Auyán, surrounded by species that only live there.

*When a huntress first encounters someone else in the forest, she hears twigs snapping. The sound echoes from trunk to trunk. Time slows to a standstill. Beams slant in through leaves, splash her shoulders. Then fear comes, like a pump in the corner of a room. The huntress realises she is not in the forest of her father – she is in her father. He has swallowed her.*

Dominique looks around and dashes straight back out. 'Please don't go,' Juan says. Please come back.'

'I can't . . .' she says. 'I'm sorry.'

'I could make you tea? Or rum?'

'No,' she says.

'You were so brave on the mountain,' he pleads, 'surrounded by evil spirits. And you came in the first day we met . . .'

'I'm sorry,' she says, waving goodbye and backing down the stairs. 'I'm so sorry!'

# EPILOGUE

*T*HERE IS A *sunlit sinkhole on Auyán-tepui, its floor carpeted with ruby pitcher plants. Juan shows me the cockroaches drowning in their vases. We watch them struggle, some wriggling, others half-digested. Beyond the pitchers is a swamp of sundews, flies trapped in their honey-dew leaves. Juan steps around them not to disturb their strange gardens. He points to one which has caught a small scorpion in its sticky droplets.*

*He leads me towards the far end of the sinkhole, where the ground is crystal beneath quartz furniture. Nothing can grow from quartz, I think, but I'm wrong, because already I can see strap leaves that shine like mirrors, so that they reflect a dazzling blue sky, and beyond them, a green cushion beckons.*

*But it isn't a cushion because now I can make out a bone-white skull, a long bill, the backbone and remains of wings, a few primaries still waving in the wind. 'I call this a death garden', Juan says. 'The tiny bird is so peaceful. A good grave for Tukui.'*

*The hummingbird's body is bursting with moss the colour of your room, Papa, when Juan had painted it green and filled it with plants. I entered it with him that first time as if it was your carnivorous body, then I could never be there again. The hummingbird's bones gleam like quartz – millipedes that live only here have crawled over you, polishing you with their feet. I think of all the flowers your bill has pierced. Perhaps that's why the moss has grown over you, its roots embroidering your bill shut. The moss in your ribcage is a forest* glimpsed from a plane, the miniature orchid of your heart a glossy purple wound.

Here are your attendants: a yellow and black spiny spider, a yellow and black poison frog, a black scorpion. A green butterfly lands to feed on your remaining micro-juices. A bushmaster curls below like a guardian. Juan says others come to sniff the death garden: coatis, porcupines, and once, an ocelot, but until now he's the only human who has seen it.

※

I sit on a rock to talk to you for the last time, my hummingbird father. You are with me in my Lost World.

We've climbed down the sinkhole, to the forest in its bed, where there are creatures who live nowhere else on earth. The trees may be stunted, but their branches are tree boas that sway to sky music. Each tree trunk is a door I open to your room where the pygmy owl hoots a warning. I have climbed inside such trees and hidden in their wardrobes, my face pressed against bats that whispered directions. I have tried your clothes on in your changing rooms and looked in the quicksilver river for my reflection, but it was warped like a cracked mirror. Papa, I have tried on your suits of leaves and your suits of bark. I have worn your shoes that know the forest like deer, their muzzles stitched with laces.

I have sat on my chair made of rock quartz while you sat on your red armchair stuffed with the blood of creatures. Your armchair of flayed skins, sewn from ocelots and tamarins. I have watched you eat as the ghosts of margays chased capuchin monkeys around the canopy of your room, leaping from spokes of your fan to your light shade, from the huge television to the clock that's always stuck at 4, the time you announced the death of my mother.

While you slipped into bed, I sat wanting to leave, not wishing to hurt you if I stayed. But I neither left, nor hurt you, even though I sat on my chair until it burst into flame. My hard chair like the seat in a plane, small as a gnat as it banked against the cliffs of Auyán. My hands gripped the seat as I dropped through turbulence, and your face loomed in front of me again, as long as a kilometre-high waterfall, while you changed into an archangel. 'No daughter hurts an archangel,' I sang, through closed lips, so I wouldn't wake you.

I saw your rug rise into the air and become a carpet of pitcher plants. I saw the pitchers were the last water flasks on earth. One had a mouse drowned in its juice, another a frog, most contained cockroaches piled on top of each other down the long tapering tubes, like the meal we had just eaten, that we were digesting. I saw that your room was half cloud and half tobacco smoke. I sat there like a girl who wanted to become a tobacco shaman, who lives in a hut made of the bones of children. But still you snored and I did not dare leave.

Should I have left, Papa?

Now I have passed through the tarnished mirror in your kitchen, into its mercurial air. I live on an island in the sky. I have dedicated my life to painting Auyán. To painting all the sky islands and their fauna and flora. Before they vanish. Around me the forests burn and the rivers glow radioactive. Around me the gold miners dredge each riverbed for nuggets. Even the lowland jaguar glows now, his coat of putrefying stars.

Juan is by my side. He tells me that even his people, who once worshipped the trees like gods, have started to dredge for gold, because they have to eat. The tourists no longer come and they cannot guide. But his people have forgotten how to hunt and farm and their teachers, the trees, are charred. He breaks down when he says this, the only time I see him weep.

We live on our rain-drenched raft and tend its hanging galleries of orchids that feed on clouds. We watch the sky rivers turn strange colours and I think sometimes that we are living in my paintings. That the Lost World has died. Like you, Papa, like all the fathers who poisoned their children. We talk about the jaguar we heard one night, long ago, outside our tent. I've taken casts of his paw prints and painted the dew inside, which fell that morning when the musician-wren sang her solitary song. I've painted the animals that only live up here, trying to make them come back.

❧

I've retreated on a rope ladder down a vertical funnel into a chasm big enough to hold Notre-Dame, where I found a virgin forest of stalagmites with broderie leaves and pearl arches. The first time, I emerged from the petrified forest as if from a dream. Juan says no one has gone there before us, that we are safe there.

I've descended into quartzite caves miles long, with their underground rivers – the River of a Thousand Columns and Oilbird River, named after the birds that are just legends now. Juan and I have walked along galleries of crystals, with opal stalactites and floors of silica desert roses. The walls are pink and the rivers red. There are pillars of stacked plates from a banquet, draperies of angel wings, clusters of cathedral organs. Sometimes a breeze penetrates from the upper world and notes play, then fade and it's silent again.

Juan says our caves are called Imawarí Yeutá – the Cave where the Gods Live. But we are inside the gods, inside bodies of dead animals. We look up to the roof and see clouds made of stone, and sometimes the roof seems like billowing smoke or mushroom clouds. There are meadows of crystal grass and a jardin of mineral roses. Juan catches blind cave fish for us to eat in the lower galleries, where the rivers still roar with cascades.

*I don't know how long we can survive down here, safe from the storms in the upper world. If I hadn't seen your face in Angel Falls, I'd still be out there, Papa. If I could have forgiven you when I heard the bell Emmanuel's voice, I might have stayed in Paris, but as soon as the last note stopped, I started to fear you again. So I had to leave your city and live here, in this sanctuary, painting the forms that appear as I walk its corridors, so like our cellar but beautiful and immense. All I know is that you led me here, Papa. It was you who made me return to the Lost World and meet Juan. And this redeems you.*

# ACKNOWLEDGEMENTS

I would like to thank P. Cesáreo de Armellada for his *Diccionario Pemón* (Universidad Católica Andrés Bello, Caracas, 1981) and his *Tauron Panton: Cuentos y leyendas de los indios Pemón* (Ediciones Abya-Yala, Quito, Ecuador, 1989), both invaluable sources for my references to Pemón language, myth, and culture. Other books that were crucial for information on the Pemón were: *Order Without Government: The Society of the Pemon Indians of Venezuela*, by David John Thomas (University of Illinois Press, 1945); *Panton Pata Pemonton: Histoires de la Terre des Hommes* by Elba Este-Clauteaux (L'Harmattan, Paris, 1997); and *Légendes indiennes du Venezuela* by R. Zocchetti (L'Harmattan, Paris, 1985). I would also like to thank three Pemón-Kamaracoto guides on my second journey, in 1993, to Auyán-tepui: José/Kumara, Atanasio/Parkia and Juan/Eimasensen, thank you for your help and patiently teaching me some Pemón phrases.

I'm indebted to Stewart McPherson for his research into the unique tepuis flora, in his book *Lost Worlds of the Guiana Highlands* (Redfern Natural History Productions, 2008), which informed my descriptions of the flora of Auyán-tepui, and for his 'death garden' (Figure 170) photographed by Andreas Fleischmann, which I refer to in my epilogue. I am also indebted to the explorers Francesco Sauro, Freddy Vergara, Antonio De Vivo and Jo De Waele, for their account of their 2013 discoveries in the interior of Auyán-tepui: *Imawarí Yeutá: A New Giant Cave System in the Quartz Sandstones of the Auyan Tepui, Bolivar State, Venezuela* (16th International Congress of Speleology, Proceedings. 2.), which I drew on for my epilogue.

A word on the Pemón name for Angel Falls before Jimmie Angel 'discovered' them in 1933: I've chosen the one his niece Karen Angel believes to be correct in her biography of her uncle, *Angel's Flight* (Lulu Publishing, 2019), where she states that the Pemón elders' name for it is Churún-Vená, not the sometimes-used Kerepakupa-Méru, which is possibly a waterfall further in the canyon.

I am deeply grateful for the encouragement and editing from my agent Jon Curzon at Artellus, and for inspired suggestions by my editor Jennifer Hamilton-Emery at Salt Publishing. Big thanks to Chris Hamilton-Emery and Jen at Salt and all the team, for their trust and faith in bringing my novel to readers, and a special thank you to Chris for the beautiful cover. With love as ever to my first reader my husband Brian Fraser.